RAVISH ME
WITH RUBIES

RAVISH ME
WITH RUBIES

JANE FEATHER

THORNDIKE PRESS
A part of Gale, a Cengage Company

LIBRARY OF CONGRESS CIP DATA ON FILE.
CATALOGUING IN PUBLICATION FOR THIS BOOK
IS AVAILABLE FROM THE LIBRARY OF CONGRESS.

ISBN-13: 978-1-4328-8787-2 (hardcover alk. paper)

Published in 2021 by arrangement with Zebra Books, an imprint of Kensington Publishing Corp.

Printed in Mexico
Print Number: 01   Print Year: 2021

RAVISH ME
WITH RUBIES

CHAPTER ONE

It was a warm, late May afternoon when Petra Rutherford crossed Parliament Square and approached St. Stephen's Porch at the Palace of Westminster. The police officer on duty in front of the great oak door regarded her with a suspicious frown.

"Can I help you, madam?"

Petra's smile was bland. She was well aware that it was her purple, green and white silk scarf that drew the man's frown. "I have an appointment to take tea on the Terrace with the Right Honorable Mr. Rutherford." She handed the officer her engraved card.

He took it and silently opened the door for her. The Sergeant at Arms stepped forward instantly to take the card handed to him by the policeman. "If you would care to follow me, madam."

Petra knew the way well enough but she also understood the rigid, frequently arcane rules and rituals that informed all activities in the Houses of Parliament. She followed the man through St. Stephen's Hall and into the ornate Central Lobby situated halfway between the House of Commons and the House of Lords.

"If you'll take a seat, Miss Rutherford, I will send a card messenger to inform the Honorable Member of your arrival." He gestured to the padded benches around the hall.

"Thank you." Petra glanced around the crowded lobby, looking for anyone she might know. It wouldn't be unusual for a friend or acquaintance to be visiting a member of Parliament at teatime.

"Petra . . ." She turned at her brother's voice. Jonathan hurried across the marble floor toward her. "I was waiting for you on the terrace." His smile became a frown as he reached her. "Did you have to wear the scarf, Petra? It's a red rag to a bull in here."

"I did have to wear it, Joth, for that very reason. I'm sorry if it sullies the sanctity of these hallowed halls, but you support the cause so you should be proud to acknowledge your sister's participation."

He shook his head. "I don't *not* support women's suffrage, but I dislike drawing attention and making a fuss, and there's someone I most particularly want you to meet and be nice to this afternoon."

"Oh?" She looked at him curiously. "Someone I don't know?"

"Well, I believe you did know him slightly, but a long time ago," her brother said with a vaguely dismissive wave of his hand. "I want to persuade him to support a bill that I'm presenting to Parliament and I need reinforcements. Just offer your sweetest smile and be as charming as you possibly can."

"You mean use my feminine wiles on him, flutter my eyelashes and blind him with flattery?" she asked, half laughing.

"I know better than to expect that from my sister, however helpful it would be. Just be pleasant and charming, I know you can do that much for all your radical inclinations," Jonathan stated. "Let's go for tea. I don't want him to be waiting for us." He offered his arm and Petra allowed him to escort her out of the hall and onto the long terrace overlooking the river.

"Your table is over here, Mr. Rutherford. Good afternoon, madam. How nice to see you again." The rotund figure of the head waiter barreled up to them as soon as they stepped onto the terrace. His eyes flicked to Petra's scarf and then turned aside, his smile of greeting fixed upon his round countenance.

"Good afternoon, Mr. Jackson." Petra greeted him with a warm smile of her own as if she had not noticed that discreetly averted glance. She had known what she was doing, wearing the colors of the Women's Social and Political Union so blatantly in this bastion of male power and privilege, but as she was not about to make a scene, her protest was silent and polite. It would still ruffle feathers, though.

She followed the waiter and her brother through the tables where conversation was low-voiced and whose occupants concentrated on the matter in hand, showing no interest in those around them. The table was set for three, she noticed, as she took her seat facing the Thames. Jonathan took the seat opposite leaving the one next to her free.

"So who is your mysterious guest, Joth?" she inquired, shaking out her napkin and laying it across her lap.

"He's a member of the House of Lords . . ." He broke off as a waiter set a teapot, milk jug, a saucer of sliced lemons and a sugar bowl on the table, followed by a tray of smoked salmon and cucumber sandwiches, and a cloth-covered basket of warm scones. A dish of clotted cream and a cut glass jar of raspberry jam followed them.

Petra waited until tea was poured. She reached for the sugar tongs and dropped a lump into her bone china teacup blazoned with the arms of Westminster. "I'm intrigued, Joth." She stirred the sugar into her tea, regarding her brother with an inquiring smile.

Her brother frowned, glanced anxiously around. "Couldn't you put the scarf in your handbag?"

Petra's gaze followed his. "No one seems interested in us, let alone bothered."

"You know full well everyone will have remarked it. *Please* take it off, Petra." His hazel eyes, mirror images of his sister's, pleaded. "This afternoon is important to me."

Petra shrugged and untied the scarf, folding it carefully before sliding it into her handbag.

"Oh, don't take it off on my account." Petra hadn't heard that voice in almost ten years.

She turned her head to the side, feeling the old dislike rising from a deeply mortifying past.

"Lord Ashton," she said distantly, staring at the man who had been her nemesis since the days when she was just trying her wings in the adult world. He looked older, which was only to be expected, at least ten years older, and there was a hint of silver at his temples. His black hair was as thick as ever, though, and carefully styled, brushed off his broad forehead. His eyebrows, black as pitch, arched above dark brown eyes that if Petra didn't know better could be described as soulful and empathetic. But she did know better. The aquiline nose and well-shaped mouth would to most eyes qualify Guy Granville, Lord Ashton, as a handsome man. But Petra's eyes in this instance were not *most* people's.

"Lord Ashton, I'm so happy you could join us," Jonathan said, half rising from his chair as he indicated the seat next to his sister. "I think you may have met my sister, Petra."

"I have indeed. Although I must say you've grown some, Miss Rutherford, since last we met." His smile, showing even white teeth, was both warm and almost complicit, as if he was sharing an old and happy memory.

Petra met the smile with stony indifference. "It would be strange if I had not, Lord Ashton. Ten years is a long time."

He inclined his head in acknowledgment.

"Particularly the ten between fourteen and twenty-four. So, tell me what the grown-up Miss Rutherford is doing with her time these days, apart, of course, from making noise with the suffragists."

Petra swallowed hard. Her mind was working furiously. She had never expected to meet this man again in the usual course of everyday life, oh, maybe a fleeting glimpse across a drawing room at a route party or some such, but Guy Granville moved in a very different social set from her own. He was ten years older for one thing. But that distance had not prevented her from knowing a great deal about the man. His fierce opposition to women's suffrage was well known, he had written articles against it in the *Times*, and his name frequently appeared in the gossip columns as an unrepentant philanderer. She took a sip of tea and reached for a scone.

"Cat got your tongue, Miss Rutherford?" His tone was gently mocking, his amused gaze watching as she deliberately split the scone and spread clotted cream and raspberry jam on both halves.

Oh, how that tone made her toes curl, that gleam of mockery in his eyes turned her stomach. But she was no longer the naïve, unsophisticated girl who had inadvertently given him so much sport ten years ago. Jonathan wanted her to charm Guy Granville, Baron Ashton. She could do that, and she would relish every minute until the moment came to put in the knife.

Petra took a bite of her scone, slowly licking a speck of cream from her lips as she met the baron's gaze. "How wonderful that our paths have crossed again, Lord Ashton. Perhaps we can dispense with such formality, though. After all, we were once so very well acquainted." She picked up the platter of sandwiches, the smile of an attentive hostess on her lips. "Do you care for one, Guy? The smoked salmon are particularly good."

She caught the flicker of surprise in his eyes, the instant of quick calculation as he took in her smile and tone, then he reached out an elegant white hand to take a sandwich and she remembered with a jolt those long slender fingers, the beautifully manicured nails.

"Thank you, Petra," he said, his smile neutral although his eyes were sharply assessing as she held his gaze, a faint smile on her own lips and her head tilted at an angle that was distinctly challenging. Little Petra Rutherford had most definitely grown up, Guy thought. Meeting that challenge from those clear hazel eyes could be very interesting. He inclined his head as if confirming something and turned to her brother.

"So, Rutherford, you have something you wish to discuss with me?" He sipped his tea.

"Yes, yes, I do. Thank you so much for coming, Lord Ashton," Joth began, then stopped as the baron raised an arresting hand.

"Let's dispense with the formalities, Rutherford. Just Granville will do."

Jonathan nodded and caught his sister's eye. She gave him a reassuring smile. "I'm guessing that my brother has parliamentary business that concerns his Somersetshire constituents. You do, after all, represent the county in the Lords."

"That's certainly true, to a certain extent. But I'm not dependent on the voters of Somerset for my seat in the House of Lords."

"Of course you're not," Petra returned sharply. "But you have an ethical and moral obligation to work on their behalf."

Jonathan was beginning to wish he'd left his sister out of this meeting. She was supposed to be flattering Lord Ashton, not putting his back up. "To get back to the point," he said firmly, a little louder than he'd intended.

"Yes, please do." His lordship waved an inviting hand.

Jonathan took a breath. "I want to present a bill to the Commons that will set up a unified authority to develop a pumping system for draining all the Somerset Levels. There are so many different areas of the moors, all with different systems, most of which have failed miserably and the soil in most cases is no longer fit for arable use. It can't be planted for cattle to graze because it's too soft and waterlogged, a cow would sink . . ."

"Some farmers have planted clover though and sheep have managed to graze, they're too light to sink," Petra put in, helping herself to a cucumber sandwich.

"True, but that doesn't deal with the problem of winter flooding. It's so bad sometimes that people have to evacuate their houses and farms and head for the hills," her brother stated. "It's not safe to live in some of the areas along the rivers, King's Sedgemoor is particularly vulnerable. An efficient, unified drainage system across the whole area would have tremendous benefits. And I was hoping, Granville, that I could count on your support in the House of Lords."

Guy leaned back in his chair, casually

crossing his legs, letting the afternoon sun fall on his upturned face. "Somerset folk don't respond too well to government authorities," he observed. "I can hear the objections now to the idea of some amorphous single authority with the power to mess with their lands, even if it is for their own benefit."

Jonathan flushed. "I have traveled around the county seeking the opinion of eligible voters. There's some resistance, I agree, but when it's explained carefully exactly what will be the result of decent drainage most of them seem willing to accept the idea."

Guy sat up straight. "In that case, dear boy, I suggest you go ahead and see how your parliamentary colleagues react. I won't say anything against your bill in the Lords." He stood up. "Thank you for the tea." He turned slightly toward Petra. "Miss Rutherford, Petra, it was delightful to renew our acquaintance. I trust I may call upon you in Brook Street sometime." He lifted a questioning brow but the accompanying smile showed that he was in no doubt as to her answer.

"How delightful," she returned with a responding smile, extending her hand in farewell.

Guy lifted it to his lips without actually

17

touching her skin, offering a gallant bow before striding toward the doors leading back to the Central Lobby, pausing now and again to exchange a word of greeting with various tea takers on the terrace.

"Odious man," Petra declared in a fierce undertone. "Oh, how I detest him."

"Why?" Her brother looked at her in astonishment. "You barely know him." A smile tugged at his lips. "I know he does have something of a reputation with the ladies." His tone was faintly admiring.

"You think playing fast and loose with some poor woman's feelings is to be smiled at?" Petra demanded. "How could you, Joth?"

He looked somewhat abashed but said defensively, "Well, as far as I hear, the women flock to him."

"More fool them," his sister said. She glanced at her watch. "Joth, I have to go. I have a dress fitting at five o'clock, and then I'm going to dinner at the Criterion."

"Who with? Can I come?"

"Diana and Fenella, and their other halves. Of course you can come, Joth. I would have said earlier but I thought you'd probably be engaged with friends, or at your club."

He shook his head. "I wasn't sure how the

18

meeting with Granville would go, so I didn't make any arrangements in case he suggested . . . oh, well, I thought maybe he might wish to talk more about the bill."

"I don't get the impression he takes such matters seriously," Petra said, getting to her feet. "Never mind. He did say he wouldn't stand in your way, at least." She bent to kiss his brow. "His loss is my gain. I'm delighted to have your escort. We should leave by seven thirty."

"I'll be ready." He raised a hand in farewell as his sister threaded her way through the tables.

Petra was more than happy to have her brother's company that evening. Although she was as close as ever to her two dearest friends, they'd known each other since they were schoolgirls, these days she sometimes felt a bit like an outsider when Fenella and Diana were with their husbands. It wasn't that she didn't like Rupert or Edward, quite the opposite, in fact, and they were clearly just right for Diana and Fenella, but once in a while she wondered if perhaps they felt she was a bit de trop. Not that any of them ever gave her that impression.

But still it would be good to have a partner of her own at dinner, even if it was her brother. She stepped out onto St. Stephen's

Porch and hailed a cab coming around
Parliament Square.

CHAPTER TWO

"Are you ready, Joth?" Petra entered the drawing room of the Rutherford town house on Brook Street just after seven o'clock that evening.

"Ready to go whenever you are. Sherry, first?" Her brother lifted the cut glass decanter in invitation.

"Oh, yes, please. We have plenty of time." She took the glass and said with a smile, "You look very elegant, brother. Evening dress suits you."

"Why, thank you." Her brother swept her a flourishing bow. "And may I return the compliment. That green silk . . . what do they call it? Apple? . . . well, whatever they call it, it's a wonderful color for you."

Petra laughed and curtsied. "Flattery has never been your forte, Joth, so I'll accept the compliment with gratitude." She sipped her sherry, wandering to the windows looking over the street below. "It's a lovely evening. D'you think it's too far to walk?"

Jonathan ran a speculative glance over her. "Definitely in those shoes."

She lifted a foot clad in cream satin embroidered with glass beads. "I have to have the heel, otherwise I'm so short people don't even know I'm here."

Jonathan laughed. "My dear girl, no one could ever miss you. You may be small but you're completely unignorable. You always wear something distinctive. That tangerine shawl, for instance. I don't know why it goes with that apple green but it does. And it draws the eye. People can't help noticing you."

"I think you will make some lucky woman a very satisfactory husband," Petra declared with a chuckle. "You always know exactly what to say."

Jonathan shook his head and refilled his whisky glass. "Talking of knowing what to say, what *was* going on between you and Granville this afternoon? I didn't think you knew each other beyond a passing acquaintance but you both gave the impression that you had some history between you. I was hoping you'd be all sweetness and light but you were as scratchy as a cross cat."

Petra hesitated. She'd never talked of that summer with anyone, but it was far enough in the past now, surely, for the memory to be no longer so painful.

"I'm sorry. I was taken by surprise," she said. "It was one summer, ten years ago. I was fourteen and had just put up my hair and started to go out into county society. Ma thought it would be good practice for when I had my come-out." She looked into her glass for a moment as if conjuring her past self in its pale gold depths. "You weren't around . . . I think you'd gone to Italy with a school friend's family. Anyway, Guy Granville was at Ashton Court with some of his London friends, having a summer house party, and we met." She looked up with a half smile. "To cut a long story short, he decided to cultivate me, escorting me at parties, dancing, playing croquet, making me feel so grown-up with all the attention. I was so young, Joth. Utterly naïve. I couldn't see then that he was just amusing himself."

Jonathan looked outraged. "He didn't try to seduce you, or anything like that, did he?"

Petra shook her head. "Not really . . . he kissed me once or twice." She turned back to the window, remembering how those kisses had made her feel. The memory *was* still painful and she put it from her. "He left Somerset without a word. One evening

23

he was dancing with me, walking in the moonlight around the lake . . . all very romantic, and the next morning he'd gone . . . to the Riviera apparently where the company would be more stimulating." She turned back to him with a rueful smile.

"My pride was hurt, as you might imagine, so I really didn't want to see him again."

"But you said he could call upon you here."

"Yes . . . I don't know what I was thinking. I had some idea of . . . Oh, never mind. It was foolish." She set down her empty glass. "We should go."

Her brother inclined his head in acknowledgment. He knew better than to press his sister when she made it clear she didn't want to talk anymore. He was intrigued, however. He draped her light evening cloak around her shoulders and held the door for her, following her down the stairs to the hall.

"Do you think Ma and Pa are enjoying themselves in Baden-Baden?" Petra asked as they stepped out into the warm evening. "I can't see Pa taking the waters, can you?"

"Only if it's liberally diluted with whisky," her brother returned with a chuckle. He waved down a passing hackney. "But you know our mother, she'll be perfectly happy

24

gossiping with her friends and complaining about how foul the water tastes."

"And making up for it with lavish dinners," Petra said with an affectionate smile. Sir Percy Rutherford and his wife, Lady Cecilia, were fond but benignly neglectful parents, happy to leave the upbringing of their children to nannies, governesses and boarding schools. Once they no longer required that supervision, their offspring were encouraged to pursue their own lives as they wished, never deprived of anything except timely advice. It had occurred to Petra with hindsight that her mother could probably have saved her from the dreadful mortification of her girlish infatuation with Lord Ashton if she'd troubled to take an interest in what her daughter was doing during that summer in the country.

The hackney turned onto Piccadilly, the pavements crowded with people from all walks of life taking the early summer air on a beautiful evening: shopgirls, maids on their evening off, barrow boys and street vendors, all jostling for space. The strains of a harmonica from a busker on the pavement filled the air as Jonathan and Petra stepped down from the cab outside the grand entrance to the Criterion. Jonathan dropped a coin into the musician's upturned cloth cap before ushering his sister through the Criterion's ornate doors into the marble entrance hall. Voices rose and fell from the Long Bar at the rear of the hall.

They climbed the wide staircase to the first-floor dining room where they were greeted by a frock-coated majordomo. "Colonel Lacy's party is already here, sir. May I take your cloak, Miss Rutherford?" He gestured to a liveried attendant, who immediately took Petra's cloak and her brother's hat, evening gloves and white scarf.

The majordomo led them across the marbled dining room to a table beside one of the long windows overlooking the bustle of Piccadilly.

"Forgive the gate-crasher intruder?" Jonathan said in smiling greeting as he brushed a kiss on the cheeks of the two women sitting at the table. "Rupert . . . Edward . . ." He held out his hand in greeting to the two men who had risen at the Rutherfords' approach.

"Delighted you could join us, Jonathan," Colonel Rupert Lacey said, before turning to greet Petra, who was embracing her friends. He kissed her and pulled out her chair for her.

"Champagne, Petra?" Edward Tremayne

26

gestured to a waiter to fill her glass.

"Yes, lovely, Edward, thank you." Petra looked around the table. "I haven't seen you in weeks."

"Only two weeks, dearest," Diana corrected. "Rupert and I were in Hampshire talking with Kimberley Diamond's trainer." Her eyes shone as she looked around the table. "He thinks she's ready for a big race. He's been trying her out on some local courses at very minor events, keeping her out of the public eye while she trained. He thinks we should spring her on the public at Ascot. Isn't that exciting?"

"Which race?" Fenella inquired, taking a sip of her champagne.

"The Queen Anne Stakes," Rupert replied.

"Yes, and we're going to have a big party in the Royal Enclosure," Diana said eagerly. "You'll all be there, of course."

"Of course we will," Petra and Fenella assured her almost in unison.

Fenella picked up her menu. "What do we usually eat here?"

Her husband glanced at his menu before regarding his wife with a half smile. "If I tell you what you usually eat you'll accuse me of telling you what to order," he said.

Fenella laughed. "He's only saying that

because once I said how nice it was to dine with a man who didn't tell me what I wanted to eat."

"Oh, Rupert does that all the time," Diana declared. "I'm quite used to it now."

"In that case," her husband said, "You'll be having the foie gras and coq au vin."

"Impossible man," Diana said. "As it happens it's exactly what I'd like."

Petra joined in the general amusement but once again she felt that stab of aloneness, of being an outsider in this circle. It was different when it was just herself and Diana and Fenella, then it was like the old days. *But was it?* Even as she asked herself the question she knew the answer. It wasn't quite the same. Marriage had added another dimension to her friends' lives, a different prism through which they viewed life. And Petra didn't have that dimension, or that prism.

Diana said suddenly, "I have to visit the ladies' room."

"Me too." Fenella pushed back her chair. "They're so splendidly luxurious here. Coming, Petra?"

Petra pushed back her own chair. "Yes, I'm coming."

Rupert watched the three of them weave their way through the tables. "Why do they always do that?" he asked.

"It's almost tribal," Edward said. "A kind of pack response."

"All for one and one for all." Jonathan added his pennyworth. "But I think Diana had something on her mind that she wanted to talk about with the other two."

"It was a rather sudden departure," Rupert agreed.

Edward shrugged. "Individually I understand them, but collectively . . ." He shook his head. "A very different matter."

The men had not seen what Diana had, attuned as she was to both her friends' moods. She had noticed the flash of sadness in Petra's hazel eyes, the sudden loss of vivacity on her mobile countenance. And she had responded automatically. If something was upsetting her friend, then something had to be done about it.

The opulence of the Criterion itself was carried into the ladies' room, where jugs of iris perfumed the air, and plush couches, gleaming vanities and gilded mirrors offered a cushioned sanctuary for its clients. An attendant in a black dress and crisply starched apron stood ready to repair a torn flounce, sew a loose button, hand out softly scented towels.

Diana cast a quick glance around and

29

said, "Good, we're alone for a moment." She sat down on one of the deeply cushioned couches and gestured to her friends to join her. "What's troubling you, Petra? You looked stricken suddenly."

"Yes, I noticed it too," Fenella said. "Has something happened, darling?" She put a comforting hand over Petra's.

Petra had always been cursed with a too expressive countenance. She had never been able to keep her emotions from showing on her face, or in her eyes. But she had no intention of telling her friends the real reason for that moment of sadness. However, she had an alternative account on offer.

"Have you come across Guy Granville?"

"Lord Ashton . . . only by repute," Fenella said with a slight frown. "He's something of a philanderer, isn't he?"

"According to the scandal sheets," Diana said. "I've seen him around, but he's not a regular on the society circuit. According to Rupert, he has his own exclusive circle who consider themselves too important to enjoy society's frivolity."

"He doesn't make any secret of his opposition to women's suffrage," Fenella said, still frowning. "He's always writing about it, and sending letters to the *Times*."

"All true," Petra responded. "Once upon a time I thought I was in love with him."

"What?" her friends demanded in unison.

She gave them a lighthearted account of the summer of Guy Granville, giving little indication of the depth of her hurt and mortification, before saying, "Anyway, I met him again this afternoon at Westminster. Joth invited him to tea because he wants his help with some legislation about draining the Levels, and he wanted me to turn on the charm, soften him up, as it were. Of course, he didn't know that I was probably the last person willing to do that."

"So what did you do?"

"I wasn't very friendly," Petra told them with a laugh. She was already feeling much better. "But then I had a vague idea that I might lead him on a little. Get him interested and then . . ."

"Drop him," Diana finished for her. "Sauce for the gander, as it were."

"Precisely," Petra declared. She stood up. "We really should go back to the table, the men will be wondering what we're doing."

"They'll probably have ordered for us," Fenella said with a laugh. "And perfectly entitled to do so in the circumstances."

She went to the mirror to adjust a hairpin in the thick chignon on her neck. Petra examined her complexion for flaws, dusting a little powder on her small nose, lamenting, "I wish I could get rid of those freckles."

"Nonsense," Diana said. "They're part of you. It's just a scattering on your nose. They go with your hair."

Petra was actually rather proud of her hair. It was thick, straight and a rich chestnut brown with streaks of a darker red. She wore it this evening in two plaits looped around her ears, beautifully set off by emerald eardrops and a necklace of the same.

"Come on, we *must* get back," Fenella urged, dropping a coin into a saucer for the attendant on her way to the door.

"Yes, we'll talk about revenge on the baron when we have time to discuss it properly," Diana stated, hurrying after her. "Shall we have coffee tomorrow?"

"Come to Brook Street," Petra invited, now totally restored to her usual lively humor. "We'll plan a strategy."

They returned to the table, where their escorts were visibly impatient and, having finished the champagne, most of the way through a bottle of Bordeaux. "We'd about given you up," Rupert said, standing up to pull back his wife's chair.

"Apologies," Fenella said, offering Edward a guilty smile as she took the chair he held for her. "We started talking about something and the time just ran away with us."

"Nothing new about that," Rupert said dryly. "If you're now here to stay perhaps we could order?"

"I really am sorry. It was my fault," Petra said without offering any further explanation. She picked up her menu again, glancing up at the attentive waiter. "I think I'd like the asparagus soup and then the rack of lamb, please."

CHAPTER THREE

Guy Granville walked into the marble hall on the ground floor of the Criterion, handing his hat and silver-knobbed cane to an attendant as he scrutinized the drinkers at the Long Bar at the rear of the hall. He raised a hand, acknowledging the greeting waves from a group of people sitting at a table, brandy goblets in front of them.

He was about to make his way across the hall when a familiar voice made him pause. He turned to look toward the grand staircase, where a small group was descending from the restaurant above. Petra Rutherford was in front, her head turned to the woman just behind her. She radiated vivacity and he remembered how that had been the first thing he'd noticed about her ten years ago, when she had caught his eye flinging herself into the steps of the Eight-some Reel in the ballroom of the Assembly Rooms in Bath, her sparkling hazel eyes laughing up at her partner, strands of that richly hued copper hair escaping its pins with the liveliness of the dance. She hadn't grown any taller since then, he thought with a half smile. She was still small but vivid, impossible to ignore or completely forget.

He stepped to the bottom of the staircase, one hand resting on the domed newel post as he waited for the party to reach him.

"Miss Petra Rutherford," he said, with a bow. "What a delightful surprise . . . twice in one day." Before she could gather her wits to respond, he had raised her hand, brought it to his lips, and then held it as she stepped off the stair and into the hall. "Gentlemen, ladies." He inclined his head in greeting to Petra's companions. "A good dinner, I hope."

"Excellent, thank you, Granville," Jonathan said. "Are you dining here yourself?"

"No, just meeting some friends in the bar," Guy answered, gesturing to the group across the hall. "I heard your voice, Petra, and had to say hello."

"Hello, Guy," Petra responded as coolly as she could. She still felt the residual pressure of his hand as he'd held on to hers a little too firmly and for just a moment longer than necessary, and she was for a moment unable to think of what to say next.

When it seemed she had nothing further to say, Guy offered a general good night and turned to make his way over to his friends.

"That wasn't very friendly, my dear," Rupert said with a slight raised eyebrow. "Has Lord Ashton offended you?"

Petra shrugged and laughed lightly. "Oh, years ago he did, and I haven't seen him to talk to since then, except this afternoon and just now." She shook her head. "I haven't decided whether I still dislike him as intensely as I used to." She watched Guy's arrival at his friends' table. A strikingly tall, elegant woman offered a languid hand in greeting and he raised it to his lips before bending to kiss her cheek. There was something about the seemingly ordinary salutation that sent prickles along Petra's spine.

"Who's that? The woman with Guy? Does anyone know?"

"That, dear Petra, is the Viscomtesse Clothilde Delmont," Edward informed her in a low voice. "Something of a mystery woman, but it's rumored that there's no mystery between herself and Granville. They're very well acquainted with each other's secrets."

"She's his mistress, you mean?" Petra asked, forcing herself to look away before anyone noticed her interest.

"So it's believed."

"She certainly stands out in a crowd," Diana observed. She frowned. "Something to be considered in our strategizing."

"What strategizing?" Rupert asked suspiciously. "What are you three cooking up now?"

"Absolutely nothing," his wife responded with a bland smile. "Nothing to concern you anyway, my love."

"If that's supposed to reassure me, it most certainly does not," Rupert declared, putting an arm around her shoulders and easing her toward the entrance. "It's time we went home. Say good night now."

Diana grinned. "Such a masterful man . . . Good night, all. I'll see you tomorrow at Petra's, Fenella."

"I'll expect you both around eleven." Petra blew her a farewell kiss, following with her brother, Fenella and Edward out into still thronged Piccadilly.

"We'll walk home," Fenella said, kissing her friend. "Shepherd Street is only around the corner."

Petra waved them goodbye as they disappeared into the crowd. "Let's walk home too, Joth. It's such a gorgeous night and I don't feel in the least tired. If my shoes bother me, I'll take them off and carry them."

Her brother hesitated a little awkwardly, "I was hoping you wouldn't mind taking a cab home without me. A group of us had planned to meet at the Reform later this evening. Asquith is going to be there."

"Then of course you must go," Petra said immediately. "You'll talk politics with the chancellor all night, and I wouldn't dream of standing in your way. I'll walk a little bit along Piccadilly and hail a cab the rest of the way home. Go on," she urged, seeing his hesitation. "I'll be perfectly fine. It's quite safe with all these people around."

Jonathan looked around, in two minds. There was no real reason for his sister not to take an unaccompanied stroll on a major thoroughfare on a summer night, but it seemed unchivalrous to abandon her. However, there was no knowing how long Asquith, the chancellor of the exchequer, would be at the Reform Club that night, and Jonathan was an ambitious young man. A rising Liberal politician had to ensure that the great and the good of his party took notice of him.

"If you're sure . . ."

"Of course I am." She gave him a little shove. "Go."

He smiled ruefully as he kissed her. "All right, but I feel horribly guilty."

"That'll pass as soon as you're in the fray," Petra retorted. She waved him away and set off along Piccadilly towards Berkeley Street. She'd decide when she got to the corner whether to hail a cab or carry on walking toward Berkeley Square and on to Brook Street.

She was glad that her brother had left her to make her own way home. The solitary walk might help to clear her head and ease the strange restlessness that her renewed encounter with Guy Granville had caused. It had never occurred to her that seeing him again after that long-ago debacle would make her feel anything other than a chilly indifference at best and a deep loathing at worst. Instead, she felt disturbed and out of sorts. And for some reason she couldn't lose the image of him greeting the elegant Frenchwoman. There had been something about his seemingly casual kiss of greeting that, even across the room, shouted of intimacy, a secret, passionate intimacy.

They were lovers, so what? It was nothing to do with her. But somehow Petra couldn't manage to convince herself of that. In the ten years since she'd talked to him, Guy had probably had dozens of lovers. His reputation as a philanderer was well known. She hadn't thought twice about it when she could only expect to catch the occasional glimpse of him moving within his own social circles, quite separate from her own. But he'd stepped back into her life and his manner toward her was far from that of a casual old acquaintance, even if it wasn't obvious to anyone else. She could still feel the warmth of his hand against her palm, still feel his deep brown eyes fixed upon her face expressing something other than mild interest.

She had reached the corner with Berkeley Street without noticing the distance she'd walked, but now her feet in the high-heeled shoes were hurting. She wasn't tired, apart from her feet, home was less than half a mile away and the evening was still pleasant. There were fewer pedestrians around now that she'd left the busyness of Piccadilly behind but the streetlamps were lit along Berkeley Street and around the square at the end, and the houses lining the street threw reassuring arcs of golden light onto the pavement.

Impulsively she took off her shoes and set off up the street, carrying them. The pavement felt pleasantly cool beneath her feet and she strode out toward the square enjoy-

ing the sense of freedom. A hackney over-
took her as she neared the railings of the
square garden and pulled up to the curb a
few houses along. Its passenger stepped
down, reaching up to pay the driver.

Even if she hadn't been thinking of him a
few minutes earlier, Petra would have
recognized Guy immediately. He stood
under the gas lamp shining over the double
front doors of a handsome double-fronted
mansion. Petra hesitated, waiting for him to
go into the house, but he remained on the
pavement, tapping his cane against his leg
as he looked down the street toward her.

Her heart seemed to speed up. He was
obviously waiting for her to reach him. For
a second she toyed with the idea of turning
back, going around the opposite side of the
square to avoid passing him, and immediately realized how stupid that would be. She
had absolutely no reason to avoid him. She
wasn't trespassing, she was as much entitled
to be on the square as anyone, not that there
was anyone else around, as far as a quick
glance revealed.

She squared her shoulders and walked a
little faster toward him. "Good evening
again," she called cheerfully, when she was
a few feet from him. "You didn't stay long
with your friends at the bar."

"No," he agreed. "Why are you walking alone?"

"Because I wish to. It's a beautiful night," she returned, hackles rising at the rather peremptory tone.

"I won't argue with that. Where's your brother?"

"Going about his own business," she responded, an edge to her voice.

"He allowed you to walk home alone?"

"I don't need my brother's permission to do anything." Petra made no attempt now to conceal her irritation. Whatever nervousness she'd felt earlier had dissipated under this cross-examination. "Good evening, Lord Ashton." She made to walk past him but he put a hand on her arm.

"If you were my sister I would not leave you to walk the city streets alone at this time of night."

"Then it's fortunate for both of us that I'm not." She shook off his hand and started to walk away.

"Indubitably," he returned with a dry smile. Then he frowned, taking in her appearance properly for the first time. "Just a minute, Petra. Are you intending to walk all the way to Brook Street in your stockinged feet?" He stepped up beside her as she continued on her way, trying very hard not to hobble.

"Yes, why not?"

"I'd have thought that was obvious," he answered. "You might step in something nasty or sharp. There are loose stones all over the place."

Why did he have to sound so reasonable, so rational? Why couldn't he have said something infuriating about it being inappropriate or irresponsible, or just wrong for a woman of her position to walk barefoot through the streets of London? All of which would have been perfectly true, but she would have felt entitled to object to such objections. Instead Petra said nothing, merely increased her speed, hoping for a nonchalant stride, her shoes dangling carelessly from her hands, trying to ignore him as he continued to keep pace with her.

But there was too much of him to ignore, even when he wasn't saying anything. "I really don't need an escort, Guy. I'm sure you must have better things to do."

"As it happens I don't find that I do," he said. "Your stockings are shredded."

As if she wasn't aware of that fact, or for the sharply unfriendly ground beneath her bare feet, Petra thought, seething silently. She caught her foot in a tree root pushing up through the cracks of the paving stones and momentarily off-balance grabbed the iron railings in front of the house she was passing to steady herself, but not before Guy had caught her around the waist, pulling her against him, bringing them both to a stop.

"Dear girl, why won't you accept that this is ridiculous and let me hail a cab?"

A lamentable stubborn streak had bedeviled Petra since the nursery. Every reasonable bone in her body said she should yield and be grateful, but she couldn't bring herself to give in. She pushed away his supporting arm and walked on, once more trying not to limp.

Guy watched her for a moment. She had always been a spirited creature, even as a girl. Her size didn't diminish that spirit in the least. And her girlhood promise had certainly been fulfilled, he reflected with a half smile, watching her striding along in her stockinged feet. Her chestnut hair gleamed, richly burnished under the streetlights, and those hazel eyes snapped as fiercely now as they had done all those years ago when something had annoyed her. At the moment, it seemed, he was the cause of her annoyance, but she really couldn't walk alone carrying her shoes through the nighttime streets of Mayfair.

44

He followed just behind her as Petra reached the corner of the square, preparing to limp across Mount Street, picking her way over the dirty paving. A hackney came up behind Guy and he flagged it down.

"Wait just a minute," he said to the driver, then strode quickly to where Petra was about to step into the crossing. He caught her arm. "Don't argue, Petra. If you're not careful you'll walk straight through that pile of horse dung in the middle of the road. Brook Street is two streets away and you really can't walk it without shoes." Still holding her arm he turned to the hackney that eased forward to draw up beside them. He opened the door. "Get in, please."

It was the only rational, sensible thing to do, Petra knew. Her bare feet were not standing up well to the grit and grime of London pavements. But every ounce of her wanted to resist his assumption of control. It reminded her too vividly of the past when she had somehow accepted his direction because, foolish child that she'd been, she'd believed his dictates were evidence of his caring. He was older, wiser, more experienced than herself, still a schoolgirl, and his every word carried the weight of that superiority.

She'd grown out of that illusion quickly

enough, Petra thought grimly, but she was no longer foolish. She stepped up into the hackney without acknowledging Guy's assistance. He stepped inside behind her, pulling the door closed.

"It's not necessary to see me to my door," she protested. "I can take myself home."

"Maybe so," he agreed, leaning back against the cracked leather squabs, watching her from beneath half-closed eyelids. "But I like to finish what I started, and I'm not lacking in chivalry."

"Oh, really?" Petra demanded. "Since when did you acquire that quality?"

Guy sat upright, his eyes opening fully. "I beg your pardon?"

"Oh, I think you heard me." Petra was regretting her remark, but she couldn't see how to back away from it. "Ten years ago, chivalry was not your forte, as I recall."

His frown deepened as he cast a quick glance through the cab window. He banged on the roof of the cab with the knob of his cane and it drew to a halt outside the Rutherfords' house on Brook Street. "We'll talk about this in a minute," he promised, swinging open the cab door and jumping to the ground. He paid the driver while Petra stepped gingerly down to the pavement, still clutching her shoes. A helping hand to alight

46

would have been appreciated, she thought. Much more so than the other unwanted helping hands he'd offered in the last half hour.

She walked up the short flight of steps to the front door, tucking a shoe under her arm as she fumbled to open the drawstring of the silk pouch that held her keys. Guy came up behind her, twitched the bag out of her grasp, deftly loosened the neck and took out the keys. He held the bunch up to the lamp above the door, selected one and maneuvered it into the lock. The door swung open onto the deserted hall. Without a word he extricated the key from the lock, dropped the set into her bag and handed it back to her.

The whole business had happened so fast and so smoothly that Petra hadn't had time to react. She was still searching for coherence as he urged her into the square hall with a hand at her waist and closed the door behind them. She took a breath and managed to say, "I don't mean to be inhospitable, but I'm going to bed."

"Not until you've explained what you meant," he stated, his voice clipped. "We can stand here in the hall while you explain yourself, if you wish, but explain yourself you will."

CHAPTER FOUR

Petra gathered her thoughts in the suddenly menacing silence. The household had all gone to bed. She and her brother were much less demanding than the elder Rutherfords and never kept the staff waiting up for them at night, which meant she had no diversion to hand. If Foster, the butler, had still been up and about she could easily have fobbed off her unwelcome visitor. As it was, she could see no way out of this uncomfortable conversation.

She hadn't meant to let her tongue run away with her, but it had and she'd accused Guy of behaving badly. He was entitled to an explanation, although she couldn't understand how he didn't seem to know what pain he'd caused her. But perhaps he'd forgotten all about her. Out of sight out of mind. She must have meant so little to him it hadn't occurred to him that she had feelings of her own. The bitter reflection restored her confidence. She was entirely justified in wishing Guy Granville, Lord Ashton, to Hades.

"There's no need to stand here, and the marble's cold on my feet. Come into the library." She turned and led the way to the library at the back of the house.

Foster had left two sconced gas lamps turned down low on either side of the mantel, and a copper jug of sunflowers stood in the empty hearth. Charged decanters were arrayed on the sideboard, cut glass tumblers beside them, together with a cheese board under a glass dome and a biscuit barrel in case the younger members of the family or their guests had need of late-night sustenance.

She dropped her shoes on the floor and walked across the thick Aubusson carpet, her sore feet sinking gratefully into the deep pile. "Cognac? Or whisky?" She laid a hand on the decanters on the sideboard, turning to face him with a bland smile of invitation.

He tossed his hat and cane onto a pier table. "Cognac, please."

Petra poured two goblets and handed him one before curling into the corner of a deeply cushioned sofa, drawing her feet up. She examined their filthy soles, looking for scrapes or cuts. "Good, it just seems to be dirt," she remarked, abandoning her examination and taking a sip from her goblet.

"How very fortunate," Guy said dryly, standing with his back to the sunflowers, cradling his goblet between his hands. "I accept that that's not a very chivalrous response, but in the circumstances it's difficult to think of something more suitable. What an insane thing to do."

"It struck me as eminently sane," she retorted. "It was a solution to a problem."

He shrugged. "So? What's all this about chivalry, or rather my lack of it?"

Maybe it was better to have it out. It wouldn't diminish her wish for revenge, but clearing the decks might make it easier for her. Revenge was simple and clear, the old muddled anger would only confuse things. She regarded him over the lip of her glass. "What did you think you were doing all those years ago, Guy? Did you set out to make me think I was in love with you just for a game?"

He looked astounded. "You weren't in love with me, for God's sake. You were a child, a schoolgirl."

"And perfectly capable of thinking myself in love. I was just ripe for the plucking," she said. "A perfect toy for your games."

"You were lovely," he said slowly.

50

"Sweet . . . no," he corrected himself, "not sweet, that's too pale a description for you. You had spirit and a lively mind, you laughed so much. I loved to hear you laugh. And, yes, you were an innocent. I didn't think I took advantage of that innocence, though. You seemed well able to respond to me in kind."

"And when you had had enough playtime with me, you just went away," she stated flatly. "Without a word."

Guy frowned, trying to remember what had seemed so unimportant to him at the time, but clearly so important to Petra. "Oh, yes, I remember now. Surely I mentioned that I had an invitation to go to Nice with some friends. That was always the case, from the beginning of the summer. I never intended to stay in Ashton for the entire summer. You must have realized that."

She shook her head. "No, why would I realize it? You never mentioned it, otherwise I wouldn't have been so . . ." She stopped, the memory of her emotional distress at the time too painful and humiliating to dwell on.

Guy looked at her in puzzlement. "But my dear girl, I was twenty-four, having a few weeks in the country. I had spent a year touring Europe after coming down from

Oxford, and was starting to think about what I was going to do in the real world. You surely couldn't have thought that I'd stay rusticating in Somerset."

Petra sipped her cognac. She had had enough of the conversation, all it was doing was making her mortification even worse. Of course she'd believed he would stay throughout that summer, how could he not? He was in love with her, as she'd thought, until he disappeared and she understood that love hadn't come anywhere near what he'd felt for her, if indeed he'd felt anything.

"I don't know what I thought. But as far as I'm concerned you led me to trust you and I was too much of a simpleton to realize that you were simply amusing yourself." She uncurled from the sofa and crossed to the sideboard to refill her glass.

"Then I can only say how sorry I am," Guy said slowly. "I promise you it was never my intention to hurt you. I still don't quite understand. . . ." He let the words fade, realizing that they were only going to make things worse.

She shrugged, turning toward him with the decanter raised in mute invitation. Despite the dismissive shrug, Guy saw the stricken vulnerability in her hazel eyes, the remembered pain of a long-ago hurt. Impulsively he set down his glass, crossed to her in two long strides. He took the decanter from her and replaced it on the sideboard. "I am so sorry," he murmured, running a finger across her lips before lowering his head and brushing light kisses on her eyelids. He caressed the curve of her cheek, then lifted her chin on his forefinger.

Petra was frozen, she wanted to slap his hands away, thrust him from her, and yet she couldn't seem to make the necessary moves. His mouth touched hers, gently at first, his tongue tasting her lips. And when she didn't object the kiss became stronger, more demanding. He wasn't holding her, except for the fingertip beneath her chin. The slightest move would put distance between them and yet she couldn't make that move. Until abruptly she took control of herself and moved her head sideways, breaking the contact.

Guy raised his head, a smile playing over his mouth. "Just as sweet and delicious as I remember." He reached for her hand, enclosing it between his palms, twining his fingers with hers, saying with a wickedly inviting smile, "All-grown-up Petra . . . I can't think why I've allowed you to drift out of my life, but I intend to make up for lost time." He touched his lips to the corner of her mouth. "Will you have dinner with me on Wednesday?"

Petra struggled with her composure. She was outraged that he thought he could kiss it all away just as he had done once all those years ago, when he'd picked her up after her horse, balking at a difficult jump, had unseated her. Although, as she recalled that incident with the clarity of hindsight, as soon as he'd picked her up off the ground and dusted her off, he'd immediately turned his attention to her horse . . . and spent a lot longer checking the animal's forelocks for swelling and sprains than he had on Petra's bruises. And she hadn't minded at all, so intoxicated was she by Guy Granville's attention, however cursory.

The elegant image of the French vicomtesse abruptly popped into her mind and her anger surged anew. How dared he think he could start up a flirtation with her again, after everything she'd said, and particularly now, when he was in an open liaison with another woman? She inhaled sharply and immediately caught the scent of him, a hint of lemon verbena, a musky earthiness beneath. It flooded her with sensual memory and absently she touched her lips, feeling the residual sensation of his kiss.

54

"Wake up," Guy said, still smiling. "I seem to have put you to sleep."

Petra gave herself a vigorous mental shake. "Of course you haven't," she stated. "But I've been ready for my bed this last hour. Let me show you out."

"You haven't answered my question," he prompted, not moving as she walked to the door.

"What question?" She looked at him blankly, deliberately keeping all expression from her countenance.

"I asked if you'd have dinner with me on Wednesday." He raised an inquiring eyebrow.

"No," she said shortly, and then realized how very rude she sounded. Behaving like an ill-bred schoolgirl would merely increase her present disadvantage. "No, I'm sorry. I'm otherwise engaged on Wednesday."

He bowed in acceptance, picking up his hat and cane from the pier table. "Another time, then." He walked past her as she held the door for him. "I suggest you soak your feet in warm water before you put them between the sheets."

Petra's eyes widened in disbelief. "You are all condescension, my lord."

He laughed, opening the front door. "Don't forget to lock up behind me." His laughter drifted back down the street as he strode toward Berkeley Square.

Petra shot the bolts on the door with almost vicious satisfaction and taking her cognac with her limped her way upstairs. Her bed was turned down, the gas lamp throwing a soft golden glow over the comfortable bedroom. She peeled off her ruined stockings, discarded her dress and petticoat and sat on the edge of the bathtub in the adjoining bathroom, turning on the hot tap, wriggling her toes under the soothing stream as she sipped the cognac.

She was all at sixes and sevens, she thought crossly. The purity of her dislike for Guy Granville was now sullied with unwanted responses to his physical presence and a host of memories of the good times that summer. Oh, she could still conjure the bad aftermath, but now the good intruded on the clarity of that long-ago hurt. But he was still arrogant, still condescending, still too sure of the effect he had on women, all women, she remembered now. It had been the same ten years ago, but she had been so flattered to be the focus of his attention she hadn't given a second thought to his flirtations with anyone else. And there had been plenty of them, she thought with the inconvenience of hindsight.

Gingerly Petra stepped onto the bath mat and hopped to the dresser stool to dry her feet. At least they were now clean, although still sore. She brushed her teeth, shrugged into her nightgown, unpinned her hair and pulled a cursory brush through the chestnut tangle, drained her glass, turned out the gas and slipped into bed.

"Lordy, Miss Petra, what 'appened to your stockings?"

Petra opened her eyes onto her now sun-filled bedroom and struggled up against the pillows. "I had to walk home without my shoes, Dottie," she mumbled to her maid, who was looking aghast at the strips of shredded silk she'd picked up off the floor.

"Whatever for?" the girl asked, discarding the ruined stockings and picking up the apple-green gown Petra had dropped over a chair.

"Heels," Petra said succinctly, leaning sideways to take the cup of tea on her bedside table. "They hurt my feet."

"Not made for walking." Dottie pointed out the obvious as she hung the dress in the wardrobe. "Will you go downstairs for breakfast?"

Petra glanced at the pretty ormolu clock on the mantel. It was gone nine o'clock and

Diana and Fenella would be here at eleven. "No, I'll have an egg and some toast and coffee up here, please. Could you run my bath?"

She sipped her tea, considering the events of the previous evening, and found that she was still as confused by her feelings as ever. When she thought of how he smiled that condescending smile, of the lightly patronizing tone of his voice, she felt only the familiar intense dislike, but then her body let her down. Her body remembered the feel and the scent of him, the warmth of his eyes when they were fixed upon her, as if they saw only her, and no one else existed outside the charmed circle of his gaze. And she went all gooey, Petra thought disgustedly, setting her empty cup aside.

She pushed aside the covers and stood up, wincing a little as her feet hit the ground. She wriggled her toes experimentally against the carpet. How stupid could she be, she reflected with the same disgust. Of course her feet were bruised even if they weren't cut. And that was bound to affect her plans for the day.

"Dottie, do we have any witch hazel or arnica?" she asked, going into the bathroom. "My feet are a bit bruised."

"I'll bring you some, miss." Dottie

straightened from testing the temperature of the bathwater. "I think there's arnica in the still room. What clothes shall I put out for you this morning?"

Petra considered. "The bronze silk shirt and cream skirt, I think. I'm expecting guests later this morning so I won't be going out until this afternoon."

She lay back in the hot water, reflecting on how much about the previous evening's encounter she wanted to share with Diana and Fenella. Not so long ago the question would never have arisen, she'd have told them everything, down to the smallest detail, but things were a little different now. They would still want to know, still be interested in whatever was going on in Petra's life, but now there were aspects of their own married lives that they would not share with one another. Petra understood that, and she would never pry into those marital nooks and crannies, but she felt that her own life was still an open book for her friends; she had no one whose secrets with herself were sacrosanct.

And that made her wonder if her own affairs seemed trivial now to her friends. But they could still amuse themselves, still play the games that had always given them so much fun. Developing a plan of well-deserved revenge on Guy Granville would be a happy diversion. After that kiss, which he'd treated with such careless flippancy, the baron deserved everything they could come up with.

Petra rose dripping from the water and reached for a bath towel. Her spirits were restored and she was hungry. She dried rapidly and, pushing her arms into the wide kimono sleeves of a silk negligee, went back to the bedroom.

Dottie was setting a round table in the bow window that looked over the small walled garden at the rear of the house. The fragrance of fresh coffee mingled with the heady scent of wall flowers rising from the bed beneath the open window. A bee buzzed lazily in the wisteria framing the window. Petra sat down and shook out her napkin. "Thank you, Dottie. I seem to be ravenous." She tapped the top of her egg to crack the shell.

"I found witch hazel," Dottie said, shaking a small bottle. "Mrs. Evans said it's better than arnica for bruises."

"Mrs. Evans is always right," Petra said with a chuckle. The housekeeper had been with the Rutherford family since she and Jonathan were children and her word was always law.

"If you rest your foot on this stool, Miss Petra, I'll put some on for you." Dottie pushed a velvet stool to the table, drew the cork on the bottle and sprinkled some of the liquid onto a gauze pad.

Petra obliged, offering up first one foot and then the other for her maid to daub with the soaked gauze. "That feels so cool and soothing. Thank you, Dottie."

"They don't look too bad to me," the girl said, peering closely at the soles of Petra's feet. "Why'd you go and do something daft like that, Miss Petra?"

Dottie, who was about the same age as her mistress and had been looking after her since Petra had first put up her hair, never stood on ceremony and Petra never thought twice about the informality of their relationship.

"Maybe I'd had a glass of wine too many," she offered with a grin, buttering a slice of toast. "It seemed perfectly logical at the time."

Dottie laughed, shaking her head as she began to lay out undergarments on the bed before turning to the wardrobe for the shirt and skirt. "I went along to the meeting at Caxton Hall last night, miss. Mrs. Emmeline Pankhurst was speaking. She said we was a suffrage army in the field. I never thought of it like that before . . . an army . . . means fighting, don't it?" She paused in the act of smoothing the folds of the skirt. "Makes me a bit uneasy, miss, if I tell the truth. Don't see meself marchin' into battle."

"No, and you won't have to, Dottie. No one will have to do anything they don't want to do," Petra reassured. "There are other ways of supporting the cause. Leafletting, joining a parade, going to meetings."

"Well, I don't mind doing any of that," the girl said, laying the skirt carefully on the bed. "But there was talk of throwin' things at the police an' stuff. I don't hold with any o' that. It's as much as my job's worth."

"Your job's always safe, Dottie," Petra said. But she knew what the maid meant. Working-class supporters of the cause were particularly vulnerable if their support became known to their employers, who were more likely to be against the idea of women's suffrage than in favor of it. Petra wasn't even sure where her mother stood on the subject, or indeed her father. Her best guess was that they were probably totally indifferent to the whole issue. Politics had never engaged either of them. Their only son's political aspirations were a puzzle and when Joth was elected to Parliament they had offered bemused congratulations, thrown a dinner party in his honor, and as far as Petra knew never mentioned the matter again.

CHAPTER FIVE

"Interesting choice of footwear, darling," Diana declared as she entered the small parlor in Brook Street that Petra had appropriated as her own.

Petra laughed, extending a leg and wriggling her toes in the soft furry slippers. "My feet need coddling," she explained. "I abused them badly last evening."

"Oh, tell me more." Diana, sensing a good story, cast aside her straw hat and gloves and took a seat in a deep armchair opposite the sofa where Petra sat.

"It seemed like a good idea at the time," Petra said ruefully. She reached behind her for the bellpull on the wall beside the fireplace. "Let's get coffee."

Fenella arrived with the parlor maid and the coffee. She too looked askance at her friend's slippers.

"Thank you, Mary. Leave the tray here and I'll pour," Petra instructed the maid.

"Well, here's the story of my stubborn idiocy," she said, taking up the silver pot and pouring a fragrant stream into the three cups.

"I suppose, if Guy hadn't inserted himself so autocratically into the situation, I would have hailed a cab sooner," she finished. "And if he hadn't forced me into the cab I probably would never have accused him of lack of chivalry and opened that whole can of worms."

"Are you sorry you did?" Fenella asked, leaning forward to refill her cup.

Petra shook her head. "Not really." She had told most of the truth of the previous evening's events, but not quite all. She couldn't bring herself to discuss her inconvenient physical reaction to the baron's kiss and the host of sensual memories it had evoked. "It's actually a relief to have let it go finally. It was a rancid resentment that I'd been holding for too long."

"Mmm," Diana murmured. "So you've given up thoughts of revenge?"

"Not exactly," Petra confessed. "But it doesn't feel so grimly vengeful. I just feel like giving him a taste of his own medicine, but more as a game rather than something deadly serious. If you see what I mean."

"Absolutely," Fenella said. "And a little

gentle payback seems a much healthier plan, rather than a full-blown Shakespearean vengeance."

Petra laughed. "That was never my intention. I'd just held on to my anger too long. But now it's gone, or the historical anger anyway. I still resent his condescension. It's as if he still sees me as the besotted schoolgirl on her summer holidays."

"Well, we can soon put a stop to that," Diana stated. "We need to —" A light rat-a-tat on the door interrupted her.

Petra knew her brother's knock and was not surprised when he pushed open the door. But she was surprised to see his companion. Guy Granville came in just behind Jonathan.

"Ladies, good morning," Joth said cheerfully. "I met Granville on the doorstep. He was coming to ask after Petra and her feet. I can't imagine why, but looking at your slippers, sister dear, I'm guessing there's a good reason."

"Oh, for heaven's sake," Petra said, unable to conceal her exasperation. "There's nothing the matter with my feet. I'm wearing slippers because I'm not going out this morning and they're comfortable."

"I'm delighted to hear it," Guy said, taking her hand and lightly brushing it with his lips. "Mrs. Lacey, Mrs. Tremayne." He bowed to Diana and Fenella.

"Granville and I are going to lunch at the Savoy. We'd be delighted to have your company, if you all have no other plans," Joth said with an expansive gesture. "I have a meeting in the House later this afternoon and Granville is going to offer his support for my Levels drainage bill in the Lords this evening, so we need a good lunch for fortification."

Petra smiled. Jonathan was always so enthusiastic and uninhibited. He never tried to conceal his pleasure, his enthusiasms, or his angers, she reflected. He had no artifice about him at all. Sometimes she worried he might be hurt by his openness, particularly in matters of the heart, but so far he seemed to have had smooth sailing in that regard.

"May I second the invitation?" Guy said, taking a seat on the sofa next to Petra as she gestured faintly in invitation. He turned toward her. "If you're sure your feet are up to wearing ordinary shoes."

"If you don't stop talking about my feet, Lord Ashton, I shall retreat to my bedroom, wrap myself in a cashmere shawl and soak them in a mustard bath for the rest of the day," she retorted.

He laughed. "Very well. I shall never mention them again. Do say you'll come for lunch, Petra?"

The personal feel of the request in front of her friends took her aback. It seemed as if he was somehow staking a claim to her personal consideration. A general invitation, supported by her brother, was one thing, quite unexceptionable, but there was implied intimacy in his voice that bordered on the particular.

Diana coughed discreetly and Fenella said somewhat hesitantly, "I have a play reading to go to this afternoon."

"But you have to have lunch," Diana stated, catching Petra's urgent glance. "I have an appointment later, but I can certainly join you for lunch."

"Yes," Fenella agreed. "I'd be delighted."

"Good." Joth pulled the bell rope. "Sherry or claret, Granville? I know these three will have sherry."

"So predictable," Petra said with a mock sigh. "Come upstairs with me," she gestured to her friends as she uncurled herself from the sofa and stood up, glad that she could do so without wincing. "I need to find shoes." She walked to the door, showing no sign of discomfort. Although she was aware of her bruised soles, she would not give Guy the satisfaction.

Fenella and Diana followed her. "Foster, could you send sherry up to my room," Petra asked as the butler appeared in answer to Jonathan's summons.

"Right away, Miss Petra."

Petra hurried up the stairs to her bedroom, her friends on her heels. "So, what do you think is going on?" she asked, closing the door behind them with a decisive click.

"Well, it seems to me that Lord Ashton is interested in pursuing something with Miss Petra Rutherford," Diana said, sitting on the daybed beneath the window. "What d'you think, Fenella?"

"The same," Fenella said, frowning a little. "But it seems a bit like he's playing a game. He seems to be smiling to himself."

"Exactly," Petra agreed, peering into her wardrobe at the array of neatly paired shoes. "These should do." She backed out with a pair of soft bronze kid shoes with a small heel. "It's his manner, and now I think of it, it was exactly the same ten years ago. But I found it attractive then," she added a trifle glumly. "More fool me."

"He certainly seems somewhat complacent," Diana stated. "I always find infuriating that air of superior certainty that some men have, and Lord Ashton has it in spades. It might be amusing to see if we could deflate him a little."

Petra shook her head. "D'you really think that's possible?"

"I don't see why not," Fenella said, and then fell silent as Dottie came in with the sherry.

"Do you need my help, Miss Petra?" Dottie set down the tray. "Should I get the witch hazel again?"

"No, I think my feet are much better, thank you, Dottie." Petra sat down to slip her feet into the kid shoes. She wriggled her toes experimentally before standing up. "If I avoid walking on hard surfaces as far as possible I'll be fine," she concluded, after taking a few steps. "That'll be all, Dottie, thank you."

She passed around the sherry glasses as the maid left, then took a deep draft from her own glass. "What's your idea, Fenella?"

"Much like what you hinted at before. Guy Granville's interested in you and makes no secret of it. He's so accustomed to women falling all over themselves for his attention, I imagine he'd be somewhat piqued by one who appeared to treat him with a degree of indifference. Not hostility," she said, "just a casual, take-him-or-leave-him attitude. Perfectly friendly but make him realize that when you spend time with him

70

it's only because it suits you."

"I use him as he used me," Petra said with a little nod of satisfaction.

"And then we find you another suitor," Diana said, her eyes gleaming with enthusiasm. "You start slowly, a little playful flirtation, and then you increase your evident interest in the new man and . . ." She smiled. "I'm willing to bet that his lordship will not like playing second fiddle."

"No," Petra agreed, taking a smaller sip of her sherry. "No, I'm sure he won't."

"Don't forget Madame La Vicomtesse," Diana put in, moving to the dressing table, taking up Petra's silver comb to tuck a stray wisp of hair behind her ears, where diamond studs glistened in the sunlight from the open window.

"No, and if she's his mistress, why would he be interested in me?" Petra asked.

"The vicomtesse spends quite a lot of the time away from London," Fenella said, her fingers readjusting the elegant rose silk scarf at her throat. The unusual sapphires on the bracelet at her wrist seemed to change color as her hands changed position in the light. "I'm guessing Granville would think pursuing a flirtation with you while the Frenchwoman is unavailable is perfectly acceptable."

"Variety is the spice of life, after all," Diana added with a cynical twist of her lips. "Are we ready?"

"In a moment, if I could borrow my comb back." Petra moved to the dressing table, holding her comb as she examined her reflection critically. "Can I get away with leaving my hair like this?" She hadn't troubled with her coiffure that morning as she hadn't intended to leave the house, and had simply pulled her thick luxuriant locks into a fat knot on the nape of her neck. Unruly strands that had escaped the pins wisped around her face.

"It gives you a rather delightfully careless air," Diana said. "It suits you. You've never wanted to look perfect, there's always something a little outré about you. It's your style."

"Outré," Petra said, grimacing. "Is that supposed to be a compliment?"

"Take it as such, dearest. It's merely a statement of fact. It's you, anything else would be artificial." Diana drank the last of her sherry. "If we're ready, let the games begin."

Petra adjusted several hairpins, took a light copper–colored bolero jacket from her wardrobe and followed her friends back downstairs.

"Foster has sent someone to fetch a couple of hackneys for us," Jonathan told them as they reentered the parlor. "They should be here by now." He set down his empty glass, flung out an all-encompassing arm in the direction of his sister and her friends and swept them out into the hall. Guy finished his whisky in a more leisurely fashion before following them outside, where two cabs awaited, one seating four comfortably, the other only two.

"Rutherford, you escort Mrs. Lacey and Mrs. Tremayne. Your sister and I will take the second one."

Petra opened her mouth to object but her brother was already handing Diana and Fenella into the larger of the cabs. Guy had taken her elbow and was turning her toward the smaller vehicle before she could summon a reasonable protest. She climbed up into the carriage wondering how he had managed so smoothly and swiftly to maneuver four independent-minded people into the positions he'd chosen for them.

"There now," Guy said with a note of satisfaction, taking his seat beside her. "You look a little put out, Petra. Are you?"

She shook her head. It was a perfectly sensible traveling arrangement, there was no point feeling manipulated, even if she had been. Besides, she was supposed to be showing only a careless, friendly indifference to the man; expressing annoyance would give him the opposite impression.

"Of course not. How could anyone be put out on such a glorious day?" She gave him a bland smile, folding her hands in her lap. "I'm surprised you don't have one of those motors, Guy. I would have thought you'd have been one of the first to drive one."

He raised an eyebrow. "Why do you assume I haven't one?"

"Because you're sitting in a hackney," she responded.

"As it happens I do own a motor, but I don't use it around town. There's too much horse traffic."

"I can see your point," Petra said agreeably. "Do you keep it at Ashton Court?"

"I do." He turned his head to look at her. "Perhaps later this summer, after the Season, I'll persuade you to join a small house party at Ashton Court and I'll show you the pleasures of a leisurely drive around the countryside. It's very pretty around there."

"I know it is," she said. "I live there myself, if you remember."

"Ah, yes, so you do. How unchivalrous of me to forget."

"Oh, I wouldn't say that," she responded

with a mock frown. "You can't be expected to remember everything, after all it's been ten years since we last spoke. I'm sure you haven't given that summer a second thought."

Guy's eyebrows lifted. "Petra, how long am I going to pay for an act that I freely admit now was both discourteous and unthinking?"

"You brought it up," she pointed out. "You mentioned chivalry, or rather its lack." She smiled suddenly. "Shall we consign the past to the devil? It was a long time ago and I certainly was a very different person then."

"I'd like to think I was too," he said. "So yes, let's please call a truce. I would like very much to get to know the grown-up Miss Rutherford, if you'll allow me to?" He laid a hand on her knee, his head tilted as he regarded her quizzically.

Petra remembered just in time that she was receiving the undivided attention of an expert seducer. His moves were practiced and presumably he was accustomed to their success. She lifted his hand and gave it back to him with a calm deliberation. "If we continue to see each other around town, Guy, I'm sure we'll become better acquainted."

Something flashed in the dark depths of

his eyes, then he inclined his head in mute acknowledgment, saying nothing more until the carriage drew up underneath the portico of the Savoy. He jumped down, reaching up a hand to help her alight.

"Thank you." Petra took his hand, jumping lightly to the cobbled carriageway before the ornate doors to the hotel. She shook out the folds of her skirt, waiting as the hackney in front disgorged its passengers.

"If you're agreeable, Petra, we thought we'd like to lunch in the River Room rather than the Grill," Diana said, coming over to her. "The river's so lively on a day like this."

"Absolutely," Petra agreed. "Is that all right with you, Guy?" She offered him a friendly smile.

"Your wish, my dear girl, will always be my command," he returned with an exaggerated flourish. "Rutherford, I'm going ahead to see about a table, if you'd like to escort the ladies."

Petra glanced at Diana and Fenella, who both raised inquiring eyebrows. "How was the drive?" Diana asked quietly as Jonathan finished paying their cab driver.

"Interesting," Petra returned as softly. "But if I'm to pull this off I'll have to keep my guard up."

She touched a finger to her lips in warning as Jonathan came up. "Shall we go?" He gestured they should go ahead of him as the doorman opened the double doors and they stepped into the hotel's cool, high-ceilinged lobby.

Guy was talking to the maître d'hôtel outside the entrance to the River Room. He waved them over. "How fortunate, Christophe has a window table for us."

"If you'd like to come this way, my lord, mesdames, monsieur." Christophe walked through the busy dining room. At first glance, it seemed to Petra that all the tables were occupied, but the maître d'hôtel moved unerringly to the far end of the dining room where a table stood in semi-seclusion in a window embrasure overlooking the river.

They took their seats and almost immediately a waiter appeared with a bottle, which he showed to Guy, who glanced at it and nodded. "I thought a cool glass of Puligny-Montrachet might be welcome to start with."

The pale straw–colored wine was poured into crystal glasses, the bottle ensconced in an ice bucket on a side table, and Guy raised his glass. "To present company."

It was a perfect toast, elegant, courteous and inclusive. "To present company," Petra returned with the rest of them. She took a sip of the crisp, cold liquid, reflecting that Guy must have ordered the wine at the same time he had somehow arranged this private table on the spur of the moment in a full restaurant. "Weren't we lucky to be able to get this table?" she observed, watching Guy over the lip of her glass.

"Ah, well," Guy said with a little smile, "I happen to know that Christophe keeps this particular table free just in case someone he likes comes in unexpectedly."

"And, of course, he likes Lord Ashton," Petra said, shaking her head in feigned wonder.

"Lord Ashton goes out of his way to express his appreciation for any little courtesies that Christophe does for him," Guy said bluntly. "Don't pretend you don't know how our world works, my dear." He took another sip and then said, "Now, I hope you understand that you're all my guests. I took the liberty of ordering lunch for us. Charles here will tell us the menu." He gestured invitingly to a waiter who now stood at attention beside the table.

Guy was insisting on playing host, therefore it was entirely reasonable that he should order the menu just as if they were in his own dining room. Nevertheless, Petra felt that a proper invitation would have been nice. She cast a quick speaking glance toward Diana and Fenella sitting across the round table from her. They both flicked their eyes in instant response.

Jonathan cleared his throat and his sister understood immediately that he was put out. Obviously, he had not expected to find himself lunching at Guy's expense and it put him in an awkward position. As he'd understood, he and Guy were having lunch together and together had invited the women. But he couldn't protest now without causing the table general embarrassment. It was yet another example of how Guy Granville managed his affairs without giving a thought to how his actions might affect anyone else, Petra thought grimly.

CHAPTER SIX

Try as she might, Petra could not fault Guy's menu or his hosting skills. He was an easy conversationalist, an attentive host, and no fault could be found with oysters, poached Christchurch salmon with a delicate watercress mousseline, buttered new potatoes and tender spring peas, followed by baby strawberries with thick clotted cream.

"What a perfect summer lunch," Fenella said, putting down her spoon with a sigh of repletion. "Thank you, Guy."

"And I thank you, Fenella, for gracing my table," he returned with a smile. He glanced at Petra, who dabbed at her mouth with her napkin before offering her own approbation.

At some point during lunch, Petra had noticed that Guy had dropped formality when addressing her friends, and if they'd noticed they hadn't objected but simply followed suit. It was yet another example of the ease with which he managed situations. She was still annoyed for her brother at the way Guy had usurped the role of host without so much as a word of consultation.

"Lunch was delicious," she said neutrally. "Thank you."

Guy frowned at her, a question in his dark eyes, but Diana jumped in with her own thanks, redirecting the conversation. Petra let the small talk swirl around her until the party began to break up. She saw her brother discreetly touch Guy's elbow, drawing him to one side, away from the women gathering their possessions.

Petra watched them for a moment. Joth was talking earnestly, seeming to remonstrate with the baron.

"What's going on?" Diana asked in a whisper, drawing on her elbow-length pale silk gloves.

"Joth thought he was also hosting this lunch. Guy took him by surprise," Petra told her sotto voce. "I know it made him feel small and subordinate. Which is something his lordship is very good at doing." Her voice was tight with annoyance.

"Ah." Diana nodded her comprehension but said nothing as the two men turned back to the table.

"Ladies, I must love you and leave you, I'm afraid. I'm expected in the House." Joth kissed them goodbye with the familiarity of long acquaintance. "Granville, I'll see you later tonight." He held out his hand.

"Indeed." Guy shook his hand. "I'll see your sister safely to her door."

"That will not be necessary," Petra said swiftly. "I have things to do this afternoon. What about you, Diana? I know Fenella has her play reading."

"Yes, I'm already late," Fenella said, extending her hand to Guy. "Thank you again for lunch." She kissed her friends and left them with a jaunty wave.

"I must go too. I have to visit my great-aunt and she gets very crotchety if I'm later than I promised. Thank you again for lunch, Guy. Petra, I'll see you this evening at the Andersons?"

"Oh, yes, of course. I forgot their party was tonight." Petra frowned. "Thanks for reminding me." She kissed Diana goodbye.

"What do you have to do this afternoon?" Guy asked, handing her her gloves and handbag.

As it happened, Petra had no plans for the afternoon and didn't want any either. "Oh, just things," she said vaguely, waving a distracted hand. "Thank you for lunch." She turned to leave the dining room.

Guy followed her and paused in the hotel foyer, watching as she seemed to hesitate at the entrance, as if deciding what to do next. After a moment she seemed to make up her mind, saying something to the liveried doorman before going out under the portico. The doorman blew on his whistle and a hansom cab approached immediately.

Guy sidestepped quickly around the doorman and opened the cab door himself. "Miss Rutherford . . ." He gestured invitingly.

"Are you stalking me?" Petra demanded in an indignant undertone, conscious of the attentive doorman.

"Of course I'm not. Whatever gave you that idea? Are you getting in, or not?"

Petra stepped up into the cab and was not surprised when Guy followed her, settling on the seat next to her. "Where should I tell him to take you?" he asked pleasantly.

Petra leaned forward to the cabbie. "Brook Street, please." She sat back again reflecting that if the man wouldn't take a gentle hint it was going to be difficult to pursue her intended course of bland indifference to his attentions.

"I've upset you in some way," Guy said without preamble. "Since we agreed to let bygones be bygones, I'm at a loss to know what I've done now. So tell me, please."

"Very well." She turned her head to look at him. "You made my brother uncomfortable. He assumed he had invited us to lunch and you swept the ground from beneath his feet. You must surely understand that he looks up to you to a certain extent, you're older than he is and you sit in the Lords. He's a very junior member of Parliament and you outrank him in age and status and you made that clear."

"Yes," he agreed calmly. "I did. It was thoughtless and when he pointed it out to me, I apologized for it. I think, Petra, that your brother is quite capable of fighting his own battles. He expressed his discomfort to me and I did what I could to make amends. Do you think he would appreciate your going to bat for him? I would think that he might find it a little mortifying."

Petra was silent, the wind completely taken from her sails. He was of course right. Joth would hate to feel that his sister thought she had to fight his battles. After a moment she said hesitantly, "You're right, of course. But it was thoughtless of you, and Joth and I are very close. He's only two years older than I am and we grew up very much left to our own devices. At least in the holidays.

84

We've always stuck up for each other."

Guy smiled, disarming as always. "He's a very lucky man to have you in his corner."

"And I'm lucky to have him in mine," Petra said swiftly, resisting the charm of that smile.

"Point taken. But in my defense, my only intention was to give you, your brother and your friends pleasure." He shook his head. "I seem to walk through a minefield of thoughtlessness in your company. It doesn't seem to happen with anyone else."

"Perhaps no one else has the courage to tell you."

His lips twisted into a wry grin. "Touché, Miss Rutherford. That is one very sharp tongue you've developed."

"I've always had it," she told him. "But ten years ago I was too young to see when I needed to use it."

"And again." He threw up his hand in a fencer's gesture acknowledging a hit. "So, what now?"

"What do you mean?"

"Are we to be at odds forever, or can we put this bone of contention behind us too?"

"I don't like being at odds with people," Petra replied obliquely as the cab pulled up outside her house.

Guy jumped down, reached up to take her

by the waist and swung her to the ground. He held her for a moment, his hands on her waist, looking down into her upturned face. "I suppose I can take some comfort from that." Swiftly he bent and kissed her mouth. The kiss was firm but fleeting and he'd lifted his head almost before Petra realized what had happened.

"Kiss and make up," he said. His eyes seemed to deepen and glow as he still held her at the waist, still looking down at her, his mouth soft. "You are quite lovely, Petra. Thank you for having lunch with me."

Petra struggled with the surge of unwanted feelings. His tenderness had thrown her off guard, the desirous glow in his dark brown eyes made her want to throw caution to the devil. Her anger, irritation, resentment fell away and for a moment she wanted him to kiss her, to lose herself in his kiss, to feel his body hard against hers.

She stepped away from him, shaking her head as if to dispel cobwebs. "Thank you for lunch, Guy." She turned and hurried up the steps to her front door, which opened before she could get out her key. "Thank you, Foster," she murmured hurrying into the sanctuary of her house feeling as if she'd escaped a monster, but Guy Granville was not the monster.

Guy waited until she was inside, then climbed back into the cab. "Westminster," he instructed the driver, and sat back with a slight smile, his fingertips running thoughtfully over his lips where he could still feel the soft, pliable shape of Petra's mouth. She'd interested him ten years ago, as a girl on the cusp of womanhood, with her eagerness to experience whatever came her way. He remembered how she had responded to his careful lovemaking with an openness and enthusiasm that he had found quite delightful. She had rather more armor now, but he had recognized for a moment while he was kissing her that same swift, sensual response. She'd quashed it quickly but he hadn't been mistaken.

Would Miss Rutherford be willing to play a little flirtatious game, he wondered. He found her both challenging and enticing, and it would be entertaining to find out if he could overcome whatever resistance their earlier history had caused.

Lord Ashton had never been able to resist a challenge.

Petra gained the tranquility of her bedroom with a sigh of relief. She seemed to be on very slippery ground when it came to Guy Granville and she didn't like the feeling at all. Games were one thing, but playing with fire was quite another. She was beginning to wonder if the strategy she had concocted with her friends was going to prove more difficult to put into play than she'd so blithely assumed.

Two things were clear: Guy would not be easily manipulated and her own treacherous responses would not be easy to restrain. Maybe she should just give up the idea, but her spirit recoiled at the thought of leaving him in control of the field after what had passed between them. He was still arrogant, he still pursued his own path regardless of whose feelings he insulted on his way. He was the epitome of the overly privileged aristocrat who had never questioned his position or his right to do exactly as he pleased, when and where he pleased.

Of course, Petra was obliged to admit that she and Jonathan too were the product of that privileged upbringing, but somehow she didn't think either she or her brother were quite so ruthlessly self-centered. Or at least, she thought, kicking off her shoes, it was to be hoped they weren't. One didn't always see oneself as others saw one.

She lay down on the bed, closing her eyes on the disconcerting reflection. She was sleepy after the wine at lunchtime, another perfect choice by their perfect host, she thought, wishing perversely that she hadn't enjoyed it so much.

Dottie's arrival woke her from a deeply refreshing nap, her spirits as refreshed as her body. She sat up, yawning. "What time is it, Dottie?"

"Just gone six, Miss Petra. It's time you was dressing for dinner. I was waiting for you to ring, but when you didn't I thought I'd best come an' see."

"I'm glad you did. Viscount Aldershot is supposed to be taking me for dinner before a party later. He'll be here around seven thirty." She swung herself off the bed, feeling for the buttons of her crumpled skirt. "The lavender silk, I think, with that wonderful purple feather boa," she decided, stepping out of the skirt and beginning to unbutton her shirt. "I'm in the mood for flamboyance." She walked into the bathroom, unpinning her hair as she went. "I think I'd like to do my hair in a pompadour this evening. You do it so well, Dottie."

"Right you are, miss." The maid began to select garments from the wardrobe, laying them out on the bed. "Will you wear the silver comb in your hair?"

"Yes, and the silver ear studs," Petra called back from the bathroom.

Half an hour later she examined Dottie's handiwork in her dresser mirror. Her rich auburn locks were piled up over pads on top of her head and twisted into a thick, elaborate chignon on her nape. Petra liked the style which, she thought, gave her much needed height. She stood up to step into the lavender brocade evening gown and Dottie fastened the plain purple sash at her waist, adjusting the low sweep of the neckline. She opened the jewel box on the dresser. "Pearls, Miss Petra?"

Petra considered, her fingers trawling through the glistening contents of the casket. "Too demure," she decided. "I like the emerald pendant to go with the lavender and purple. It's a striking combination."

Dottie made no demur, she trusted her mistress's dress sense, even when she insisted on putting together colors that traditionally would not be considered compatible. She fastened the emerald pendant and nodded as the large, deep stone nestled against the whiteness of Petra's throat.

Petra swung the feather boa around her shoulders, catching the edges on her elbows, and twirled in front of the pier glass. She nodded her satisfaction. The complete look was exactly as she'd envisioned. Charlie Aldershot would be appropriately captivated.

90

Not that it took much to captivate the viscount, she reflected, making her way downstairs. She'd known him all her life and enjoyed his friendly company, but sometimes Charlie seemed to think that more was expected of him and every time he ventured beyond the easy friendly kiss she would gently remind him of the time when Joth had thrown him into the duck pond for breaking the bow of his archery set. It usually reminded him of where things stood between them.

The doorbell rang as she reached the hall and she waited for Foster to open the door. "Lord Aldershot, good evening, sir."

"Evening, Foster. Is Miss —"

"Yes, she is," Petra chimed in, gliding across the marble floor to greet him with a kiss on the cheek. "How lovely to see you, Charlie." She gave him her cheek. "Would you like a drink before we leave?"

"No, I think we should go right away, if you don't mind." He ran an appreciative eye over her. "Only you could wear that boa, Petra."

"I'll take that as a compliment, thank you." She dropped a mock curtsy. "I'm quite ready if you are. Did you bring the barouche?"

"I did, it awaits my lady's pleasure." He

gestured in invitation as Foster opened the front door.

Charlie handed Petra up into the open carriage and followed to sit beside her. "Trocadero all right?"

"Lovely," Petra agreed, hoping she could do justice to dinner after her River Room lunch. Well, she'd be dancing off any excess at the party afterward, she reflected, and she'd need her strength for an energetic evening.

The Andersons' house on Grosvenor Square was ablaze with light in every window. As the barouche drew up after dinner, the doors stood open to the street and the sounds of music and voices drifted across the leafy square. Footmen stood on the pavement outside the open doors ready to direct carriages to the mews and to escort their occupants into the house.

Petra and her escort walked up the wide sweep of the horseshoe staircase to where their hosts waited to greet them. The double doors to the glittering ballroom behind them stood open. As she waited her turn to greet her hosts Petra glanced quickly inside the ballroom to see if she could identify anyone in the moving throng. She caught sight of Diana's dark head bobbing amongst the dancers.

"Lady Anderson, Sir John."

"Petra, my dear, delighted you could join us. Have you heard from your parents recently?" Lady Anderson asked. "I understood your dear mother was not enjoying the waters. Lady Cartland has just returned from Baden-Baden where she spent several days with your parents."

Petra, who hadn't heard anything from her mother in weeks, murmured something vaguely suitable in response and moved away, Charlie at her side. "It's embarrassing," she said in a low voice, "but my mother is an appalling correspondent. She only ever writes if she has something most particular to tell us, or to ask us. It doesn't surprise me that she doesn't appreciate the healing qualities of the spa water, in fact I'm surprised they haven't moved on to somewhere more lively, like the South of France."

She had no scruples about revealing anything about her parents to Charlie; he'd known them most of his life and he responded to this confidence with a grin. "I can't imagine your mother enjoying Baden-Baden, it's far too staid for her, she's so glamorous and lively. When I first met her I couldn't believe she was actually anyone's mother, and it's still hard."

"I know what you mean," Petra said with feeling. They stood for a moment at the entrance to the ballroom getting their bearings. Her gaze swept over the throng and alighted on a dancing couple at the far side of the dance floor. They were a striking pair, Lord Ashton and the Viscomtesse Clothilde Delmont, moving across the floor with practiced ease, seemingly deep in animated conversation.

Chapter Seven

Petra took a glass of champagne from the tray offered by a passing footman and watched the dancers. The orchestra was playing a lively two-step and her foot tapped involuntarily to the rhythm.

"Shall we dance?" Charlie asked.

"Yes, please." She took a sip from her glass, set it aside on a pier table, took Charlie's hand and moved with him onto the dance floor. Her feet moved of their own accord and it was easy to maintain a conversation with Charlie while acknowledging friends and acquaintances circling the floor with them. She was acutely aware of Guy Granville as he and his partner seemed to come closer with each sweep of the dance floor. Was he deliberately steering his partner in Petra's direction, or was it simply part of the inevitable rhythm and movement of the dance?

Her question was soon answered. "Good

evening, Miss Rutherford." Guy and his partner were beside them.

She looked sideways as if surprised at seeing him there. "Why, Guy, fancy seeing you here. I thought you were to be in the Lords this evening. Charlie, are you acquainted with Lord Ashton?"

"Not personally," Charlie said, bowing his head in greeting. "But of course I know who you are, sir. I read your columns in the *Times* regularly. Charles Aldershot at your service."

Guy returned the nod with a polite smile of acknowledgment, before drawing his partner forward. "Clothilde, may I introduce Miss Petra Rutherford, and her partner, Viscount Aldershot. The Viscomtesse Delmont."

The tall Frenchwoman's smile seemed distant to Petra, who felt rather insignificant beside the other woman's height and elegance. Nevertheless she managed a friendly smile. "I'm delighted to make your acquaintance, Lady Delmont."

"Indeed," the woman said. "Charming." She looked at her partner. "I would like champagne, Guy."

"Of course," he responded. "Until later, Petra." His dark eyes held a glow in their depths, one she recognized from those moments just before he kissed her. She felt her cheeks warm and with a quick half smile turned back to Charlie to resume the dance.

"How do you know Lord Ashton?" Charlie asked.

"He's a neighbor, in a manner of speaking," she replied carelessly. "His family seat is a few miles away from my home in Somerset. Joth is trying to persuade him to support a bill he wants to put up in the House about draining the Somerset Levels." She frowned. "I thought Guy was supposed to be in the Lords tonight, supporting Joth's bill. If he's let him down . . ."

She let the sentence fade as she saw Charlie's expression sharpen with interest. "Oh, well," she attempted a light laugh as the music came to a stop. "Joth's dealings with Lord Ashton are his own business. Shall we go and find Diana and Rupert? I saw them go into the supper room a few minutes ago."

"As you wish." Charlie steered her to the edge of the floor. "You sounded quite fierce just then. Do you not approve of Lord Ashton?"

"I wouldn't have the temerity to have an opinion on his lordship," Petra said with another careless laugh. "He's far too lofty to move in my social orbit."

"You know each other well enough for first names," he pointed out, easing her through the throng toward the doors to the supper room.

"That's only because he and Joth are so well acquainted," she improvised. "It doesn't mean we're on close terms or anything. I hardly know the man. Oh, there's Diana waving to us." With relief she moved quickly toward the table where Diana sat with a group of friends.

"Good evening, everyone." She greeted the table at large, taking the seat that Charlie pulled out for her. "How are we enjoying ourselves?"

The conversation was general and lively and she was able to regain her equilibrium and hope that Charlie's interest in her relationship, such as it was, with Lord Ashton, would fade. Until she caught sight of Guy standing in the entrance to the room, looking around as if making up his mind. There was no sign of the vicomtesse.

Her heart jumped as she saw him move toward her, threading his way expertly but seemingly without a goal through the tables, pausing now and again to exchange a few words with people as he passed. Finally he arrived at the table where Petra sat, idly twisting her champagne glass between finger and thumb trying to look as if she hadn't noticed him.

"Miss Rutherford, may I ask for this dance?" He held out his hand, his inviting smile belying the formality of the greeting. "They're playing a waltz and I well remember how accomplished a waltzer you are."

Petra took the offered hand, trying for a bland smile. "I hope your memory hasn't exaggerated my accomplishment, Guy."

"I doubt that very much," he replied, drawing her to her feet. "If you'll excuse us, ladies, gentlemen." He led her back through the room to the dance floor.

As he clasped her hand and moved them into the dance it felt to Petra as if the last ten years had not happened. Her body seemed to adapt to his without conscious thought, following steps as memory dictated. He held her close, not close enough to draw attention but she could feel every movement of his lean, hard body, every ripple of muscle as if he had always been close to her like this, as if they always moved in step.

"You're very quiet, Petra." His voice, soft though it was, crashed into her daydream, bringing her back to the present.

She looked up. "Oh, I was enjoying the music. I'm sorry if I'm being unsociable."

"Oh, I wouldn't say that. I'm enjoying the feel of you too much to find fault of any kind. It's amazing how vividly memory can come back."

"Yes," Petra agreed, knowing that her body was moving too fluidly with his to make denial credible. "I thought you were to be in the Lords tonight. Joth was counting on your support, wasn't he?" The question was designed to break the spell, but somehow she couldn't produce a convincing note of provocation.

"As it happens, the reading of your brother's bill was postponed. The chancellor had something more urgent to bring before the House."

"Oh. I see."

"There really is no need to fight your brother's corner with me, dear girl," he said, sounding amused. "I believe Jonathan will go far. His dedication to his constituency is to be admired, and, if I might say so, somewhat unusual in the present crop of young politicians."

"Jonathan never does anything by halves," she said, willing as always to sing her brother's praises.

"No doubt. But, do you think once in a while we could talk about something other than your estimable brother?" The note of amusement was still in his voice and she could hear his smile in the lightly teasing tone. It wasn't possible to take umbrage.

"Yes, of course. I don't mean to be a bore."

He laughed. "Oh, Petra, I don't believe you could ever be boring." He turned them in the dance toward an anteroom opening off the floor, guiding her steps out of the dancers.

"What are we doing here?" Petra asked, looking around the room. Judging by the deep armchairs and velvet-covered sofas it was intended as a refuge from the ballroom for fatigued ladies and chaperones. However, it was presently deserted.

"I had an overpowering urge to do this," Guy said, drawing her with him to a curtained embrasure.

Petra was ready for his kiss, her body leaning into him, her face lifting as he brought his mouth to hers. She couldn't have feigned reluctance if she'd tried, and she had no desire to do so. Her mouth was hungry for his, opening eagerly beneath the pressure of his lips, her tongue fencing with his, tasting the warm sweetness of his mouth as she inhaled his scent. It hadn't changed, she thought distractedly, his skin still smelled of lemon and sunshine, his linen of starch and the hint of lavender. His hands clasped her rib cage and she could feel the press of his fingers against her skin beneath the lavender silk, and as she moved against him she felt his erection rising.

Guy lifted his mouth from hers, looked down into her upturned face, his expression both soft and desirous. "Oh, dear, I should know better by now," he said, with a rueful smile stepping away from her body, even while keeping his hands at her waist.

Petra glanced down at his body, at the bulge of his erection, and smiled a little hesitantly. She was not overly experienced in these matters, although not lacking in knowledge. "Did I do that?"

"Yes," he said. "You did. But it's my own fault. We'll have to wait here for a few minutes." He turned away to look out of the window.

"Maybe you shouldn't be flirting with me when you're here with your mistress," Petra suggested, deliberately hoping to break the charged atmosphere. "Where is Lady Delmont?"

"Lady Delmont is no concern of yours, Petra." Judging by the sharpness of his voice her deflection had worked.

"Perhaps not, but if she's your mistress, should you be kissing someone else?"

Guy turned back, his expression no longer soft, but annoyed. "What makes you think Clothilde is my mistress?"

"It's received wisdom in society."

"Then received wisdom should mind its own business," he retorted. "It's not always correct. I suggest you return to the ballroom and Lord Aldershot."

Petra went immediately, hiding her discomfort at having pried where she had no business, but glad nevertheless that her flat-footed questions had destroyed the dangerous intimacy of those moments. Had he implied that the Frenchwoman was no longer his mistress? It had sounded like it. But he hadn't completely denied it either. Puzzling over the conundrum she strolled with apparent insouciance around the dance floor toward the supper room, where she assumed Charlie was still to be found.

"What happened to your partner?" Diana inquired with a mischievous smile as Petra returned to her seat at the table.

"Nothing," Petra replied cheerfully. "We danced, the music finished, and I excused myself to come back to Charlie."

"Well, now you're back, would you like to dance again? It sounds as if the orchestra's playing another waltz." Charlie pushed back his chair, ready to stand up.

"Oh, if you don't mind, Charlie, I'd like to sit this one out," she said, putting a hand on his arm. "I'd like some champagne and one of those lobster thingies. Could you get me one, please?" Her smile was cajoling.

"Yes, of course. I'll be right back." He moved toward the buffet table.

"Why isn't Fenella here tonight?" Petra asked into the moment of silence.

"Edward has a play showing somewhere in Chiswick," Diana told her. "It was a rather sudden engagement, but apparently he decided on the spur of the moment to see how it would play to a different kind of audience."

"And Fenella has a part, of course."

"Of course," Diana agreed. "Anything to do with the theatre that involves Edward involves his wife. They're two of a kind, those two."

Petra nodded in acknowledgment, aware once again of that little stab of envy. Edward and Fenella could fight like cat and dog, but there was never any question of their commitment to each other, of the deep love and loyalty that went along with their naturally challenging natures and their shared passion for the theatre.

"I managed to nab the last two of the lobster thingies." Charlie reappeared, setting a plate in front of Petra with a fresh goblet of champagne.

"Thank you, you're a dear." She smiled up at him. "Have one."

He shook his head. "No, I had several while you were dancing with Granville."

Petra wondered if Guy would reappear as the evening progressed, but there was no sign of him, or of Clothilde Delmont. It was well after midnight when the party broke up and she stood outside in the cool of the night waiting for Charlie's driver to bring around the barouche. She climbed in, arranging her skirts around her, waving farewell to Diana and Rupert, who were waiting for their own carriage.

"That was a good evening," Charlie said, settling beside her. "Straight home?" he asked.

"No, let's drive around for a little," she suggested. "It's such a beautiful night and I'm not terribly sleepy. Probably because I had a nap this afternoon," she added with a laugh. "Are you tired?"

"Not in the least," he responded gallantly. He leaned forward to speak to the coachman on his box. "Fred, just drive for a little, maybe down to Berkeley Square, along Piccadilly perhaps. Unless" — he turned to

Petra — "unless you'd rather go into the Park?"

Petra shook her head, "No, it's not fair to keep Fred up too long. Just ten minutes or so." She leaned back contentedly against Charlie's encircling arm.

"I wish I thought you meant something by leaning against me like that," he said with a mock sigh.

"Oh, Charlie, you know I love you, you're one of my dearest friends, but . . ."

"But," he said with another sigh. The carriage had just entered Berkeley Square and was rounding a corner of the garden when something shot out through the railings, darting into the street, between the hooves of the horse, which reared up in the traces with a high whinny of alarm.

"Whoa, steady there," Fred said, wrestling with the reins, trying to bring the frantic horse under control. As he did so the same creature that had shot out from the square suddenly turned and raced back chased by something small and black. Fred had almost gained control of the horse when the racing pair hurtled between its legs and the animal reared again, hooves flailing as it jerked forward.

The two-wheeled carriage, unbalanced, tilted at a sharp angle, hovering for an agonizing moment on one wheel. Charlie grabbed at the edge of the door too late. He tumbled into the street. Petra, off balance, half fell, half jumped down behind him, just as the horse backed up, bringing its hooves to the ground again. The right wheel rolled over Charlie as he lay momentarily stunned in the road.

His shriek of pain resounded through the hitherto quiet square. Fred, cursing, leaped to the ground, grabbing the horse by the bridle, trying to pull it forward to get the wheel off Charlie's body.

Petra struggled up to her knees beside Charlie. "Oh, God," she muttered seeing the odd angle of his arm, the blood welling from his side. "Get the damn wheel off him, Fred," she yelled, trying to lift it off him herself. With a sickening jolt the wheel finally moved forward off the body and onto the road again. Petra gasped in horror at the bleeding wound it left behind. She yanked up her lavender skirts and ripped the thin silk of her petticoat, pressing the strip into the wound, desperate to staunch the blood.

"Here, let me do it." Suddenly Guy was kneeling beside her. He pulled the white silk evening scarf from his neck and swiftly substituted it for the already soaked strip of her petticoat. "Keep pressing down."

Petra did so, stunned by the rapidity of the unfolding horror. She pressed hard on Charlie's side, watching the blood well up, soaking the silk scarf. She took folds of her skirt and added them to the bloody scarf, pressing with all her strength. Charlie was gray, his eyelids fluttering, but other than that and the welling blood gave no signs that he was conscious, or even alive.

She glanced up to see Guy leading the trembling horse far away from Charlie, all the while giving sharp orders to Fred, who, shaking with shock himself, went to check the animal. Guy came back, kneeling once more beside Charlie.

"Are you hurt? You're bleeding."

She shook her head. "I don't think I'm hurt, maybe a scratch. I think the blood is Charlie's."

He nodded and pressed a finger to Charlie's neck. "His pulse is strong. But I think he might have broken his arm when he fell." Gently he touched the strangely angled arm and Charlie's eyes opened as he groaned.

"Charlie, darling, be still." Petra leaned over him, still pressing down on his side. "You're hurt. We have to get you to a doctor."

"Give me that boa," Guy instructed. He

took the feather boa from her and fashioned a sling, deftly looping it around the injured man's neck, securing the arm against his chest. "I'll be back in a moment. Keep the pressure on." He hurried across the street and Petra realized that the accident had happened right outside his house.

He reappeared within minutes with two footmen carrying a flat board that looked to Petra like a door. Following Guy's orders they set it down beside Charlie and then the three men lifted him and put him on the board in a movement so swift Charlie uttered only one stifled groan of pain, his eyelids closing again.

"You can take your hand away for the moment," Guy said to Petra as the three men hoisted the board. "Come with us." They carried the injured man across the road and into the cool depths of Granville House.

"Set him down on the billiard table," Guy instructed, gesturing to the open double doors to a room at the rear of the hall. "It'll be easier to see to his injuries." He turned to the butler, who, showing no sign of having been dragged untimely from his bed, was setting a basin of hot water and a pile of white napkins on the sideboard in the billiard room. "Has Ferguson gone for the doctor?"

"Yes, m'lord. Ten minutes ago. He should be here soon." The butler looked at Petra, bloody and bedraggled, her face white. "I'll send for Mrs. Carter, ma'am. She'll know what to do for you."

"No, please don't wake anyone. I don't need anything," Petra said swiftly.

Guy shrugged out of his coat, tossing it over a chair. "Do as Miss Rutherford says, Babbit. But bring cognac." He rolled up his sleeves and bent over Charlie again, resuming his pressure on the wound.

"Will he be all right?" Petra asked, coming to stand beside him.

He looked up. "I'm no doctor, and it's a nasty wound. As far as I can see, the wheel gashed his chest, probably broke some ribs. There's a lot of blood, but his pulse is still strong." He frowned. "How much of that blood is yours and not Aldershot's?"

She shook her head, looking at her red hands and blood-soaked skirt. "I scraped my knee when I fell, but it's nothing. The carriage tilted and threw Charlie out and then the horse backed up and the wheel ran over him. It's all his blood."

Babbit came back with a decanter and glasses. "The doctor's here, my lord."

A man in a black coat over what looked suspiciously like striped pajama trousers

110

came in on the butler's heels. He set down his bag and bent over Charlie. "What happened?"

"A wheel went over him," Petra told him, taking the glass that Babbit handed her.

The doctor merely grunted and got on with business. After half an hour, he washed his bloody hands in the refreshed basin of hot water. "He'll do, my lord. I've strapped the broken ribs and the wound's not as deep as I feared. I've cleaned it and as long as infection doesn't set in, the bones will knit on their own. The arm needs a proper cast, I'll be back in the morning to do that. Meantime, I've given him laudanum for the pain, enough, I hope, to put him to sleep for a few hours."

He turned his attention to Petra. "What about you, ma'am? Are you hurt?"

She shook her head. Her knees were sore, bruised and scraped from her tumble from the carriage, and she seemed to ache in every bone. "Nothing that a hot bath and my bed won't cure, Doctor."

"Right. Well, I'll leave you a sleeping draft." He took a vial from his bag and set it on the billiard table.

Babbit saw the doctor out while Guy gave instructions to the two burly footmen to take Lord Aldershot to the blue bedroom.

"Who should we notify?" he asked Petra.

"His sister, Lady Vernon. She lives in Eaton Square. Charlie lives alone in Belgrave Square since his mother died last year."

Guy gave instructions to Babbit to send a messenger to Eaton Square, then he rolled his sleeves down again before pocketing the vial with the sleeping draft. "Let's get you home to bed."

CHAPTER EIGHT

"Do you think we'll be able to get a hackney at this time in the morning?" Petra asked, sounding doubtful. "It's not too far to walk."

Guy didn't trouble to answer her. "Get someone to bring the carriage round, Babbit, as quickly as possible. I'll drive myself."

"Yes, m'lord." The butler disappeared and his voice could be heard issuing rapid instructions in the hall.

"Your whole household seems to have been roused from their beds," Petra observed wearily.

"Sit down before you fall down," Guy said sharply, catching her as she swayed. He pushed her down into a chair and knelt on the carpet, pushing up her blood-stained skirts ignoring her faint protests and her feeble efforts to stop him.

"Your knee's got a nasty scrape," he said, getting to his feet. "And it's going to bruise badly." He dipped a cloth in the cooling

113

water in the basin and knelt again, carefully cleaning the wound on her knee. "Let me see your hands."

Petra gave them to him, too tired to resist. He turned them over and washed the blood from her palms, observing, "Well, it's not all Aldershot's blood. You must have scraped them when you fell, bruised them too." He pushed back onto his heels and stood up. "You'll need to treat yourself gently for the next day or two, my dear."

"The carriage is here, sir."

"Thank you, Babbit . . . come, Petra." He put an arm around her waist and half lifted her from her chair.

"I can walk," she said, pulling away from him.

"Of course you can." But he kept a steadying hand on her waist as he steered her out to the Square.

A blackbird's full-throated song filled the air and Petra paused, listening. "It's such a joyous sound," she said. "He's calling for a mate. Listen." She held up an arresting hand and almost immediately the blackbird's song was answered with another paean of joy. They listened to the duet for a few moments before Guy lifted her into the waiting carriage.

He took up the reins and the sleepy groom

climbed onto the step at the rear of the two-wheeled carriage. When they reached Brook Street Guy handed the reins to the groom and stepped down, catching Petra as she attempted to jump to the pavement. "You don't have to prove anything to me," he chided. "Where's your key?"

She didn't have anything to prove, of course, Petra acknowledged. It was just that she felt if she was to stay on equal footing with Guy she couldn't afford to show any weakness. The problem now was that she felt as weak as a kitten, the shock of the accident and Charlie's injuries finally taking their toll. She gave Guy her drawstring purse without a word.

Inside the dimly lit hall, Guy looked around. "Is your maid waiting up for you?"

"No, of course not. It's gone three in the morning," she said, shocked. "Everyone's asleep."

"Well, we need to wake someone up," he said. "You need help getting to bed."

"Nonsense," she protested. "I'm quite capable of looking after myself."

"Unfortunately, dear girl, on this particular night I beg to differ." He looked at her with a measure of exasperation. "You are so stubborn. However, so am I. I'll give you a choice, either you wake someone to help

115

you to bed, or you accept my help. Which is it to be?"

"Oh, for heaven's sake." Petra glared at him. He merely looked back at her, unmoving. "Very well," she said after a long moment. "I'll ring for Dottie when I get upstairs."

He nodded. "Then let's go." He turned to the stairs, his hand on her arm.

Petra pulled away. "You don't have to come with me, Guy."

"Oh, I think I do," he responded, moving her inexorably to the stairs. "I want to see this Dottie in person."

"Don't you trust me?" she demanded, mounting the stairs willy-nilly.

"Not in this matter," he replied pleasantly. They reached the head of the stairs. "Where to now?"

Defeated, Petra gestured to the stairs to the bedroom floor and led the way to her own door. Guy opened it and ushered her into the softly lit, curtained room. He nodded his approval and reached unerringly for the bell rope beside the fireplace, pulling it once and then twice.

"That should produce results," he observed amiably.

"People will think there's a fire," she

116

declared. "You don't need to wait any longer."

"No, probably I don't," Guy agreed, taking the doctor's vial from his pocket and setting it on the dresser. "I strongly suggest that you take that. A good night's sleep will help the bruises." He didn't wait for a response, going to the door. "I'll come by later this morning to see how you are."

"You're too kind," Petra muttered, and was rewarded with a soft chuckle as he left her, leaving the door slightly ajar.

Dottie, her hair in curling papers, appeared in the corridor from the back stairs hastily tying the sash of her dressing gown. She stopped dead at the sight of the man emerging from her mistress's bedroom, her eyes widening.

"Your mistress was in an accident," Guy explained. "She needs to be helped to bed. Oh, and see if you can encourage her to take the sleeping draft. It's on the dresser."

"An *accident*." Dottie's hand flew to her mouth, then she ran to the open door of Petra's room. Satisfied that he'd done all he could, Guy continued down the stairs to the front door.

He was crossing the hall when the door opened and Jonathan came in, yawning. He stopped in the open doorway. "Granville?"

"Yes, you may look askance, Rutherford," Guy said easily. "Your sister was in a carriage accident . . . no, no, she's not seriously hurt." He held up an arresting hand as Jonathan's mouth opened in shock. "But Aldershot is injured. It happened fortuitously outside my house, so I was able to help. Petra's both shocked and exhausted. I brought her home and she's upstairs with her maid."

"How . . . what . . ." Jonathan stammered.

"I'm sure Petra will tell you everything. I'll be by later this morning." Guy put a reassuring hand on Jonathan's shoulder as he passed him in the doorway and went out into the faint light of the false dawn.

Jonathan took the stairs two at a time and burst into his sister's room without ceremony. "What happened, Petra? I just saw Granville."

"Then I daresay he told you all you need to know," Petra said, yawning. "Go away, Joth. Can't you see I'm only half dressed."

Her brother belatedly took in her state of undress and backed out of the room, apologizing profusely as he did so. Petra sighed and slid into bed as Dottie held up the crisp white sheets. She sank into the feather mattress with a groan. "Thank you, Dottie. Go back to bed now. I'll ring when I need you."

118

Her eyes had closed before Dottie could even offer the sleeping draft.

"Petra, dearest, what happened . . . are you all right? Oh, poor Charlie. It's all over town." Diana and Fenella came into Petra's bedroom on a rush of words just before noon.

Petra, propped on a mound of pillows and sipping hot chocolate, greeted them with a faint smile. "What's all over town, or, rather, how could it be all over town?"

"Serena Vernon," Fenella informed her, sitting on the edge of the bed. "Charlie's sister. You know how her tongue runs away with her."

"Yes, apparently she told Lizzie Greenward, who told —"

"Spare me the gossip mongering," Petra begged. "Do you at least know how Charlie is?"

Diana sat on the other side of the bed. "Apparently, Serena wanted to take him back to Eaton Square, but Guy wouldn't let her until the doctor said it was safe to do so. She was very put out. So what happened exactly?"

Her friends listened to Petra's unvarnished narrative without interruption. "How are *you* feeling?" Diana asked when Petra fell silent.

"Like hell, quite frankly," Petra responded. "I ache as if I've been on the rack, and my knee's swollen and bruised, and my elbow too, somehow. I must have fallen from the carriage harder than I realized. I was just so frightened for Charlie." She leaned sideways to set down her chocolate cup. "I need to get up and go and see how he is. It was awful . . . so much blood and his arm at the most horrid angle." She pushed aside the covers and swung her legs off the mattress. "Ouch."

"Do you think that's a good idea?" Fenella asked.

"It's most definitely *not* a good idea," Guy Granville stated, coming into the room with Jonathan. He held a bunch of sweet-smelling freesias, laying them on the foot of the bed. "Your brother said you were holding court from your bed this morning so I came to give you an update on the patient."

Petra shot an irritated look at her brother, who seemed not to notice. Dottie, who had been mending a tear in a flounce on one of Petra's gowns, set aside her work and hurried to the bed. Hastily she helped Petra to get back under the covers, plumping the pillows at her back before draping a cashmere shawl discreetly over her shoulders.

"Thank you, Dottie. I appear to be holding a levee," she remarked pointedly.

"I'll put the flowers in water, Miss Petra. Is there anything I can get you?"

"No, I'm getting up in a minute. Would you run me a bath?"

Dottie curtsied and left with the freesias. Her mistress was more than adequately chaperoned by her brother, not to mention her two friends.

"So, how is Charlie?" Petra asked directly.

"In pain, too much to be moved just yet, much to his sister's annoyance. But the doctor set the arm this morning and there's no infection in the wound so far. He's sedated and I hope sleep and quiet will work its healing magic," Guy told her. "How are *your* bruises and scrapes, dear girl?"

"Tiresome," she responded. "But I intend to get up." The statement sounded more like a challenge, she thought, as if she was expecting Guy to object. Which was silly, she told herself. He had no right to object, no say at all in any decisions she made for herself. Still she caught herself waiting for an objection.

"I'm sure you know best," he said easily. "I'll leave you to your toilette, then." He moved away to the door. Joth said quickly,

"I have to be somewhere too, Petra, but I can come back later if you need company."

"No, I won't need company," she reassured him, waving him away with a smile.

The door closed on the two men and Petra had the oddest sensation of an absence in the air, a void left by Guy's departure. Perhaps she'd hit her head last night without noticing and now she was hallucinating.

"Guy seems quite at home in your bedroom," Diana observed with a wicked smile. "You certainly seem remarkably at ease with each other now."

Petra grimaced. "He just seems to take over," she said. "I don't think it ever occurs to him that he might be unwelcome, or that perhaps it's not a good time. . . ." She sighed. "I don't quite know how to explain it. Guy Granville is a force in his own right."

Fenella gave her a shrewd look. "Maybe it's my imagination but you don't seem to be fighting against that force with much conviction, dearest."

"It doesn't seem to do any good," Petra said flatly, still keeping her own counsel on the subject of her own physical responses to the force that was Lord Ashton.

"Was it like that ten years ago?" Diana asked.

"I was too young to realize what was going on," Petra answered. "I thought he was wonderful, God's gift specially to me. Of course I followed his lead, hanging on his every word. And he seems to think nothing's changed and I'm supposed to be still like that."

"Then I think you'd better put him straight," Fenella stated. "For both your sakes." She got off the bed. "I have to go." She bent to kiss Petra's cheek. "You aren't an impressionable schoolgirl any longer, Petra darling."

Petra shook her head with a tiny laugh of agreement. "I know, but he makes me forget that I'm not sometimes. He doesn't seem to leave any room for me to assert myself."

"Well, that won't help the plan to ensnare his lordship in your toils," Diana pointed out.

"No, I still appear to be snared in his." Petra shook her head, defeated. But only for a moment, with renewed vigor she declared, "But I can still play the game. In fact, if he thinks I'm still as malleable and yielding as I was ten years ago, it might be even more of an unpleasant surprise for him when he sees who I really am. I'll shatter his preconceived notions like crystal on concrete. That'll teach him to make assumptions."

"Bravo." Diana laughed. "That's more like

123

you. I could almost imagine playing such a game with his lofty lordship myself, if I didn't have enough masculine attitude in my life already. Talking of which, or do I mean whose, Rupert is expecting me to organize the invitations and details for our Kimberley Diamond lunch party at Royal Ascot. Should we invite Guy, Petra?"

"Absolutely," she said, without hesitation. "It's time for me to initiate things. Maybe I'll casually let slip that I asked you to invite him, what do you think?"

"I think it's an excellent idea," Diana said. "I'll send out the invitations this afternoon. Guy will get his this evening and you can work your mischief any time after that." She gathered up her scattered belongings. "Are you going my way, Fenella?"

"As far as Oxford Street."

Petra leaned back against the pillows in the sudden quiet of her bedroom as the door closed on her friends. Despite her aches and pains she was restless. Staying in bed had never appealed. She kicked off the covers and stood up, stretching.

"Your bath's all ready, Miss Petra." Dottie came in from the bathroom, a cloud of steam in her wake. "You'll not be going out, of course."

"On the contrary, Dottie. I am definitely

going out. I have something to do. I'll have lunch and go out afterward, just for an hour or so." She walked into the steam, saying over her shoulder, "The gray suit, I think, with the red shirt."

She slipped gingerly into the bath, wincing as the hot water stung the abrasions on her knees and hands. She should count her blessings, she reflected, thinking of poor Charlie. As soon as she was dressed and had had lunch she would stroll round to Berkeley Square and see how he was doing. A box of his favorite pralines would go down well, she decided. One of the footmen could run to Mulberry's in Bond Street and fetch her a box to take with her.

CHAPTER NINE

Refreshed after her bath, her abrasions liberally dressed with some magic ointment from Mrs. Evans's still room, Petra was finishing a light lunch when Foster came into her parlor with a prettily wrapped box. "The pralines, Miss Petra."

"Oh, excellent, Foster, thank you. Viscount Aldershot is very partial to them. I hope they'll cheer him up." She scrunched her napkin on the table as she got up. "I'm going to deliver them to him at Lord Ashton's house in Berkeley Square, could you tell Mr. Jonathan if he comes home and wants to know where I am?"

"Certainly, ma'am. Should I send the lad for a hackney?"

"No, I'll walk, it's only a couple of streets away and it's a pleasant afternoon."

Foster bowed and held the door for her as she left the parlor, taking the box of pralines with her, and headed back to her bedroom for her hat and gloves. She took stock of herself in the mirror as she pinned a straw hat into the heavy braided knot on top of her head. Rather paler than usual, she decided, which made the scattering of freckles across her nose stand out more than she cared for. A certain heaviness under her hazel eyes. Only to be expected after such a short night of alarums and excursions, aches and pains, Petra concluded, turning away from the mirror, drawing on her gray kid gloves.

She dropped the box of sweets into a straw handbag and hastened downstairs, out into the sunny afternoon. She strolled to Berkeley Square, enjoying the summer air, despite its lacing of city smells, horse dung and odiferous garbage receptacles in the basement areas of the town houses she passed. As always the lingering sensation of coal dust hung in the atmosphere, coating everything with a film, more like a miasma, of sooty smut.

Babbit, the Granville butler, opened the door to Petra's knock. "Miss Rutherford." He greeted her warmly, holding the door wide. "I trust you suffered no ill effects from last night."

"Not really, Babbit. I'm so sorry you were disturbed at such a dreadful hour." She stepped into the galleried hall. It looked different in the daylight, the softness of gaslight yielding to bright sunlight from the windows on either side of the doors and the stained glass transom over them, the marble and gilded cornices, the grand sweep of the horseshoe staircase giving an overall impression of established grandeur.

"No trouble at all, Miss Rutherford. I'm afraid his lordship is not at home."

"Actually I've come to see how Lord Aldershot is today. I understand the doctor doesn't want him moved for a while."

"That is so, ma'am. I'll take you up to his room. If you'd follow me."

Petra followed the man upstairs to the bedroom floor and into a large, sunny bedroom at the rear of the house, away from street noise. Charlie was in bed, slumped against a mound of pillows, his arm in a sling across his bandaged chest.

"Oh, Charlie, dearest, I'm so, so sorry," Petra said, hurrying to the bedside. "I feel so guilty."

"Good God, Petra, why would you feel guilty?" he asked, struggling higher on his pillows, giving her a wan smile.

"Well, if I hadn't wanted to drive around a bit we wouldn't have come into the square and that cat, if it was a cat, wouldn't have frightened the horse and the carriage wouldn't have tipped —"

"And I wouldn't have fallen out," Charlie finished for her with a gallant grin. "Fate, dear girl. It had nothing to do with you."

"Can I bring you some refreshment, my lord?" Babbit asked, still standing in the doorway.

"Petra?" Charlie invited.

"Tea, please, Babbit. Is there anything else you'd like, Charlie?"

"Just tea."

The butler withdrew and Petra set the box of pralines on the bed. "You probably don't feel like these at the moment, but when you feel better . . ."

"My favorites, thank you." Charlie reached for the box with his good arm and then subsided with a stifled groan. "I keep forgetting these damned ribs. According to the sawbones they'll take months to knit back together again. I'm going to be stuck like this forever." He closed his eyes for a moment, then opened them and took a deep breath, struggling again to pull himself higher on the pillows.

"Let me help." Petra bent over him, trying to support him with one arm while pulling up the pillows with the other.

"Babbit said you were here, Petra." Guy

came into the room followed by a footman with a tray of tea. "Let me do that. You arrange the pillows." He reached around her, hoisting Charlie higher with a swift deftness that caused the patient very little discomfort, while Petra plumped up the pillows and piled them behind him.

"Thank you." Charlie heaved a sigh of mingled relief and frustration. "I can't stand feeling this helpless."

"You'll get stronger every day." Petra poured tea and brought a cup to him. "Shall I hold it?"

"No, I can do that at least for myself." He extended his good hand and took the cup, lifting it rather shakily to his lips. Neither Petra nor Guy made the mistake of offering to help.

Guy took his own cup from Petra and sat in a chair by the bed while she perched on the edge of the bed. "So Serena came to visit you this morning?" she said with a meaningful glance.

"Oh, I have one boon to ask of you, Granville. Please, under no circumstances allow my sister to carry me off," Charlie said with a mock groan. "While I'm bedridden and weak as a kitten she'll try to take charge and if anything will keep me on my bed for eternity it will be that."

130

Guy laughed. "I can safely promise you that I am proof against all managing sisters. You'll leave my house only when you're ready and willing to do so."

"Serena means well," Petra ventured. "But she can be overbearing."

"An understatement," Charlie responded.

"Your sister is in Scotland, isn't she, Guy?" Petra asked. "She married the Duke of Brandon, didn't she?"

"She did, and has the most enormous brood of children," Guy said. "I have at least five nieces and three nephews."

"Do you spend much time with them?" Petra found she was very curious to find out more about Baron Ashton. Ten years ago she'd been so immersed in the actual fact of the man himself anything else hadn't interested her, but now she very much wanted to know what, or who, had contributed to making him the man he was. His family could prove fertile ground for exploration.

"I go to Innes in August for the opening of the grouse shooting and when I can for the salmon fishing in the spring," he answered. "But I'm not always able to do so." He shrugged lightly and leaned over to take the cup from Charlie, whose eyes were closing periodically. "I think we should leave the patient to sleep, don't you?"

"Yes, of course." Petra slid off the bed. "If you'll lift him, I'll put the pillows down a little."

Guy obliged and she readjusted the pillows. "Is that all right, Charlie? Are you comfortable?"

"As much as I can be at the moment," he responded, wincing.

"Take a spoonful of this." Guy poured liquid from a medicine bottle onto a spoon and held it to Charlie's lips.

Charlie obediently swallowed the dose and closed his eyes. "I'm sorry to be such a pathetic invalid," he murmured.

Petra laughed and kissed his forehead. "I'll come back tomorrow and we'll play piquet if you're up for it. Backgammon if you're not." She followed Guy to the door, which he was holding open for her.

"Come into the library," he said as they reached the gallery overlooking the hall. He ushered her down the stairs with an all-encompassing gesture.

Petra wasn't sure whether a tête-à-tête in the library was her best move when she hadn't had time to marshal her guns. The next steps in the game she was supposed to be playing were not yet mapped out, but as they reached the grand hall, Guy's hand on her waist, warm, intimate, imperious, propelled her toward double doors at the rear.

"What can I get you, Petra? More tea, if you must. Sherry, madeira, a glass of claret?" He went to the sideboard where decanters were ranged like soldiers. "Or, a glass of champagne? Perfect for this time of day." He rang the bell even as he spoke.

Petra glanced at the tall case clock. It was almost five o'clock and champagne, crisp and dry, was very appealing. She wandered across to one wall of floor-to-ceiling books, idly glancing at the titles on the leather-bound spines. She'd expected the usual heavy Greek and Latin tomes, encyclopedias, reference books, dictionaries, all generally to be found in a gentleman's library, and they were certainly all there, but she was fascinated to see Thackeray and Austen, Trollope and Scott, Gaskell, Hardy and Dickens represented, all easily accessible on the lower shelves. Somehow she hadn't thought of Guy as someone who would while away the hours with a good book. Salmon fishing and grouse shooting, certainly, but long evenings alone by the fire immersed in Dickens's London? Another interesting piece to add to the slowly forming picture of Lord Ashton.

Guy perched on the massive mahogany

desk in the bay window, one leg swinging casually, watching Petra as she wandered along the shelves. He raised a quizzical eyebrow. "A penny for them?"

Petra turned back from the shelves. "I wasn't expecting such an array of novels," she answered frankly.

"Why is that? Do you think it strange that men in general read such books, or me in particular?"

"Both, I suppose," she said. "I don't think I've ever considered what men in general might read for pleasure, I know that my brother has read some Walter Scott, but I can't imagine him reading Jane Austen or Mrs. Gaskell, or most of these." She gestured to the shelves behind her. "They have a too small and generally too domestic canvas for a man's more . . ." She hesitated, looking for the word. "More muscular interests, I suppose."

Guy laughed slightly. "I enjoy the sharpness of some of the social observations and the quick wit of much of the dialogue in many of them. And I find reading women novelists rather illuminating. They give me —" He broke off as Babbit came in with the champagne. "Thank you, just leave it on the sideboard, I'll deal with it."

The door closed on the butler and he

busied himself with the cork, easing it carefully from the bottle so that it came free with barely a pop. He lifted a glass from the tray, holding it at a slight angle as he poured the pale bubbles so that the wine didn't froth over the top of the glass.

"You were saying?" Petra prompted him, taking the glass he handed her.

He frowned as he poured the second glass. "Oh, yes . . . I was saying that I find reading women writers illuminating. Their work gives me a greater understanding of what your sex generally finds interesting and important. Both of which tend to be much broader than the impression men generally garner from the usual run of social encounters."

Petra absorbed this, gazing down into the effervescence in her glass. "I can see how that could be," she said thoughtfully.

"A toast." Guy lifted his glass. "To a greater understanding."

Petra drank the toast before asking, "A greater understanding of what exactly?"

"Ah." Guy regarded her over the lip of his glass. "I very much want to understand you, Petra. A lot happens to people in ten years, and while I still recognize in you the girl you were, it's clear to me that you were barely formed. And now . . ." He shook his

135

head with a small smile.

"Now?" she prompted, very curious to hear what he would say.

"Now, while I appreciate no one is ever their finished self, for as long as we breathe we keep growing and changing, you are very different from what, or rather who, you were. And I want to learn who you truly are because I am already deeply drawn to that person."

So much for playing games, Petra thought. How could she possibly indulge in her vengeful little scheme in the face of such candor? Even if she still wanted to. And she wasn't at all sure about that anymore. She took a sip of champagne to give herself a moment's breathing space. Something was required of her, some answering statement and there was only one way she could truthfully respond.

"Perhaps, if you were to kiss me again it might help to clarify my thoughts," she said.

"With the greatest of pleasure." Guy set aside his glass, reached for hers and put it on the desk. "It might be easier without the hat."

"Oh, yes." Petra caught her bottom lip between her teeth, her fingers quivering a little as she pulled out the long hatpins before tossing the straw hat onto a chair.

Guy took her hands in his, drawing her in to him, cupping her face, tilting it up. For a moment his face hovered over hers, his dark eyes holding her gaze, until Petra felt she was losing herself in those dark pools. As his mouth took hers and his hold tightened on her slight frame, his hands moved down her back in long, seductive strokes. Without taking his mouth from hers, he lifted her against him and with a deft twist of his body sat down on a leather chesterfield holding her across his body, his hands now roaming freely, cupping her breasts, a finger teasing the nipples beneath the thin silk of her blouse so that they rose hard against the silk.

Petra's fingers caressed his face, twisted in his hair as she reached against him, no longer capable of coherent thought, lost in the urgent heat of these moments when her senses were flooded with the scent of his skin, the pressure of his hands, the warmth of his breath. She felt his fingers on the tiny pearl buttons of her silk shirt and then the cool caress of the air on her bared skin. She caught her breath as his fingers moved over the rounded flesh, flicked at the erect nipples. His hand moved to her back, under the loosened shirt, and played an intimate tune along her spine, before flattening to slide up to her neck in a warm firm clasp, all the while his mouth held hers, his tongue engaged with hers in a dance of delight, in a darting exploration of the contours and recesses of her mouth until she could no longer separate herself from the tantalizing invader.

At last he lifted his head and smiled down at her, a finger stroking her swollen kiss-reddened lips, lightly caressing her flushed cheeks. "Any clarification?"

Petra's gaze was still unfocused as she murmured, "Not really. A little more might help."

Guy's expression changed, his gaze sharpened. He inclined his head in mute acknowledgment and brought his mouth down to hers, but this time his lips were hard and firm, demanding in their pressure and Petra felt herself rising to the challenge of this kiss, her fingers tangling in his hair as she half lifted herself against him, pressing her mouth into his, opening her lips again for his tongue, even as she pushed her own into his mouth for her own exploration. She was barely aware of how it happened but suddenly she was lying on her back on the sofa, Guy kneeling on the floor beside her. His hands were on her body, sliding the blouse from her shoulders, baring her breasts for his kisses, long leisurely strokes of his tongue over the soft mounds, kissing her erect nipples, lightly grazing the aching points with his teeth. There was a moment when he raised his head, looked a question even as his fingers teased her nipples. There was a moment when she nodded silently to the mute question, and then she slipped into a world where only sensation ruled and her body's responses were both strange to her and utterly right.

Her hands helped him as he undressed her, barely lifting his mouth from hers until finally she lay naked on the sofa, aware of the soft cool of the leather beneath her as he came over her, kneeling astride her, lifting her legs onto his shoulders so that his hands had free access to the soft moist folds of her sex. Her body leaped beneath his touch and she gripped her bottom lip between her teeth as his finger slid within her, delicately probing, sending waves of hot sensation darting through her belly. The single thrust of his penis when he finally entered her seemed to fill her to the full and she lay still, not breathing as her body grew accustomed to the strange invasion, to expand around him, and when he started to move, slowly, gently, within her she moved to his rhythm without conscious will.

He left her body suddenly and she felt bereft, hanging on the brink of something but she wasn't sure what, and then she felt his fingers again bringing that strange hovering sensation to fulfillment and waves of pleasure swept through her belly and loins, leaving her weak and smiling.

Guy slid off the sofa and bent to kiss her. "How do you feel?"

"Strange and wonderful," Petra responded, still smiling. She reached up to touch his face. "I didn't know what to expect the first time."

"I didn't hurt you?"

She shook her head and struggled to sit up. "Not in the least. But I expect I lost my maidenhead years ago. I've been riding astride since I was fifteen, except hunting or in Hyde Park. Oh, and I have a bicycle in the country."

"Such a modern woman," he teased gently. He extended a hand to pull her to her feet. "Let's put your clothes back on." He bent to pick up her discarded stockings.

"Pour me some more champagne while I put myself back together," Petra said.

"As you command, ma'am." He bowed, which, given his own semi-clad condition, made her laugh.

She seemed clumsier than usual, her

fingers fumbling with the buttons of her chemise and shirt, and her heart was beating faster than usual. Petra closed her eyes for a moment, trying to center herself. She'd assumed that her first experience of the mystery of sex would take place on her wedding night. Not that she'd given its timing much thought. Now she wanted to go home and reflect on the significance of the last hour. She took the champagne glass Guy offered her and sipped the cool, crisp bubbles.

Guy looked at her with concern. "You're looking tired, sweetheart, and I imagine those bruises are probably troubling you. There's nothing I'd like better than to tuck you up in my bed right now, but with Charlie in the house . . ."

"Yes, of course," she said, draining her glass, feeling somewhat vague and uncoordinated. "I am engaged to join a party at the Haymarket this evening. I need to go home."

Guy went to the door and opened it. "Babbit, send someone for a hackney."

"I can walk," she suggested without conviction.

Guy ignored the comment, placing her straw hat carefully on her disheveled head, equally carefully inserting the pins. "It's not perfect but it'll do for the moment," he

141

declared, taking her arm. "Ordinarily, after lovemaking, one enjoys the afterglow during a certain period of relaxation. It's a shame present circumstances don't allow for that," he commented dryly. "Next time, I'll be rather more prepared."

"Next time?" Petra queried, rousing herself from her stupor.

"Oh, yes, my sweet," he said softly. "There will most certainly be a next time." With an arm around her shoulders, he eased her out of the library, across the hall and into the waiting hackney.

Petra leaned against his encircling arm as the carriage took them the short distance to Brook Street. The only thing she knew for certain was that there would be no excursion to the Haymarket for her tonight. There was far too much to think about, not least what this afternoon meant for the future.

CHAPTER TEN

Over the next weeks society at large became accustomed to seeing Petra Rutherford in the company of Guy Granville. Rupert Lacey came back to Cavendish Square one evening and entered his wife's bedroom as usual without ceremony. "Do you know what's going on with Granville and Petra, Diana?"

Diana swiveled on her dressing stool. "They enjoy each other's company."

Rupert surveyed her, his eyes narrowed. "Don't be obtuse, wife."

Diana laughed. "I admit it seems to go deeper than that."

"Well, Granville's reputation with women isn't going to do Petra's much good," Rupert said bluntly. "Is she his mistress?"

Diana considered the question. "I haven't asked her," she said after a moment's thought. "And she hasn't volunteered the information. So, quite honestly, I don't know."

Rupert frowned. "That's not like Petra. I thought you three shared your most intimate secrets."

Diana's fingers trawled through the open jewelry box on her dresser while she thought how to respond. She and Fenella had both remarked upon how unusually reticent Petra was about her dealings with Guy. She'd dismissed any inquiries with a light laugh and the statement that she was enjoying herself and saw no reason to change anything. She had admitted that her plot to give him a dose of his own medicine had fallen by the wayside, but had reassured her friends that her eyes were wide open when it came to Guy's dubious reputation. He wouldn't blindside her again. However, the paucity of her confidences troubled her friends. They both understood that Petra was in uncharted waters and was sailing them alone. But neither would either of them press for confidences she was not ready to share. It wasn't the way their friendship had ever been. They were there for one another when needed, but respected one another's privacy.

"Petra knows Guy's reputation," she said finally. "She knows what she's doing."

"Well, I hope so. They're taking odds in the clubs that she's his mistress and that as soon as Granville thinks things have gone far enough, and he might be expected to declare himself, he'll do what he always does and disappear abroad. Probably into the ever-open arms of Clothilde Delmont."

Diana frowned. "I don't get the impression Petra's afraid of that."

"Maybe not, but she's not experienced in the ways of the Lord Ashtons of this world," Rupert said dryly. "I think you should warn her, or at least drop a few hints. I'd hate to see her hurt."

"I don't think she'll let that happen to her again," Diana told him.

"Oh? When did it first happen?"

"Ten years ago. Petra's no naïf, Rupert. She knows what Guy's like, or at least *was* like. I think she's on her guard."

"Well, let's hope so. I must get dressed for dinner." He bent and kissed his wife lightly before disappearing through the connecting door to his dressing room.

Diana stared thoughtfully into the mirror. Why *was* Petra so unforthcoming about her relationship with Guy? She didn't conceal the pleasure she took in his company and indeed he was faultlessly attentive to her, almost always at her side in public. They seemed to share a private way of communicating, as so many couples did, and it was true that her friends and acquaintances had imperceptibly come to accept them as a couple. The next step was inevitable for most people in that situation. There would be an engagement. But Petra didn't seem at all concerned about the future, just appeared to be wholeheartedly enjoying the present. And her friends couldn't begrudge her that.

But it was true that society was speculating. And it was true that Guy Granville had a reputation as a philanderer.

Diana sighed. Rupert was right. She and Fenella owed it to their long friendship to bring up at the very least the subject of what Petra expected to happen next.

Petra stretched languidly in Guy's big four-poster bed. The afternoon sun streamed through the open windows throwing bars of light across her naked body as she lay only half covered by the sheet.

"Now that is a most wonderfully wanton sight." Guy turned from the window coming over to the bed. "You have the air of a most contented and indolent cat, my sweet."

Petra smiled, rolling onto her side, propping herself on her elbow, her head resting on her hand as her eyes greedily devoured his nakedness. She didn't think she would ever have enough of that lean muscularity, the flat belly, his long thighs and his delicious bottom. "Come back." She patted the mattress in invitation. "I haven't finished my dish of cream yet."

"Oh, you are a witchy woman," he declared, his eyes taking on a smoky hue. "And heaven help me, but I can't resist you." He came down on the bed beside her, sliding his arms beneath her as he rolled onto his back bringing her with him so she lay on top of him, her hazel eyes laughing down at him.

"What now?" she asked, moving her hips seductively against his loins. Her mouth hovered over his, her tongue suggestively moistening her lips before moving in quick little darts against his, touching the corner of his mouth, outlining the shape of his mouth with the tip.

"You seem to be doing very well on your own," Guy murmured, his hands stroking the length of her back, caressing the curve of her bottom, as she captured his mouth with hers, her tongue demanding entrance, before moving on a seductive exploration of the warm sweet cavern.

He lifted his hips, his penis pressing

upward, insistent against the soft mound of her sex. She shifted slightly, opening her thighs for him, her breath coming fast as she felt him slip within her welcoming body, claiming her for his own. It was a glorious possession and she reveled in every deepening thrust within the tight sheath, moving with his rhythm.

"Kneel up. You'll have more control," he instructed softly, clasping her hips.

Petra did as he said, kneeling astride him. She looked down at the point where their bodies were joined, at the hard pulsing penis pushing into her opened body, and thought she'd never seen anything so gloriously erotic. She lifted her hips, then very slowly brought them down again, enclosing him inch by inch, reveling in his low moan of pleasure. A heady rush of pure sensual triumph washed through her at the knowledge of how much power she had to give or deny his pleasure at this moment. She was now in possession, Guy belonged to her in these moments and as her climax rushed upon her she leaned forward, changing the angle of her possession, heard his joyous cry at the moment of his release. Her own cry blended with his as she fell forward on his body, her forehead resting on his shoulder, her legs straightening as the wonderful weakness washed through her, turning her limbs to jelly.

Guy held her gently, too drained by climax himself to do more than stroke her back in gratitude. "Oh, witchy woman, indeed," he managed finally. "You unman me, sweetheart."

"Do I?" Petra murmured into the hollow of his neck, thrilling to the idea. She had realized from the beginning that sex was an act of power and possession, it needed a possessor and one willing to be possessed. Until this moment it had seemed axiomatic that men were the possessors, their female partners the willingly possessed in the act of love. But Guy had just shown her that the parts could be switched with even greater pleasure for both partners.

"I didn't know it could be like that," she said, lifting her head slightly. "I thought men were always on top."

He laughed, the muscles in his chest and stomach rippling against her skin still pressed into his. "Oh, there are many variations, sweetheart. And I intend we should try them all." He slid his arms between their bodies and lifted her, rolling her onto the bed beside him. "I could stay here all day with you, but the world is intruding."

Leaning over her, he kissed the corner of

149

her mouth, before getting off the bed. "It's almost five o'clock. Would you like some tea?"

"Yes, please. I'm thirsty after all that strenuous activity," she answered with a smug smile, leaning forward to pull the crumpled sheets up to cover her. "What are you doing this evening?" she called after him as he went into the adjacent dressing room.

"I'm engaged to dine with some friends," he responded. He pulled the bell in the dressing room and asked the answering footman for tea. Petra's presence in the four-poster bed next door was an open secret but no one ever saw her there. Her comings and goings were not secretive, but what she did when she was in the house was never made obvious. And Guy was confident in the discretion of his household staff.

Petra waited for him to go on, to tell her who his friends were, but Guy said nothing more, and she didn't feel comfortable asking further questions. For all the wonderful ease and intimacy, the sense that there were no boundaries between them when it came to shared passion, she knew if she was honest with herself that there were boundaries, hard lines that Guy drew between them. What he did when he was not with her, how close he was to the other people who inhabited his private world was a mystery, and one she was somehow wary of penetrating. It was in those moments that she was aware of the gulf of experience that lay between them.

He was in his shirtsleeves when he brought her a cup of tea. "What are your plans this evening?"

"Oh, I'm engaged to go with a party to the opera, but it's Wagner's *Lohengrin*. It's supposed to be a romantic opera but it all ends in death and dismay. I'm probably a philistine but it depresses me."

"I take your point." He returned to his dressing room and said nothing more on the subject of plans for the coming evening.

Petra drank her tea, feeling suddenly deflated. After the glories of the afternoon the prospect of an evening without Guy seemed rather drab, even though she had known they both had separate plans. It didn't help that he was humming to himself next door as he completed his dressing.

"If you can get dressed in ten minutes, I'll walk you home on my way to Curzon Street," he said, returning to the bedroom.

"Brook Street is in the opposite direction," Petra pointed out. "Anyway, I don't feel like hurrying. It's broad daylight on a June early evening so you can't have any objections to my walking two streets home."

"No, I can't," he said easily. "If that's what you want, I'll leave you to take your time." He shrugged into his jacket, brushing an invisible speck off the well-fitting shoulders.

"Why don't you have a valet?" Petra was curious. In many ways Guy was a typical wealthy member of the landed gentry, an aristocratic gentleman about town, but in many other ways he scorned the conventional trappings of that privileged life.

He shrugged. "I learned to look after myself in my travels many years ago and I've never liked the idea of a manservant dedicated to my needs."

"You never talk of those travels," she said, her curiosity still rampant. It was rare the opportunity arose to dig a little into his past.

"Oh, I found myself caught up in a little squabble in Macedonia," he said lightly. "Very important if you were living in Greece or Bulgaria a few years ago, but it didn't resonate much outside that part of the world."

"Oh." Petra leaned forward. "Did you fight? Surely not."

"Why surely not?" He raised a questioning eyebrow.

"I don't really know, it just doesn't seem

to be the kind of thing you'd do. You don't seem like a soldier, not like Rupert at least."

"Lacey chose to fight the Boers," Guy told her. "He chose the life of a career soldier. I certainly had no intention of living that life. However, I fell in with a group of Greek guerrilla fighters." He shrugged. "It was for love of a woman, if you must know, my dear. I've always been hopelessly susceptible to the charms of the fair sex, as I imagine you realize by now." He leaned over her and kissed her. "It was a long time ago."

"What happened to her?"

"She fell in love with a fiercely bearded Greek and out of love with me," he responded with a laugh. "And I left the mountains of Macedonia and came back to England to assume the life I was supposed to live." He straightened. "I have to love you and leave you, sweet Petra."

Petra blew him a kiss as he left the bedroom. That was an interesting nugget of information. She was not in the least troubled by the idea of his fighting in a foreign conflict for the sake of a woman. It struck her as rather romantic, and Guy was not in the general run of things particularly romantic. He was stimulating and amusing, a wonderful lover, courteous and generous, a little too fond of his own way but that was

153

annoying her less now. She just wished he would tell her more about himself, what he was thinking, the experiences that had made him who he now was.

But at least he'd given her something from his past this afternoon, she reflected, getting out of bed, going into the adjoining bathroom. Maybe asking more about his Macedonian adventures would give her a greater sense of who he had been then. It was a start anyway. Lovemaking was wonderful but she knew it was no longer enough. Their liaison had arisen so naturally, after their strange pact of understanding that afternoon. She couldn't remember either of them actually putting the desire into words, or making any particular arrangements, it had just happened, and it had seemed so right, inevitable, a growth from the early beginnings ten years earlier. But now she wanted more. She wanted to know more of the man than Guy Granville the lover. Much more.

Guy strolled toward Piccadilly, relishing the sense of well-being, the overall feeling of pleasure he always had after spending time with Petra. Her challenging, sometimes combative nature met and matched his own, but there were so many other dimensions to

Miss Rutherford, and he was enjoying discovering and exploring each and every one of them. He loved her openness, her lack of artifice, and the way it was tempered with a natural sophistication, a lack of guile that was tempered with a natural caution, an understated wisdom in her understanding of the world they shared. He loved the wonderful devil-may-care flamboyance that she showed in her dress and her lively wit. And he was beginning to recognize that the joy he took in her company was something quite different from the feelings he usually had for the women who shared his bed and his company for as long as it suited them both.

In fact when Guy started to think of a time when Petra's close company would suit him no longer he found it hard to imagine. And that brought him to his present errand. It was not one he relished, but in honor it was one that had to be done.

His walk brought him to an elegant terraced house on Curzon Street. He glanced up at the drawing room windows on the first floor before stepping up to the door and lifting the heavy lion's head brass knocker.

"Milord." The butler bowed him in immediately. "Madame la Vicomtesse expects you. May I take your hat?"

"Merci, Giscard." He handed his top hat and cane to the servant. "No need to announce me." He crossed the square hall and mounted the stairs, entering the double doors to the drawing room with a light alerting knock.

"Ah, Guy, I have been waiting for you for days." Clotilde Delmont glided across the blue Axminster carpet in an elegant rustle of blue and gold damask.

"Hardly days, my dear," he protested, brushing a kiss on her powdered cheek. "I have it on the best authority that you only returned to London the day before yesterday."

The lady made a flirtatious little moue as she flicked her fan open and closed. "There was a time when you would never have waited two days to visit me, *mon cher.*"

"True," Guy conceded. "But time moves on, my dear, for both of us."

Clothilde's blue eyes snapped, the flirtatious glint vanished, a sharpness in its stead. "Whatever can you mean, Guy?"

He took her hand, holding it gently but firmly. "I think you know what I mean, Clothilde. You have acquired other . . . shall we say other interests, in the last year, as have I."

She withdrew her hand from his, her lip

156

curling. "We've known each other for many years, Guy. We've amused each other when the opportunity arose, and we've both indulged ourselves elsewhere on occasion. But we have never been *bourgeois* about it." She shrugged and threw out a dismissive hand. "Such petty little concerns have never troubled you before. What has changed?"

He seemed to consider the question before saying, "I find I have acquired a new sensibility about matters like loyalty, honesty, perhaps even fidelity." He smiled at her. "Come, Clothilde, let us accept the time has come for us both. We took much pleasure in each other, but I find that I want more from a relationship than a superficial, mutually beneficial intimacy. And I fear, my dear, that you could never supply that."

"Is it that simpleton?" she demanded with a cold anger that couldn't disguise the hint of bewilderment in her voice. "The Rutherford woman that everyone's talking about? For God's sake, Guy, she knows nothing of the world, she's everything we despise about the naïve English debutante who sees only marriage and breeding in her future. She'll be a good, obedient wife to whatever man is dull enough to want a wife like that. You've always expressed contempt for such ninnies."

Guy's bark of laughter was harsh. "You don't know what you're talking about, Clothilde. And you certainly know nothing about Miss Rutherford. But if my past hasty generalizations have come back to bite me, then I accept the consequences. As I said, things change, people change."

"Well, you may have changed into a sentimental fool, Guy, but I certainly have not. I enjoyed your company precisely because you were above petty concerns." She turned away from him.

Guy saw the tiny quiver of her hands as she flicked open the silver cigarette box on a side table. He moved swiftly to pick up the engraved lighter, flicking it open. She bent her head to the light, inhaled deeply and walked away from him to the window.

"Goodbye, Guy."

"Goodbye, Clothilde." He bowed to her back and left. He hadn't expected it to be a pleasant conversation but now he realized that he had hoped for an amicable agreement to bring their liaison to a cordial close. But maybe he should have been more realistic. Clothilde was never an easy woman and her bitterness, while regrettable, was probably only to be expected. However, he couldn't deny the lightness, the sense of relief, as he walked back toward Piccadilly.

He could now with a clear conscience devote his attentions to getting to know Miss Rutherford in all her manifestations.

Something Clothilde had said troubled him though. Why hadn't he realized that Petra's name was being bandied about in the clubs and drawing rooms of Mayfair? He should have realized the danger of his attentions to her reputation, but all his liaisons hitherto had been with women who could not be touched by gossip, and who certainly wouldn't be concerned by it. The irony of his insisting she not walk home alone at night, while he recklessly played fast and loose with her reputation, was not lost on him.

CHAPTER ELEVEN

"Must we really go back inside for the second act?" Petra asked in the crowded foyer of the Covent Garden opera house. "We all know Elsa falls down dead at the end."

"At the end of the third act," Diana pointed out.

"Oh, yes. I managed to forget there are three acts," Petra said with a mock groan.

"I think you're feeling faint, Petra." Fenella took a sip of champagne. "I think we should take her home, Diana, don't you?"

Diana grinned. "Definitely. You're looking really sickly, dearest."

"Oh, am I? I do feel a little unwell." Petra drooped into a convenient armless chair, her hand pressed to her forehead. "One of my headaches is coming on."

"I'll make our excuses to Bella Carrington," Fenella said.

160

Her friends watched her thread her way through the chattering throng to where their hostess stood with some of their fellow guests in the Carringtons' party. Petra sighed and wilted convincingly as Lady Carrington looked toward her with concern. They couldn't hear the conversation between the lady and Fenella but it looked as if Fenella was more than convincing in her tale.

"She is an actress after all," Diana said with a stifled laugh as Bella patted their friend's arm and looked again toward Petra, saying something urgently to Fenella.

"Oh, I do hope she's not coming over here to see for herself," Petra whispered. "*I'm* not an actress."

"No, it's all right. Fenella seems to have put her off. Look, she's coming back alone."

"And now I feel horribly guilty," Petra said.

"All done and dusted," Fenella said brightly as she rejoined them. "Bella at first wanted us to take her carriage, but I managed to persuade her that we would manage with a hackney. Come, lean on my arm, Petra. Diana, take her other arm."

Thus supported, Petra managed to stumble from the foyer and out into the warm night. "Where shall we go now?"

"I'm a little peckish," Fenella said. "Dinner seems like a long time ago."

"Opera will do that," Petra told her. "Let's go to Gunter's. I need an ice for my head."

Diana hailed a passing cab and the women climbed up, squeezing onto the single bench. "Gunter's in Berkeley Square," Diana instructed the cabbie on the box in front.

"Berkeley Square," Diana mused. "Maybe we'll run into Guy Granville."

"I doubt it," Petra replied. "He's engaged with friends in Curzon Street."

"Curzon Street. Isn't that where the vi—" Fenella broke off as Diana pinched her leg.

"Where who?" Petra asked. "What's the matter?" she demanded, seeing her friends' discomfiture. "Where who?" she asked again.

"Clothilde Delmont has a house on Curzon Street," Diana told her.

"So what if she does?" Petra looked directly at Diana. "It's nothing to me where she lives."

"No, of course it's not." Diana was rarely flustered but her usual composure deserted her. "I'm sorry, Petra. I don't know why I'm making such a mess of this. It's just that . . . that we —"

"That we're very curious to know how

162

things stand between you and Guy," Fenella broke in. "You never talk about it, or at least not beyond the merest commonplace. And, well, it's only natural that in the absence of fact we're going to speculate."

"Oh, is that all?" Petra said with a laugh. "If I'd known you were so curious I'd have answered all your questions. But you haven't asked any."

"No," Diana agreed. "We were rather waiting for you to volunteer the details."

"When we get to Gunter's," Petra promised. "How are the arrangements going for Ascot next week?"

Diana accepted the changed subject. "Very well. Rupert and I are still arguing about whether to have poached salmon or roast partridge for lunch. What's your opinion?"

"Have both," Petra replied. "That way you'll please everyone."

"I'd rather come to that conclusion myself," Diana said.

"Russian salad and caviar," Fenella put in. "Perfect for a summer lunch."

"Strawberry shortcake and sherry trifle," Petra added. "Oh, this is making me hungry. I need something more substantial than just an ice. We can get a light supper at Gunter's."

The carriage drew up outside Gunter's on the far side of the square from Granville House. Diana paid the driver and the three of them went into the tea shop. It was busy, a warm evening brought out people strolling the square garden and the quiet residential streets. One of the round iron tables on the pavement outside the tea shop was free and they took it, ordering a few light dishes from the white-aproned waiter.

"Oh, and a bottle of Moët," Petra called after him. "We might as well make the most of our freedom from Wagner. I shall have to write a groveling apology to Bella Carrington in the morning. I'll apologize for spoiling your evenings too." She bestowed a benign smile on her companions.

"Forget that," Diana said. "Tell us what's going on with Granville."

"Have you already made love?" Fenella asked, cutting to the chase. "I don't believe in beating about the bush."

"No, you don't." Petra fell silent as the waiter opened the champagne, filling their glasses. When he'd departed she said, "To be equally blunt, yes, we have. And lovemaking is wondrous. But you both know that."

"Indeed," Diana agreed.

"You're not taking any risks?" Fenella asked hesitantly.

Petra gave a half laugh. "You really don't believe in discretion, Fenella. No, no risks. Guy uses those rubber sheaths, even though he doesn't like them. I'd be quite happy if he didn't use them."

"Not until you have a ring on your finger," Fenella said sharply.

"Oh, you're such a mother hen, dearest." Petra laughed. "Of course I'm not going to take any risks. Even if I was willing, Guy wouldn't be. He's oddly strict about some things, sometimes annoyingly conventional and rule abiding."

Diana and Fenella exchanged glances of relief and Petra went into a peal of laughter. "Oh, dear, why does everyone feel the need to watch over me, to guide my hesitant footsteps? I'm perfectly able to look after myself."

"Yes, of course you are, darling." Diana shook her head ruefully. "We have no right to think you need tutoring in this game of life we're all playing."

"How do you feel about Guy?" Fenella asked, leaning across the table. "Do you just really like him, or do you think you might *love* him?"

"To the point as always, Fenella," Diana observed.

Petra took a leisurely sip of champagne

before responding. "It's a fair question. The answer is that I'm not really sure. All I know at the moment is that I'm loving every minute of the whole adventure and I'm hungry for whatever new experiences I can have with Guy. The future is the last thing on my mind." She selected a crab tart and ate it with reflective pleasure.

"I hate to say this, but, a word to the wise, Petra. Rupert says they're taking odds in the clubs about your relationship with Guy, how far it's gone," she added delicately. "But also about whether he'll declare himself. It's never good to be the subject of gossip."

Petra's high spirits wavered for a moment. So far she had managed to ignore that most inconvenient and unfair fact of life. An unmarried woman's reputation was like gold dust. Ephemeral, blown away on a slight breeze. A man's reputation, of course, was immune from anything short of murder.

"I haven't done anything publicly to offend society's dusty morals," she said, after a moment. "I defy anyone to find something concrete to accuse me of."

"I hate to say it, darling, but Guy's reputation is enough to sully yours," Fenella pointed out. "It's the height of injustice, of course, but it's a sad fact."

"And if tongues are wagging the gossip is bound to reach your parents," Diana added.

Petra closed her eyes briefly. Scandal was the one thing she could be sure would bring her mother and father hot foot from the baths of Baden-Baden, or wherever they were now. "Joth hasn't said anything. If he had wind of any potential scandal he would have said." Although, now she thought about it, Petra wasn't so sure. Jonathan was so deeply involved in his parliamentary life, and thought Guy was the answer to his prayers when it came to legislation for Somerset, that he probably couldn't see past the end of his nose when it came to Granville and his own sister.

"I don't think it's taken wings yet," Diana said. "Rupert just thought we should warn you of the possibility that the gossips might get ahold of it."

"Well, thank him for the warning," Petra said. "I'll be as discreet as a nun from now on." She drank her champagne. "Oh, don't look so uncomfortable, both of you. I'm not in the least offended, how could I be when I know you only have my best interests at heart."

"Well, as long as you don't think of us as a pair of fussy maiden aunts," Fenella said, which had the beneficial effect of reducing the three of them to helpless laughter.

A carriage bowled past the scatter of tables on the pavement beside the square garden while they were still enjoying the joke and they took no notice when it drew to a halt a few yards farther down the street. Guy jumped down, paid the driver, and stood for a moment regarding the three laughing women with a slightly puzzled expression. What on earth could have caused three adult women to collapse in giggles in the middle of the street? He was on his way home, finding that he had little appetite for company after his uncomfortable meeting with Clothilde, and had seen the women out of the corner of his eye as the hackney passed. He stopped the carriage on impulse, intending to join them for a few minutes, but now, seeing their closeness, he felt somehow that they had thrown up a wall of exclusion around themselves and he was reluctant to intrude.

He decided to avoid them by walking through the garden to his house on the other side of the square but Petra, wiping her streaming eyes, glanced in his direction. Instantly she raised a hand, waving vigorously. "Guy, come and join us."

So much for discretion. He strolled toward them. "Something has amused you, ladies.

Dare I ask what?" He reached for a spare chair at a neighboring table and swung it around to join theirs.

"I doubt you'd find it funny," Petra said.

"Yes, we were just being a bit silly," Fenella added.

"It comes from knowing one another for so long," Diana explained. "We were school-girls together and there was a time when the silliest of things would reduce us to tears of laughter."

"Would you like champagne, Guy? I think there's a drop left in the bottle." Petra made to lift the bottle out of the ice bucket.

"No, thank you. I prefer cognac." He waved at a waiter standing in the doorway of the tea shop and gave his order. "So, what happened to Lohengrin?"

"I felt rather faint in the first interval." Petra passed a hand across her brow.

"I'm glad to find you in such rude health now," Guy said solemnly. "How unfortunate you could only manage the first act."

"Yes, wasn't it?" Petra agreed blandly. "But fortunately my strange turns don't last very long."

"That is certainly a blessing." He nodded his thanks to the waiter, who set a brandy goblet in front of him.

"How was your evening, Guy?" Petra

asked. "It's rather early to call it a night, isn't it?"

"I found I was not in the mood for blackjack," he told her. "I thought I'd have a return engagement with Mr. Pickwick." He gave her a conspiratorial smile over his goblet.

"Guy's very fond of Dickens," Petra said airily. "He likes Miss Austen too."

"I wish Edward did," Fenella lamented. "He says her subjects are inconsequential. Perhaps you could change his mind, Guy."

Guy put up his hands in a defensive gesture. "I wouldn't dream of trying to change anyone's mind about literature, and particularly not your husband's, he's too erudite a scholar." He turned to Diana. "How's the mare doing, Diana? Is her trainer confident for the Queen Anne Stakes?"

Diana grimaced. "No one's confident about anything, which isn't good news for the bookies. Kimberley Diamond is untried on a major course, although she'd done well in the local races. But we're hoping, of course, that she'll spring upon an unwary public and astonish the world."

"I look forward to seeing her triumphant," Guy said. He turned to acknowledge the waiter who set a saucer with the bill at his elbow. "I think they would like us to leave. We appear to be the last holdouts." He took a billfold from his pocket.

"No," said Diana. "You can't —"

"Don't be tiresome, Mrs. Lacey," he said calmly, laying a bill on the saucer.

Diana gasped in indignation. Her fingers twitched toward the plate and then she caught Petra's eye. Petra shook her head and Diana closed her lips firmly and gathered up her belongings. "Thank you, Lord Ashton. You are too kind."

He bowed his head with a pleasant smile. "The pleasure was all mine, ladies. It was a delightful surprise to find you on my doorstep." He beckoned the waiter again. "Send someone to find a hackney for the ladies. Petra, I'll walk you home."

Punctiliously he handed Diana and Fenella into a hackney, his dark eyes alight with amusement as Diana bade him a stiff good night. "We're hat shopping for Ascot tomorrow, Petra, don't forget," Fenella called as the carriage took off toward Piccadilly.

Petra raised a hand in farewell. "Do you like making enemies, Guy?"

"Of course not. But Diana should have known better."

"You're doing it again," she exclaimed. "It

was not your party. It was not your bill. We split restaurant bills all the time and have been doing so for years. And we would have been delighted to have bought you a cognac."

"Yes, but you see I'm rather old-fashioned in such matters." He gave an exaggerated sigh. "I fear I'm too old and set in my ways to change now." He took her hand and tucked it into his arm as they walked into the garden.

"That's arrant nonsense," Petra declared. "You fly in the face of convention all the time."

"Oh? Do I?" He looked down at her, the moonlight silvering the shadows beneath the trees. "How so?"

Petra realized too late that once again she had ventured too far. How to extricate herself? "I don't know exactly," she prevaricated. "You seem to have a very freewheeling attitude to women."

"Ah." He paused on the path. "And how is that exactly, Petra?" There was a dangerous undertone to the question.

"It matters nothing to me," she said, tossing her head. "But everyone talks about your liaison with the Frenchwoman. The Viscomtesse Delmont. It's hardly discreet."

There was a long silence as they continued

to stand beneath the trees. Then Guy said, "No, you're quite right. Clothilde and I have never troubled about discretion. But I can assure you, Petra, that where you are concerned, I am and always will be the soul of discretion." He started walking again, her hand still firmly tucked in the crook of his elbow.

Petra had nothing to say. He had just confirmed his relationship with the Frenchwoman as if it was the most natural thing in the world, and had said nothing about its being finished, or even about the possibility of its being over in the future. She was dumbfounded.

She kept her silence until they emerged from the garden on the far side of Berkeley Square and Guy closed the gate behind them as they stepped onto the street. He glanced down at her, a question in his dark gaze. He could detect no hostility in her preoccupation, but he could sense her sudden uncertainty.

"Will you come home with me?" he asked as they reached his front door.

Petra hesitated, then shook her head. "Perhaps not tonight, Guy, if you don't mind. I feel rather tired. I'm sorry."

"Dear girl, there is nothing for you to be sorry about," he said, turning their steps towards Brook Street. "Much as I would love to spend the next few hours with you in my bed, you're under no obligation. You never could be. You do understand that, Petra, don't you?"

"Yes . . . yes, of course I do. It's just that there's nothing I would like more, except that I really am tired and I don't think I'll be very good company."

Guy wasn't fooled. "Another time," he said quietly and silence fell between them until they reached the Rutherford house on Brook Street.

Petra made no demur as he took her evening bag and found her keys. She'd have been more surprised now if he had left her to open the door herself. But he didn't immediately put the key in the lock, instead stood looking down at her intently for a moment. She met his gaze with a questioning smile, waiting for his good night kiss.

Instead, Guy lightly ran a fingertip over her lips, the expression in the dark eyes grave, then he said, "You need never give Clothilde Delmont a second thought, my sweet. I promise you she is of no importance at all." Then he kissed her quickly, opened the door and stepped back off the doorstep as Foster held the door wide.

Petra was too stunned to do more than

offer a half wave of farewell before she forced a smile and word of greeting to the butler as she stepped past him into the cool dim light of the hall.

Foster removed her key from the lock before closing the door, handing the key to her. "You passed a pleasant evening, I trust, Miss Petra."

"Very pleasant, thank you, Foster." Petra dropped the key back in her bag and moved to the stairs, feeling slightly dazed. "Good night." She hurried up to her bedroom, wondering what had just happened. What lay behind Guy's declaration? He was under no obligation to make it.

CHAPTER TWELVE

"Your mind is not on hats, dearest," Diana stated, looking across the milliner's shop to where Petra was idly picking at the elaborate black ruched ribbon on a wide-brimmed straw hat. "That will most definitely not suit you."

Petra dropped the hat with a guilty flush. "No, I know. I don't like it at all," she said hastily. "But I like that ice blue silk one with the floppy brim on you. You're tall enough to carry it off."

"I'm not sure." Diana picked up the hat in question, turning it around on one hand. "What d'you think, Fenella?"

"I think it suits you very well," Fenella declared, peering at her own reflection in the large mirror, adjusting the set of a straw confection festooned with tulle flowers. "I look ridiculous." She set it aside in disgust. "Hats just don't suit me."

"This one will." Petra selected a cream

straw hat with a wide turned-back brim and a sprig of pale green leaves. "Try it."

Fenella did so and looked surprised. The wide brim framed her face in a most attractive way. "You do have an eye, Petra. I would never have believed it, but it actually does work."

"Yes, it does," Diana agreed, examining her friend's appearance.

"Well, that's me done," Fenella declared with satisfaction, handing the cream straw to the assistant. "Now what about you two?"

"I'll take the blue silk." Diana made up her mind. "It'll be set off nicely by my dark blue taffeta." She handed the hat to the assistant. "Now, Petra, let's see what we can find for you."

Petra forced herself to concentrate on the vitally important matter at hand. She couldn't go hatless to Ladies Day at Ascot. She picked out a close-fitting hat of white lace and tulle, trimmed with a bright orange ribbon and sporting two white plumes. "Let's see what this looks like." She put it on, tucking her hair up, and examined her reflection tilting her head this way and that. "I was going to wear my white silk dress, the one with the pink and orange flowers. The orange ribbon will go beautifully."

"Then I believe our work here is done,

ladies," Diana stated with satisfaction.

"And it didn't take all morning either," Fenella added with similar satisfaction. "What shall we do until lunchtime?"

"St. James's Park," Petra said promptly. "It's such a gorgeous day."

After giving the milliner directions as to where to deliver the three hatboxes, the women went out onto the Strand and started walking toward the park. The thoroughfare was busy with carriages, the pavements crowded with pedestrians and it was hard to keep up a conversation as they tried to stay abreast of one another. At one point a knot of people emerged from an alley and converged on the path in front of Petra separating her from her friends, bringing her almost to a standstill. She moved to the edge of the pavement to slide past them, stepping for a moment into the street just as a barouche swept up at a brisk pace. She jumped hastily back onto the pavement, glaring at the coachman, who was belatedly attempting to slow his horses.

Clothilde Delmont stared at her from the cushioned seat behind the coachman. Petra saw recognition flash in the other woman's blue eyes, replaced with something most unpleasant. Malice, she thought. It was malice, with a good helping of disdain.

Unconsciously, Petra put up her chin and met the other woman's stare with her own, then she forced herself to feign a smile with a nod of courteous recognition, and hurriedly stepped up to join her friends.

"Wasn't that — ?" Fenella began.

"Clothilde Delmont, yes," Petra said. "She's so incredibly elegant. No one has the right to have a neck that long."

"And that hat . . ." Diana shook her head. "It was like a tricorne, so unusual."

"I thought she looked most disagreeable," Fenella declared. "As if she'd just tasted sour milk in her coffee."

Petra laughed, trying to dispel the unease that fleeting encounter had engendered. "She didn't look very content, I must say. But we sound like a trio of gossiping cats."

"I imagine she'll be at Ascot," Diana said. "It's Ladies Day, everyone will be there."

Petra managed a casual shrug. "Even if she is, there's no reason why we should run into her. There are other enclosures, other pavilions."

"But only one Royal Enclosure," Fenella pointed out. "And somehow I don't see the vicomtesse gracing any other."

"Will it be awkward for you, Petra? Guy will have to acknowledge her," Diana asked directly.

"Of course he will, if he bumps into her," Petra replied. "And it won't be awkward in the least."

"Good," Diana said, sounding a little doubtful. "Anyway, maybe horse racing isn't her cup of tea."

Petra had little doubt that Clothilde would be at Ascot, looking impossibly elegant, impossible to ignore. Her hat would be spectacular, of course, and she would be wearing shoes with heels that would make any other woman teeter with every step. But she would glide, of course she would, over the grass and the gravel paths, tall and graceful as a swan, while lesser women picked their way over the treacherous ground in fear of making utter fools of themselves.

She could see in her mind's eye Clothilde and Guy walking side by side, perfectly matched in height, impeccably dressed, so utterly suited to each other. Whereas when she walked beside him she was like a sparrow hopping to keep up with an eagle. The image was so absurd it chased away her moment of despondency. It didn't matter what she and Guy looked like side by side as long as they enjoyed each other. And so far it was abundantly clear that they did.

■ ■ ■

Ladies Day dawned bright and warm and the crowd at Ascot was in a festive mood. Family parties picnicked under the trees and bookies shouted the odds from their stands where ordinary folk milled, an excited buzz of speculation filling the air. Hats of every size and description were on display in the stands among the regular racegoers as well as among the elite in their boxes.

Petra leaned her elbows on the edge of the Laceys' private box in the Royal Enclosure, looking out over the racecourse. The far side of the box overlooked the straight mile along which, punctually at two o'clock, the royal party would progress in their landau drawn by four Windsor Greys. Only when the royal couple were seated in the royal box could the races begin.

"More champagne?"

She turned to look up at Guy, who held a champagne bottle in invitation. "Thank you." She proffered her glass. "Diana and Rupert are on tenterhooks. I don't think I've ever seen Rupert tense before. He's always so collected."

"There's a lot at stake." Guy took her glass and refilled it. He looked across at the

181

course. "At least the ground's in good shape."

Petra laughed. "Yes, apparently Kimberley Diamond's trainer called it Goldilocks, not too soft, not too hard, not too wet, not too dry."

"Have they gone down to the owners' paddock?"

"Yes, just to wish the jockey good luck. They'll be back before the race."

"Could I have a refill, Guy, if there's any in that bottle." Fenella appeared beside Petra. "I'm beginning to feel as nervous and excited as Diana and Rupert."

"It means more to them than it might ordinarily," Petra said. "Because of Jem."

"Jem?" Guy inquired, refilling Fenella's glass.

"Diana's brother. Rupert's best friend. The filly belonged to Jem and Diana, as a colt she was a present to them both from their father, but she was particularly Jem's project. When he was killed at Mafeking his share went to Rupert." Petra grinned. "That was a real bone of contention between Diana and Rupert, d'you remember, Fenella?"

"How could I forget? Diana was mad as fire," her friend said with a chuckle. "But all's well that ends well, and now I think they both feel this race is for Jem."

182

Guy nodded, he was just beginning to understand the depths of intimacy between Petra and her friends, and their families. The layers went down very far into their shared past. Sometimes he found himself envying them their natural ease and understanding with one another. He was fond of his sister and interested in her life and her family, but he wouldn't say they were close, not in the way Petra and her brother were. And he'd never really developed any particularly close relationships with either men or women. His love affairs had been satisfying, but not particularly deep, if he was honest.

Until now.

He glanced sideways at Petra, who was laughing at something Fenella had said, her hazel eyes alight, her cheeks slightly flushed with champagne, sun and pleasure, and something seemed to come loose inside him. It felt almost like a spring breaking. If he'd ever tried to imagine the woman who would steal his heart, she wouldn't have borne the slightest resemblance to Petra Rutherford, small, vivacious, challenging, with little respect for the rites and rituals of society's dictates. She lacked artifice. What you saw was what you got, and Guy's experience with women hitherto was that a man had to assume wiles and deviousness in all their dealings. The image of Clothilde rose vividly in his mind's eye. He enjoyed matching wits with Clothilde, but he wouldn't trust her any further than he could throw her and knew she felt the same way about him.

"The Royal Procession is just starting." Jonathan's voice interrupted his thoughts as the younger man hurried across the box toward them. "Let's see if we can squeeze into a spot at the front of the box for the first race?"

"Come over here," Diana called imperatively, waving from where she now stood with Rupert in the middle of the front row of the box. "The Queen Anne Stakes are the third race."

"Oh, good, I've time to put a bet on," Petra said, fumbling in her handbag for her wallet. "Guy, will you place it for me? How much do you think?"

"How confident are you in the horse?" he asked with an amused smile.

"Oh, totally confident," she said airily, withdrawing a ten-pound note. "Ten pounds on Kimberley Diamond to win."

He took the money and shook his head. "Do you even know what the odds on her are?"

"No, but what does it matter?" she said.

"That's what I want to do."

"Very well. As my lady wishes." Still smiling, he made his way through the gathering to the bookies' stands outside the enclosure.

"Edward put five pounds on," Fenella said. "Now I feel as if we didn't have enough faith."

"Nonsense," declared Petra. "I'm just feeling impulsive. What do you think of the queen's hat?"

Fenella wrinkled her nose, watching the royal carriage approach up the Straight Mile. "Pedestrian," she stated. "I'm sure I've seen her wear it before . . . at one of the garden parties, I think."

"She's never been much interested in high fashion." They watched as the carriage disgorged its royal passengers, who took their places in the royal box. "Now that's over, the excitement can begin." Petra turned her head to look toward the entrance to the box. "It's taking Guy a long time . . . oh, there he is." She waved at him vigorously.

"Quite reasonable odds," he said, giving her the betting slip. "The filly doesn't have much of a reputation yet. If she wins, you'll make some money."

"Diana, how much did you put on Kimberley Diamond?" Petra asked. "Guy says the odds are reasonable."

Diana looked stricken. "I didn't put anything on her. I was so agitated and excited and nervous it was the last thing I thought of."

"Well, fortunately for the honor of the family, I thought to put twenty guineas on her," Rupert said, laughing.

Petra gave her attention to the racecourse, leaning her forearms on the rail, her gaze roaming over the crowds in the stands below her and across to the neighboring boxes. And her eyes met those of Clothilde Delmont, leaning forward in the neighboring box, regarding the crowds and the course. She held opera glasses on a wand in one hand, occasionally lifting them to her eyes to get a better look.

Petra turned her head away but not quickly enough. Clothilde raised the glasses and seemed to examine Petra minutely for a very long time. Even with her head turned away she could feel the stare boring into her. Deliberately she turned to look at the woman, then touched Guy's arm. "I think Lady Delmont is trying to attract your attention, Guy?"

He raised his eyebrows, then turned to look where Petra indicated. Clothilde lowered her glasses and smiled, raising a hand in a fluttering wave. Guy bowed his head in curt acknowledgment and his expression was dark as he turned abruptly away.

"That is the most fetching hat Lady Delmont is wearing," Petra said. It was a towering confection elaborately adorned with silk flowers and what looked remarkably like a bird in a gilded cage, but one couldn't be certain at this distance, Petra thought, hugging to herself Guy's clear displeasure.

"Lady Delmont's dress sense is always impeccable," Guy said coolly. "She has unerring taste."

That wasn't quite what Petra had hoped to hear but she had to admit it was only the truth. It seemed though that perhaps Guy and the lady had had a falling-out when she considered his present clear displeasure combined with what he had said to her on her doorstep about not worrying about Clothilde. But it also seemed to her that there might well be some unfinished business between them. And complications were always dangerous. Just when you thought something was settled, some twist or other would upset the apple cart.

Guy glanced down at Petra, aware of a sudden rigidity in the slight frame beside him. He saw the line of her jaw harden and frown lines deepen between her arched eyebrows. And once again he had the strange sensation of something loosening within him, followed by conviction, the absolute knowledge of what had to come next.

"Come." He took her hand, drawing her away from the front of the box.

"What? Where? Guy, the race is about to begin," Petra protested in a fierce undertone.

"Never mind that." He pulled her inexorably beside him, circling her waist with an arm, guiding her through the box. No one paid them any attention, they were all too intent now on the racecourse, binoculars in hand, and they reached the ground outside the box without notice.

"Guy, what are you doing? I want to see the race." Petra pulled back, digging her heels in. "Are you mad?"

"No, probably saner than I've been in a very long time," he responded. "I have something to say to you and it can't be said in a crowd. This way." He gave a quick pull on her hand that almost unbalanced her and she flailed for a few seconds trying to get her footing. But she was propelled along nevertheless until Guy stopped in a far corner of the Royal Enclosure, as far from the course and the spectators as it was possible to get.

"Hush, Petra," he said imperatively, as she looked ready to launch into an indignant tirade. He put a finger on her lips, keeping it there as his steady gaze held hers until she took a breath of acceptance and was still.

He smiled, running his thumb over her lips as he so often did. It made her lips tingle and she moistened them with the tip of her tongue, held by his gaze as if on the brink of something momentous. "I don't know what to do with the way you make me feel, Petra. I want to look after you, to protect you, but then your stubborn, obstinate, challenging, bristly self-assertion annoys me and I want to shake some sense into you. But you move me in a way I've never felt before, being with you fills me with joy, like the blackbird's song the other night, so my question to you, Petra Rutherford, is, will you marry me?"

CHAPTER THIRTEEN

Petra was faintly aware of the roar of the crowd somewhere in the far distance, the thunder of pounding hooves, but her world seemed to have shrunk to this encapsulated moment contained by the intense dark gaze, the fingertip warm on her lips, the soft but so momentous words in her ears. It took a long moment for the import of those words to penetrate, to fall into a sensible pattern. And as the pattern fell into shape she wondered what answer she wanted to give to his straight question.

Part of her couldn't believe she was hesitating. What woman in her right mind would turn down such an advantageous marriage proposal? An ancient title, lands, fortune . . . her parents would be pleased. They would consider they had done very well by their daughter, who had done very well for herself.

Even as these cynical thoughts played in

190

her head, she realized that she was trying to find a way to temper her need to fling herself into his arms, to shout her acceptance to the rooftops. Some warning niggle held her back from the unbridled joy his proposal brought her. Of course she wanted to marry him, of course she wanted to share her life with him. Of course she wanted that close, intimate partnership that Diana and Fenella had with their husbands. But was it safe to love Guy Granville?

Petra knew that she could not tolerate a marriage where there was ever the faintest suspicion of a lack of loyalty on either side. She could not commit herself if it was not completely and forever. Was that the same for Guy? His past spoke against it.

"Petra?" he prompted quietly. "Will you please say something?"

"Yes, oh, yes, I'm sorry. I was thinking."

His finger left her lips and his smile was puzzled as he said, "I hadn't realized my proposal would cause you so much heart searching. If you need to think further, why don't we discuss this again in a day or two."

The world fell back into place. Petra shook her head vigorously. "No. No, Guy, of course I will marry you. I love you and there's nothing I would like more than to share my life with you."

"Well, that took you long enough," he responded, his smile now teasing as he bent to kiss the corner of her mouth.

"I've never been proposed to before," she said, laughing against his mouth. "I had to get used to the idea."

"I've never proposed to anyone before," he returned, cupping her face between his hands.

"Not even to the lady guerrilla in Macedonia?"

"Most definitely not to her." He kissed her, a deep, affirmative kiss and the last faint wisp of misgiving flew into the ether. When at last they moved apart their surroundings flooded in, the raucous sounds of the crowd, cheering and applauding.

"What happened?" Petra asked. "Which horse won?"

"We'll find out if we go back." Guy slipped his hand under her arm. "Shall we keep this between ourselves for the moment?"

"Yes, of course. This is Diana's day. Oh, I do hope Kimberley Diamond won." Petra plunged into the crowd, fighting her way back to the box.

Guy shook his head in astonishment. She seemed to have forgotten the last momentous moments, or at least thrust them into the background with no difficulty. He'd rather expected that when a young lady received an acceptable proposal of marriage she would find it difficult to think of anything else and be bursting to share the news. Not so, it seemed. Or at least not where Petra Rutherford was concerned. Anyone would think she received marriage proposals on a daily basis. It certainly put him in his place. The reflection brought a reluctant smile to his lips. He doubted life with Petra would ever be boring, infuriating at times almost certainly, but boring? Never.

"Oh, where were you, Petra?" Fenella cried as Petra pushed through the excited guests in the box. "Diana and Rupert have gone down to the Winners' Enclosure. Did you see it? It was so exciting."

"Kimberley Diamond won?" Petra asked, guilt mingling with pleasure at the news.

"Yes, by a hair, just in the very final seconds, she pulled ahead. It was so exciting." Fenella stared at her. "Where *were* you? You were right here when the race started."

"Sudden call of nature," Petra improvised airily, ignoring her friend's disbelieving stare. "It couldn't wait."

"This calls for more champagne." Guy appeared opportunely, bottle in hand. "Have a drink and then we'll go and collect your winnings, Petra." He filled Fenella's glass. "Has Edward gone to collect yours?"

"Yes, a moment ago," Fenella said, regarding the pair of them with a bemused question in her eyes. Something had happened between them, but before she could say anything further, a cheer went up from the party in the box as Diana and Rupert returned. Diana's eyes were shining, and the sheen was more than pure joy and excitement, her friends could see the gloss of tears and knew she was thinking of Jem, and wishing he were beside her to revel in their filly's triumph.

"Congratulations, dearest." Petra hugged Diana tightly. "It must feel wonderful."

"It does," Diana agreed, smiling through her tears as she turned into Fenella's embrace. "Jem would have been so thrilled. Rupert . . . ?" She looked around for her husband. "Oh, what's going on now?"

An ensign in royal livery was talking to Rupert, who nodded and came over to his wife. "We've been summoned to the Royal Box, Diana. His Majesty wants to congratulate us on Kimberley Diamond's race."

"Then I suppose we had better obey the call," Diana said. "We won't be long. Don't go anywhere," she enjoined her friends, following her husband to the Royal Box.

"Well, here you are, my love. Thirty pounds." Edward materialized out of the crowd, flourishing a handful of banknotes. "Not a bad return on a fiver."

"No, indeed not." Fenella tucked the winnings into her handbag. "What about the next race? Should we put money on that?"

"If you wish," her husband said. "I've never seen the appeal of gambling just for the sake of it."

"Oh." Fenella looked a little deflated. "I thought that was quite exciting."

"Well, we're going to collect Petra's winnings," Guy said. "I'll be happy to put a bet on for you for the next race."

Fenella shook her head. "No, really I agree with Edward. It was only so exciting last time because it was Diana and Rupert's horse."

"Come then, Petra." Guy guided her through the box and out to the bookies' enclosure. They collected her winnings and Petra turned to make her way back to the others.

Guy put an arresting hand on her arm. "Do you really want to go back?" he asked. "Could we make our excuses? I feel we have some unfinished business."

Now that the excitement of the race was over, Petra forgot everything but the astounding few minutes before the race. Had Guy really proposed? Had she really said yes? The enormous significance of it all swamped her and she gazed at him, for the moment numbed into silence. Then with an almost visible shake of her head she brought herself back into the world.

"I'll send a message to Diana," she said finally. "I can't possibly go back and pretend everything's just the same as it always was."

"Good." Guy turned back to the bookies' stand. "Can you let me have a piece of paper?" The man tore a piece out of a notebook.

" 'Ere y'are, guv."

"Thanks." Guy borrowed the stub of a chewed pencil and scribbled on the paper. "Is there a lad who can take this for me to the box over there? The one with the blue and white flag." He gestured to the box, which flew the colors of Kimberley Diamond's stables, setting half a crown down with the note.

"Our Diccon'll do it." The man pocketed the coin before yelling something incomprehensible over his shoulder and a grimy boy of about ten appeared at a run. He took the note, listened to instructions, and dived into the crowd.

"What did you say?" Petra asked.

"Just that something urgent had come up and we needed to leave, and that you would explain everything when you saw them. Was that all right? I didn't see a need for an elaborate fabrication."

"No, that was fine. I'm not in the habit of lying to my friends."

"And there's no reason to in this instance, is there?"

"No, of course not." Petra laughed suddenly. "There's so much to talk about. Where shall we go?"

"Berkeley Square?"

"Yes, let's take an early train home. We can get away before the crowds. I think Diana and Rupert's party are planning to stay for the singsong around the bandstand after the last race, so no one will be back in London until much later."

The communal singsong at the end of every race day during Royal Ascot was a long-held tradition, but Petra was perfectly happy to skip the ritual this time and Guy made no demur, guiding their steps to the field where the hired hackneys awaited travelers for the station.

As luck would have it a London train steamed into the station five minutes after they arrived on the platform, and Guy half lifted Petra up the steep step into a deserted

197

first-class carriage, stepping up behind her.

She sat down on the plush bench seat, resting her head against a starched antimacassar, her head turned to the window as the train whistled shrilly and began to chug out of the station and into the countryside. The wondrous excitement she had felt earlier seeped back, filling her with a delicious sensual anticipation. Her toes curled in her elegant kid shoes, and her blood seemed to run fast through her veins. She looked across the small space to where Guy sat, arms folded, on the opposite bench, watching her with narrowed eyes.

"What are you thinking, Petra?" he asked, his voice smooth as cream, a deep note of something wonderfully wicked beneath the question.

For answer, she stood up and pulled down the blinds at the carriage window, shutting out the passing world. Guy reached across the space, taking her hands and pulling her toward him. "Lift your skirt."

She did so, hitching the delicate silk up to her hips, pushing down her drawers, kicking them off one foot impatiently, as she straddled his lap. Guy unbuttoned his trousers, his penis springing hard and erect as she sank down slowly astride him, taking him deep within her.

She caught her bottom lip with her teeth as she felt him move high inside her, his full length buried to her core, her thighs pressing hard against his. He moved his hands to her waist, holding her lightly, moving upward even as she circled her hips around him, lifting and lowering herself, her head thrown back, her eyes closed as the moment of climax crept up, hovering in the background, holding her in a suspended anticipation. Guy seemed to know exactly what she was feeling, seemed to know as the moment crept closer and her breath came fast. He stopped moving and held her still, poised on the brink of ecstasy, watching her face, watching for the moment when she could bear the suspense no longer, and at that moment, he drove upward, holding her waist firmly, bringing her down upon him as he rose within her.

Petra's world shattered. She lost all sense of herself, of her physical presence, of the rhythmic clatter of the train's iron wheels on the rails, she fell forward, her head dropping onto his shoulder until the ecstatic tempest finally rode itself out.

"I've been wanting to do that all afternoon," Guy said as she raised her head from his shoulder. He traced the curve of her cheek with a fingertip. "Heaven help me, my sweet, but I can't seem to get enough of you."

The train whistle shrilled and the train began to slow. Hastily he dropped his hands to her waist again. "Lift up now."

She did so, yanking up her drawers and smoothing down her silk skirts. "I didn't think I'd ever make love with my hat on," she observed, standing on tiptoe to look at her image in the little mirror under the overhead rack.

He laughed, adjusting his own dress as the train pulled into the gloomy, steamy, noisy chaos of Waterloo Station.

Petra hastily pulled up the window blinds. Guy moved her aside so that he could lower the window. He leaned out to open the carriage door, stepped onto the platform and held up his arms for her to jump down from the high step.

"I'm parched," she declared, accepting the invitation, and for a moment clinging to him, her arms around his neck. "It must be the champagne, don't you think?" Quickly she kissed his mouth before he let her slip through his hands to the platform.

"That or something else thirst-provoking," he said lightly. "Can you wait until we get home?"

"Yes, I suppose so. The tea'll probably be

stewed in the station café anyway."

"We'll get a cab outside and be in Berkeley Square in no time." Once again he eased her forward with a hand in the small of her back, steering her through the crowds.

A line of cabs waited on the station approach and they took the first one, an open two-seater, and by the time they turned onto Berkeley Square the post lovemaking lethargy had vanished and Petra was conscious of a restless excitement, a need to make decisions and plans without delay. Weddings could take months and months to plan, but now that the die was cast she could see nothing to be gained from waiting months to become Lady Ashton.

Babbit greeted them with some surprise. "I was not expecting you back this early, my lord. Was Mrs. Lacey's horse successful?"

"Yes, the filly won her race," Guy responded, handing his top hat, cane and gloves to the butler. "Could you bring tea to the library, please. And I expect Miss Rutherford would like to refresh herself after the train journey."

"Certainly, sir. If you'd care to come with me, ma'am, I'll send a maid to you immediately."

Petra followed the man upstairs to a pretty bedroom at the rear of the house. She unpinned her hat and examined her pale kid gloves, which were grubby with soot. A maid came bustling in with a jug of steaming hot water, which she set by the basin on the washstand. "Here's hot water, ma'am. And towels. I'll take the gloves and brush them. I'll have them clean in no time. Is there anything else I can get you?"

"No, this is fine, thank you." Petra relinquished her gloves and poured water into the basin. She peered at her reflection in the mirror with a grimace. "Trains are so dirty. I feel as if I have a layer of soot everywhere." She dipped a cloth in the basin and held it to her face with a little sigh of pleasure at the warm, clean feel of it. "That's much better."

Five minutes later, after tidying her hair and washing her hands and face, she went down to the library, wondering for a fleeting instant what it was going to feel like to be mistress of this house. And Ashton Court into the bargain. She'd only once seen the sprawling Elizabethan pile of the Ashton family seat and that had been ten years ago when she'd gone to a ball there, the ball at which Guy, for the first time, had singled her out. It seemed a very long time ago now. And she had been a very different person then, still unformed.

But it was time to put all thoughts of that time behind her, she told herself, as she crossed the hall to the library. The memories contained too much old rancor. It was over, in the past. And Guy was not the same careless, thoughtless young man of those days. They had swept the slate clean, and that was how it would stay.

A footman hurried to open the library door for her and she gave him a smile of thanks. Guy turned from a tea tray on a pier table as she came in. "Here's tea." He handed her a delicate porcelain cup. Petra drank it to the dregs and wordlessly handed it back for a refill before flopping onto a leather chesterfield and stretching her feet out with a sigh of relaxation.

Guy handed her a fresh cup of tea and stood thoughtfully in front of the empty fireplace. "I'll send your father a telegram this evening, and then, once he responds, I'll send notices to the *Times* and the *Gazette*. That should get the ball rolling. I'm assuming he'll have no objections?" He raised an amused eyebrow.

"Hardly," Petra said dryly. "Ma will be in a twitter and I'm sure they'll both be back in town within the week." She frowned, wondering how best to approach her next point. *Probably best to just come out with it,* she decided. "This may sound a bit unusual, Guy, but I really don't want a big wedding. I don't want St. George's, Hanover Square, or anything like that. I'd like to get a special license and have the ceremony in a small church with just family and close friends."

Guy looked at her, dumbfounded. "You want *what*?"

Petra was surprised at the vehemence. She spread her palms. "It's not outrageous to want a small wedding, Guy. You sound as if it's unheard of."

"In this case it is outrageous," he declared. "Of course it has to be a society wedding. It'll be the wedding of the Season. And that's just as it should be."

"No." Petra sat upright on the sofa, leaning forward for emphasis. "No, Guy, please listen. It doesn't have to be like that. It's personal, it's between ourselves. Edward and Fenella had a small, intimate family wedding, and . . . well, Rupert and Diana married over the anvil at Gretna Green, and there's nothing unmarried about any of them. And that's what I want."

"Why?" Guy demanded. "Why would you want some hole in the corner affair? I always thought a woman's wedding day was one to celebrate, a day when she's the center of attention, the cynosure of all eyes."

Petra struggled to explain. "Maybe it is for most women, Guy, but I don't like being the center of attention. I want to get married, I want to be married to you, and as soon as possible. I don't want to take months over it."

He shook his head in exasperation. "Don't you understand, Petra? A rushed, unceremonious wedding will look as if we have something to hide, as if you don't really want to be my wife."

"That's nonsense," she said with a stubborn twist to her lips. "It'll look as if we wanted a quiet and quick wedding."

"And what impression does that give?" he demanded. "Think, Petra. Think of the whispers."

She looked at him in dawning understanding. "But that's ridiculous," she exclaimed. "Why would anyone dig for a scandal?"

"Because, my dear, I do not have a lily white reputation," he stated bluntly.

Petra grimaced. "But that's got nothing to do with me. Besides, I don't give a fig for what people are saying."

"No, you've made that abundantly clear, but in this instance as it happens, *I* do." He regarded her in the ensuing silence, reading her frustration on her mobile countenance. After a moment, he sighed, saying, "I won't

205

insist on Hanover Square, or even London at all. If you prefer we will be married from your family home in Somerset. But the guest list has to have the right names on it and the customary rites have to be observed. The engagement will be formally announced, there will be an engagement party, that can be as small and intimate as you wish, but the wedding itself is a different matter. I'm sorry, my dear, but I have to insist. I know what I'm doing."

"You're riding roughshod over everything I believe in and wish for," she retorted. "Supposing I say I won't be married like that?"

There was silence in the library. Guy didn't move, merely looked at her steadily. Petra returned the look, her face set, even as she felt her heart banging against her ribs. Had she just issued an ultimatum? Finally, Guy said, "That is, of course, your prerogative, Petra. But I have to say I would be deeply sorry for it."

Petra stood up slowly. "I think I'm going home now," she said, her voice sounding as if it came from a great distance. "I'll ask Babbit for my hat and gloves." She started to walk to the door. "I'll make my own way."

Guy stepped swiftly in front of her, opened the door, and holding it half open he put his head around and called into the hall. "Babbit, Miss Rutherford needs her hat and gloves." He closed it almost completely and turned to look at her. She was very pale, her expression still set, and she made a conscious effort to stiffen her shoulders under his gaze.

"Come. I'll walk you home." He held out his hand. "Once we've both slept on it, we'll find a way out of this silly impasse."

It was the worst thing he could have said in such a lightly dismissive tone. "You think it's silly?" Petra demanded, sounding incredulous. "You can dismiss my wishes, my concerns, so flippantly." She pushed past him into the hall. "I don't want your company, Guy. I intend to walk home alone. If you insist on following me it will make everything worse." Taking her hat and gloves from Babbit, she stalked out of the house, walking quickly, almost blindly, back to Brook Street. She half expected to hear his steps behind her, but there was only a deafening silence.

How could such a glorious afternoon turn so dismal in the space of five minutes? One moment there was a whole wonderful future to anticipate, the next a wasteland.

She walked blindly into the house and up to her bedroom, closing the door behind

her and sitting numbly on the bed, making
no attempt to take off her hat and gloves.

CHAPTER FOURTEEN

Guy stepped back into the library and closed the door. He poured himself a whisky from the decanter on the sideboard and went to the French doors, staring sightlessly out at the large garden, bathed in the last rays of the setting sun.

How the hell had that gone so wrong? One minute Petra was radiant, her usual vivacious self, eager to plan for a future, and the next, she was as stubborn and mutinous as a mule. Prepared to cancel that future for something so unimportant.

But was it unimportant?

Honesty raised its inconvenient head. If it was unimportant, why was he insisting on following his own wishes? But he knew why. He had too many secrets, even if most of them were imagined. Once the engagement notice was published tongues would be wagging, the gossips would have a field day. Guy Granville, confirmed rake and bachelor, had been finally dragged to the altar, with an innocent, not quite ingénue, to boot. There would be endless speculation as to how Petra Rutherford had captured such a prize, and if society was presented with a fait accompli then the gossips would have even more to play with. Why was the wedding celebrated quietly, in secret? What were they hiding? What was wrong?

He wouldn't subject Petra to that.

He refilled his glass. He wouldn't subject himself to it either. He had never felt the slightest urge before now to couple his life with another person. He enjoyed women, but he had always managed to keep them in a separate compartment of his life. Petra had crept up on him. Insidiously she had made herself necessary to his happiness. He wanted her part of his life, he wanted to hear her laughter every day, to feel her presence in the air around him, to enjoy her radiance, bask in her sunny insouciance. Even when she exasperated him with her stubbornness, her self-determination, her refusal to compromise, he loved her for it. As a man who had little interest in making close friends, who was accustomed to consulting only his own wishes and needs and confided in no one without reservations, he wondered at Petra's ease and intimacy with her friends, at her deep-seated affection for her brother, at the openness of her manner, her ready assumption that people meant well, and that no one would deliberately set out to hurt someone else.

It inspired in him the desire to protect her from the world's unkindness, the careless cruelties and the deliberate ones. The image of Clothilde rose in his mind's eye. There was a woman capable of manifest cruelties. Beside Petra, she was a monster of selfish carelessness. And he would not allow a single barb from her malicious tongue to touch Petra. She would try to hurt her, he was under no illusions there. Clothilde did not relinquish what she considered hers without a fight, and if she could see a way to cast doubt on the integrity of this marriage, she wouldn't hesitate to do so.

It was imperative he marry Petra with all the extravagance, all the public spectacle, all the conviction of a man certain of the rightness of what he was doing. Somehow he had to make Petra understand that.

He drained his whisky glass and set it down decisively. This couldn't be left to fester, God knew what knots Petra was tying left to her own thoughts. No one would be back from the races for several hours yet, there was time to put this right before the world and his wife barged in with their opinions.

He went to a door at the back of the library and opened it into a small inner office he kept purely for his parliamentary business. It was where his secretary was usually to be found on days when Parliament was sitting, but this evening it was empty. He unlocked a drawer in the oak desk and took out a key, going to the bookcase on one wall and gently tapping the spine of a green leather tome. The section of the bookcase slid back to reveal a safe. Guy unlocked it with his key and took out a small square velvet box. He flipped it open, checked the contents, then slipped the box into his coat pocket. He locked the safe, slid the bookshelf back into place and left the office.

He left the house, bareheaded and gloveless, walking quickly to Brook Street, ordering his arguments in his head. He had to keep his temper in check, however frustrated Petra made him. He had belatedly come to the realization that if he dug his heels in, she would do the same. And he was in no mood for a playground tug-of-war.

Petra didn't know how long she sat on the bed, staring into the middle distance, still wondering what had just happened . . . how it was possible to go from the giddy heights of joy to the darkest depths of misery. She was confused and disbelieving, and yet she couldn't deny what had been said between them. Guy had been adamant and so had she. Why was it so important to him to have this big society spectacle? She had always wanted a small, intimate wedding, ever since she could remember. The traditional little girl's dream of sailing down a flower-strewn aisle in a cloud of meringue had just never appealed to her. She'd always thought that the most romantic wedding would be a special affair in a little country church in a little village, with a congregation of immediate family and her dearest friends. And afterward, the happy couple would kiss everybody goodbye at the lych-gate and head off into the sunset.

Her lips twisted into a wry grimace. Realistically, of course, it couldn't be just like that. But Guy's extravagant vision wasn't necessary either. There had to be a middle ground. She remembered what he'd said about his reputation. Maybe there would be talk, a certain amount of catty gossip and speculation if they had the wedding she wanted, but what did it matter? They would be married and the talk would die down soon enough when it became clear there was no basis for scandal. If she wasn't worried about it, and was quite prepared to face it down, there was no reason for Guy to think he had to fight the battle for her.

She jumped at a sharp rap at her door, which opened instantly, before she had time to speak. Guy stepped into the room, closing the door with a firm snap behind him.

"Guy, what are you doing here . . . . how did Foster let you come up?"

"I gave him no choice," Guy said curtly. "We can go somewhere other than your bedroom, if you wish."

Petra shook her head. "No, we can stay here." She folded her hands in her lap, and looked at him inquiringly. "Do we have to fight?"

He shook his head. "Not unless you wish to. I didn't come here with that intention."

"I don't wish to."

"Good." He perched on the deep window-sill, crossing his legs at the knee, one foot swinging carelessly as he looked at her with an air of mild exasperation. "What do you know about compromise, Petra?"

"Don't be so damned patronizing," she exclaimed, jumping off the bed. "How dare you march into my bedroom and start lecturing me on compromise. You really are

214

a complete *arse,* Guy."

The sudden shocked silence was deafening. Petra didn't move, just stared wide-eyed at him, horrified at what she'd said. Guy looked momentarily astounded, then quite suddenly began to laugh, throwing up his hands in defeat. "Yes, yes, I am, my sweet. You have every right to hurl insults at me. I came with soft words and sweet thoughts in my head and my gremlins got the better of me. Forgive me, and let us start again."

Petra hesitated, but his laugh was so infectious and the glint in his eyes so inviting that she finally managed to laugh herself. "Yes, perhaps we should. I'm sorry, I should never have called you that, but you made me so furious. What compromises did you have in mind? They can't all be on my side."

"I wasn't going to suggest that they should." He had sobered now, his expression serious again. "I am willing to agree to a small wedding from your family home in Somerset, if you are willing to agree that the engagement will be celebrated in Berkeley Square, in Granville House. I will take charge of the celebration and the guest list, which will be extensive and include every important family in town."

Petra absorbed this. She looked at it from every angle and apart from her innate dislike of big parties, she could find no fault. It would only be one evening. Slowly she nodded. "I could live with that."

"Thank the Lord for that." He gave a deep sigh of relief, getting up from the window seat, reaching into the inside pocket of his jacket. "Give me your hand, sweetheart."

She held out her right hand and he shook his head impatiently. "No, not that one. The left hand."

"Oh." Understanding dawned. She held out her left hand and watched mesmerized as he slid a star ruby, richly faceted, and deep reddish purple, onto her ring finger. "It's so beautiful," she breathed, turning her hand this way and that to catch the light in the depths of color. "And it's a perfect fit."

"I hoped it would be. My mother had small hands and slender fingers too," Guy said. "It's part of a set. History dates the Granville rubies to Tudor times but my own mother had all the pieces reset with more modern designs. There's a necklace, earrings, which are pigeon's blood rubies, a bracelet and a tiara. They are traditionally worn by Granville brides and I hope you'll wear the set on our wedding day, my love. For all that it will be a simple ceremony," he added, with a flicker of an eyebrow.

"I will be honored," Petra said simply.

Guy held out his hands to her, grasped hers and pulled her into him. "Now, my quarrelsome bride-to-be, kiss me and we'll seal our bargain."

Petra melted into him, losing herself in the warm affirmation of his kiss, only to jump apart as the door was abruptly opened. "What's going on?" Jonathan's startled voice broke the peace. "I couldn't credit it when Foster told me you were entertaining Granville alone in your bed-room. What on earth do you think you're doing?"

"Kissing, what does it look like, Joth," Petra said, unable to resist the urge to tease her brother.

"For shame, Petra," Guy chided. He took her hand and smiled at the irate but confused Jonathan. "Rutherford, I am happy to say that your sister has just agreed to be my wife." He extended his free hand.

"Oh." Jonathan took the offered hand and shook it, still bemused. "Betrothed? I . . . I . . . how did that come about? I knew you were seen around town together, but I didn't think it meant anything . . . oh, damn it, what am I saying. Congratulations, both of you." He hugged his sister. "I don't know how you got to this point, but I'm very happy for you."

Petra hugged him warmly, kissing his cheek. "Thank you, dearest. I'm very happy. See my ring." She showed him her hand. "Isn't it beautiful?"

"Stunning," Joth said simply.

"But you're the first to know about this, so don't say anything yet."

"No, no, of course not. Haven't you even told Diana and Fenella?"

"No, not yet. It only happened this afternoon. You're back early from the races."

"Yes, I wanted to read some reports on improving shipping access to Bristol harbor. Dredging needs to be done," he said. "Perhaps I could persuade you to look at them with me, Granville."

"Oh, Joth, not now," Petra exclaimed, half laughing. "Please."

Her brother flushed. "Sorry, you're quite right. Let's go down to the library and open some champagne. We should be celebrating." He walked to the door, continuing over his shoulder, "Have you notified the parents yet?"

"I was intending to send Sir Percy a telegram this evening," Guy told him, following him out of Petra's bedroom. "They're in Baden-Baden, I understand."

"No, they moved to Nice last week," Jonathan said. "I have their address downstairs. You could send the telegram from here if you wish."

Once the telegram was sent everything else would follow in the customary order. Petra paused, her foot on the top stair as the men preceded her downstairs. Every step of a society betrothal and wedding was foreordained. Her mother would fling herself into preparations, it would be as bad as Petra's debutante Season, the only time she could remember when her mother had devoted her full attention to her daughter. And Petra much preferred it when she was not the focus of her mother's waking hours. But at least the ceremony itself would be as she wished it. She could handle her mother that far.

"I'll join you both in the library in a few minutes," she called, then turned and retraced her steps. She would send the news to Diana and Fenella, so that it would be waiting for them when they got home. They could convene in the morning and this bubble in which she seemed trapped would burst with a commonsense discussion that would put everything into perspective.

The front doorbell was ringing at Brook Street before nine o'clock the next morning. Foster greeted the two visitors on the doorstep with a calm good morning. "Miss Petra hasn't come downstairs as yet, ladies. I'll send a message up to her."

"No, don't trouble yourself. We'll go straight up ourselves." Diana waved a hand vaguely and headed for the stairs, Fenella on her heels. They burst into Petra's bedroom without ceremony. "Sorry, I know it's horribly early," Diana said. "We met on the doorstep. Tell us everything at once."

"Oh, give the poor girl a chance to wake up," Fenella protested, laughing. "Not that I'm not as desperate as you to hear the whole. When did it happen, Petra?" She dropped onto the edge of the bed where Petra sat drinking her morning tea.

"All in good time," Petra said, casting a warning glance toward the bathroom door where her maid could be heard humming as she drew Petra's bath.

Diana nodded and Petra called, "Dottie, leave the bath for now. I'll ring for you when I need you."

The maid appeared from the bathroom wiping her hands on her apron. "As you wish, Miss Petra. Should I fetch coffee for the ladies?"

"In half an hour, please." Petra waited for the maid to leave the room before sliding her left hand out from under the bedclothes where she'd been concealing it. "So, what do you think?" She laid her hand on the coverlet, where the ruby glowed, its interior star sparking in the deep red.

"It's gorgeous," Diana said, taking Petra's hand to look at it closely. "Is it a family jewel?"

"Part of the Granville rubies set. Guy wants me to wear the rest of it on the wedding day."

"They're quite famous, I think," Fenella said. "I heard my mother talking about them once, I can't remember why."

"I'm afraid they'll overwhelm me." Petra looked at the ring again. "I think I can get away with the ring, but I think I'm too small and insignificant-looking to get away with the whole set at once."

"Nonsense," Diana stated, sitting on the other side of the bed from Fenella. "There's nothing insignificant about you at all. So, start from the beginning. Did the engagement have anything to do with why you both left Ascot so suddenly?"

"Yes, it did." Petra told them everything except for the quarrel about the kind of wedding they would have. She said only, "Guy wants to hold a big society engagement party in town, but the wedding will be small and in Somerset."

"I wonder how many noses this will put out of joint," Diana mused. "Clothilde Delmont's for one."

"Should I concern myself with that?" Petra asked.

"No, of course you shouldn't," Fenella responded vigorously. "The engagement will be the talk of the town for a while, it's inevitable, Guy Granville's doings are always matters for gossip and speculation, but once Sir Percy and Lady Rutherford are back in town and the planning's in full swing no one will think of anything but guest lists and speculation about the marriage settlements."

"Well, I couldn't care less about settlements," Petra declared. "I just want to ensure that I keep control of my own money. I don't need any allowance from my husband and I don't want one either."

"But Guy is said to be hugely wealthy," Diana pointed out. "Sir Percy is bound to want to negotiate something for you."

"Then I shall tell him not to bother," Petra stated. "I don't intend to be dependent in any way upon my husband. I have my trust fund from great-aunt Agatha. It's more than enough for my personal needs."

Diana and Fenella exchanged a look. Petra

intercepted it. "What was that look for? You're neither of you dependent on your husbands."

"Not financially, no," Fenella conceded. "But in all sorts of other ways, dearest. Support, love, friendship. Oh, there are countless ways Edward and I depend on each other."

Petra nodded slowly. "I understand that. I wasn't thinking in those terms. It's just . . ." Her voice faded.

"Just what, Petra?" Diana asked into the ensuing silence.

Petra sighed, feeling somewhat deflated. "Guy can be rather . . . rather opinionated."

"He wouldn't force you to do something you didn't want to do?" Fenella asked, frowning. "Surely he wouldn't."

Petra shook her head. "No, no, of course he wouldn't. But he can be very persuasive."

"So can Rupert," Diana said. "But so can I be. And so can you be, Petra."

"Yes, of course I can." She smiled, her spirits rising again. "It's only that this is all so new and I keep thinking of all sorts of aspects of marriage that I'd never considered before."

"Perhaps you should have this discussion with Guy," Diana suggested. "Just to establish some ground rules. He's older than you and he's had longer to decide what he wants out of life, he might be a bit set in his ways." She looked hesitantly at her friend.

"The more set in them he is, the harder it will be to move him," Petra said. "Yes, I see what you're saying."

"But he's not an unreasonable man," Diana said with a reassuring smile. "You never hear anyone say anything bad about him."

It was true, Petra thought. And she remembered how he'd responded with immediate understanding to Joth's complaint that he'd upstaged him at their lunch in the Savoy, and even how he'd resolved their argument the previous evening. Guy was strong-minded, firmly opinionated, used to getting his way, and if she was brutally honest, that was a pretty good description of herself. They would clash at times, probably quite fiercely at times. As did Diana and Fenella with their husbands. But she could hold her own.

Guy was not an unreasonable man. And, besides, she loved him. And she'd been out in the world quite long enough not to expect a fairy-tale marriage. She and Guy were real people, well versed in the practicalities of life. They had their differences and they understood them. But the love they had for each other, the wonderful pulsing passion they shared, those feelings overrode any differences.

CHAPTER FIFTEEN

"Do you think Pa's really injured his ankle?"
Petra asked her brother as she climbed into
the carriage outside the house in Brook
Street on a lovely evening four weeks later.
"I'm wondering if he decided he didn't
want anything to do with this engagement
party. He was distinctly snippy about the
idea of Guy's hosting it instead of himself.
I'd have thought he'd be delighted not to
have to worry about anything, he's usually
so uninterested in any of London's society
doings. But his telegram about Guy's engagement plans sounded less than enthusiastic, and then suddenly he's hurt and can't
travel."

"Well, I suspect his sense of paternal
obligation warred with inclination," Jonathan said with a chuckle. "Inclination won.
A sprained ankle on the tennis court gives
him the perfect excuse to grumble at Granville's arrangements while allowing him not

226

to participate in them. And Ma certainly wouldn't travel from the Riviera without him. So it's the best of both worlds as far as they're concerned."

"Well, I refuse to feel guilty at being glad of their absence," his sister announced. "To be honest, I wouldn't mind if they missed the wedding."

"That, sister dear, is going a step too far," Jonathan declared. "And I can assure I wouldn't relish walking you down the aisle."

"The whole business is archaic anyway," Petra grumbled. "I'd like to elope like Rupert and Diana did."

"Well, you can't," Jonathan stated as the carriage drew up outside Granville House. Lights blazed from every window although it was still light outside, and the square garden was a wonderland of lanterns strung from the trees, offering an enticing playground for anyone choosing to stroll the pathways. Liveried footmen stood waiting at the open doors to the house, from which the strains of an orchestra drifted into the evening.

Guy himself came down the steps to greet them as the carriage arrived. "You're about to be late," he chided, lifting Petra down to the pavement, holding her in the air for a moment with a teasing smile before lowering her to the ground, kissing her before turning to Jonathan. "Jonathan, good evening."

"Good evening, Granville." Jonathan shook the offered hand and followed as Guy escorted Petra, his directing hand as usual at her waist, into the house, up the splendid staircase and into the salon that ran the length of the front of the house.

Petra had rather hoped for a comment on her dress. She was pleased with the brilliant emerald taffeta with lavender silk ruffles at the neckline and edging the elbow-length sleeves. She had thought it striking, but clearly it had not immediately struck Guy. "Champagne," Guy offered, taking two glasses from the tray brought forward by a footman and handing one each to his guests. He raised his own. "To a successful evening."

Petra and her brother echoed the toast, then Petra asked, "What will make it a success, Guy?"

He looked at her for a moment with a slight smile. "You, sweetheart." He raised his glass again, his dark eyes glowing. "My congratulations. You look entrancing."

So he had noticed. She flushed with pleasure. "You look intimidatingly handsome yourself, sir." Which was only the truth. Evening dress looked remarkably good on him.

"It's not every night a man celebrates his betrothal," he said, lightly kissing her cheek. "I had hoped my sister would be able to make the journey from Scotland but one of the children has some ailment."

"Oh, I'm sorry. The child's not seriously ill I hope?"

"I don't think so. One of the usual childhood ailments, but Elinor is afraid all the children will catch it."

"Well, Joth will have to do duty as family for both sides," Petra said, smiling at her brother. "You don't mind, do you, Joth?"

"Not in the least," he said with a gallant bow. "Not for one evening, anyway."

"Let's go into dinner." Guy moved to the door. "Just the three of us, since we lack other family."

"Well, I for one am heartily glad of it," Petra said. "Although, I would really like to meet your sister, Guy."

"So you shall. I hope at the wedding, but either way we'll visit Scotland on our honeymoon. I think you and Elinor will get on well."

"We haven't discussed a honeymoon." Petra took her seat at the dining table. "I thought we might go to Florence. I'd love to spend more than a flying visit at the Uffizi."

"Then we'll do both," Guy said. "Tell me what you think of the white burgundy, Jonathan."

At ten o'clock Petra glanced behind her at the tall case clock on the gallery at the head of the staircase. At eleven she and Guy would be able to leave their post where they had been receiving guests since nine o'clock. The orchestra was playing a lively polka in the ballroom behind them and she wished for the tenth time that she could be done with this irksome courteous ritual and join the dancers.

Guy had not been joking when he said all the prominent members of society would be invited to the betrothal party. For the last hour the stream of guests ascending the staircase had been unbroken, members of Parliament and government ministers, including the prime minister, mingled with representatives of every major aristocratic family, including the royal family.

Congratulations were on every lip, but Petra detected more than a casual curiosity from many of the guests, sharply inquisitive eyes appraising her, the surreptitious whispers as the guests moved on into the ballroom, and not a few backward glances. She felt as if society at large was wondering what on earth had drawn the noble Lord Baron Ashton to the unremarkable Petra Rutherford. Her birth was more than respectable, but hardly spectacular. Sir Percy was significantly wealthy, but the Ashton fortune was known to be vast, so any dowry prospects would hardly be an incentive. She was not particularly beautiful, the most she could claim was the unusual color of her hair and a somewhat striking wardrobe.

The scrutiny and the whispers made her hold her head higher, tilt her chin with a touch of hauteur, and keep a neutral smile on her lips as she trotted out the stock phrases of welcome, her hazel eyes meeting every artificial smile with a pinprick of defiance.

Guy, for his part, was a genial host with an appropriate word of welcome for every guest. But he kept a hand resting on Petra's arm, a proprietorial gesture she found reassuring. He was obviously not oblivious to the questioning glances or the whispers. But he had warned her to expect something of the kind and she understood now his insistence on forestalling prolonged rumors and speculation by facing them down.

It was ten thirty before there was a pause

in the stream of ascending guests and Guy said softly, "Have you had enough?"

"I'd like to dance," she responded. "The music is so inviting."

"Then to hell with this. Let's dance." He swept her ahead of him into the ballroom, where a waltz had taken the place of the polka.

Guy led her onto the floor and Petra was again aware of the curious glances directed their way as they moved into the dance. Guy was a superb dance partner and she was content to let her feet follow instinctively as he held her. She was acutely aware of his body, of his scent and the pressure of his hand against her back in the low-cut ball gown. She caught sight of Diana dancing with Charlie Aldershot, whose arm was finally out of its cast and pathetically thin.

"Can we move closer to Diana and Charlie?" she asked. "I haven't seen him properly since he returned from his country convalescence."

Guy obligingly steered them both around the floor until they were dancing next to their quarry. "How's the arm, Aldershot?"

"Feeble," Charlie replied with a grimace. "But I'm working on it. Petra, I'm heartbroken, of course, but I wish you every happiness. And you, Granville. I'd give much to be in your shoes."

Petra laughed, and blew him a kiss. "You won't be a lovelorn swain for long, Charlie. Eager debutantes are lining up three deep with their tongues hanging out for your attention."

"Much as I deplore my betrothed's vulgar way of expressing herself, Aldershot, I suspect she's right," Guy said. "Do you care to exchange partners? If Diana is agreeable."

"Certainly," Diana said. "Charlie's been longing to dance with Petra ever since he arrived. And there's something I want to discuss with Guy, anyway." She gave Charlie's hand to Petra and herself took Guy's, moving easily into his hold.

"I wonder what Diana wants to talk about with Guy," Petra said, then dismissed the question. "It's so lovely to see you back in town, Charlie. Does the arm still pain you?"

"A bit achy now and again," he confessed. "But not too bad. So, you're marrying Granville." He looked at her closely. "Do you love him, Petra?"

"Yes, of course I do," she returned with a frown. "Why do you ask?"

"Forgive me, I don't have the right, I know. But I've loved you myself for at least two years and, well, he is quite a lot older than you, and he . . ."

"Has a reputation with women," Petra finished for him. "Yes, I know all about that, Charlie. And, I couldn't care less about his reputation. I love Guy, and he loves me. It's as simple as that. Although I can feel the speculation all around me. Do they think I'm marrying him for his money . . . or for his title?"

Charlie didn't immediately answer and Petra said, "So, as I thought, they're all wondering why Guy's bothering with me."

Charlie didn't contradict her. "Gossip is never pleasant." He steered her deftly around a stationary couple before saying hesitantly, "Do your parents approve of the marriage?"

Petra sighed. "Because they're not here, you mean?"

"Well, it is unusual. People do notice such things."

"If I didn't love you as a dear, dear friend, Charlie, I would resent these questions," she stated. "But to answer you, my father gave his consent very readily, but he managed to injure his ankle, which stopped them from traveling for the moment."

"I know I shouldn't be saying any of this," he replied. "But I wanted you to know that people are asking and speculating and I

234

think you should be prepared. Diana agreed."

"So you were discussing me with Diana," Petra said, sounding resigned.

"Only because we both love you."

"Yes, I know." Petra looked around the floor for Diana and Guy, wondering if Diana was having a similar conversation with him. She didn't think Guy would take kindly to such comments. She caught sight of them across the room. Guy was returning Diana to Rupert, but he looked quite unperturbed as he kissed her hand and moved away to talk with a group of men standing by the orchestra dais. So, no troubled waters then, whatever Diana had said.

"Don't be angry, Petra," Charlie said. "You look really fierce."

"Do I? I'm sorry, I'm not in the least angry. Guy had said there would be gossip, it was why he wanted a big party so there were no secrets to fuel it." She gave him a reassuring smile. "I'd like some champagne. Let's go and sit in the window over there." She gestured to a deep embrasure where two gilt chairs stood invitingly empty.

Charlie readily directed their steps there and Petra sat down, resisting the urge to fall back and stretch her legs out in front of her.

Sprawling was frowned upon at a formal ball. She tucked her feet under the chair and fanned herself while Charlie went off for champagne.

Petra's vaguely wandering gaze suddenly focused sharply as a couple entered the ballroom. Clothilde Delmont and her escort, a man Petra didn't recognize, were late arrivals and paused in the doorway, taking in the scene. Clothilde was a figure of elegant perfection, her thick dark hair carefully dressed in an elaborate pompadour, the scarlet silk folds of her gown sweeping into a train at the back, revealing at the front dainty ankles in dazzling silver satin high-heeled shoes, which together with the towering coiffure made her tall enough to dwarf Petra.

Her eye fell on Petra and with a word to her escort she moved toward the window, her fan dangling from her wrist, the silver plumes in her hair waving with every gliding step.

"Miss Rutherford, my congratulations," she said. "However did you manage it?" She sat down in the chair beside Petra, her eyes bright with malice taking in the other woman's appearance.

"Manage what, Lady Delmont?" Petra asked, smiling blandly.

236

"Oh, I think you know," Clothilde said, looking over the dancing couples on the dance floor. "I trust you won't regret it, my dear. Guy is not husband material. I doubt you'll keep him at your apron strings for many months." She flicked open her fan, turning to regard Petra with a derisive smile. "Do you have some hold over him, I wonder? As he said himself, you have so little to recommend you."

For a moment Petra thought she would lose her carefully constructed composure. Surely Guy had never discussed her with this woman? He would never be so disloyal. No, Clothilde was trying to stir up trouble and she would not allow her to think for one minute that she'd succeeded.

"Oh, I think you'll find I have hidden depths, Lady Delmont," she said, her eyes glittering with anger. She rose from her chair. "If you'll excuse me." She walked away just as Charlie pushed through a group of dancers with two glasses of champagne. "Thank you," she said, taking one from him without ceremony and drinking it down and handing him back the empty glass. "Oh, that's better. That dreadful woman makes me so angry."

"Who? Lady Delmont?" Charlie took the glass, turning to follow Petra's gaze. "I don't know her at all. She moves in very different circles."

"Yes, Guy's circles," Petra declared, then immediately regretted the indiscretion. She didn't want anyone to think she was jealous of the vicomtesse.

"Yes, I had heard that." Charlie looked at her in some consternation. "What did she say to upset you?"

"Nothing really." Petra glanced over her shoulder to where Clothilde still sat, and her gaze sharpened. Guy was striding across the dance floor toward the vicomtesse and his expression was far from pleasant. Clothilde, languidly fanning herself, smiled at him, a seductive smile that made the watching Petra's stomach lurch. She couldn't hear what was said, but stared at the couple with naked fascination.

Clothilde plied her fan in a way that left only her eyes visible as she gazed at Guy, who stood over her as he spoke. His back was to the ballroom but there was something almost menacing about the way he held himself, nothing about his stance could be interpreted as casual and friendly. After a few minutes, he turned and walked off, making his way straight to where Petra still stood with Charlie.

"Come," he said, holding out his hand to

Petra. "Let's dance."

She put her hand in his, his expression was still grim and closed, and she decided to keep quiet until he spoke first. As they moved among the dancers, he asked, "What did Lady Delmont say to you?"

"Oh, nothing much," Petra responded casually. "I don't really remember."

"Don't lie to me, Petra." His voice was clipped.

She looked up at him indignantly. "I'm not lying. I just don't think anything she said was worth repeating. And just because you're annoyed about something, there's no reason to take it out on me."

He said nothing for a moment, then a reluctant smile touched his lips. "You're right. I'm sorry. But I do want to know if she said anything to upset you."

"I'm not in the least upset," she averred, then couldn't help herself, "Why did you invite her?"

"For the same reason we're having this very public engagement celebration."

"Oh." Petra absorbed the implication, then said, "So you wanted to neutralize her, is that what you mean?"

"Exactly. I don't intend that my somewhat checkered past should cause you any hurt."

"Were you in love with the vicomtesse?"

"No. I've only ever loved one woman and I'm dancing with her right now." He drew her closer, turning them in the dance.

Petra rested her head for a second against his chest, feeling the steady thud of his heart beneath the white waistcoat. "Good," she said. She raised her head and looked around. There was no sign of Clothilde Delmont or her escort. "Do you think she's left?"

"I neither know nor care," Guy responded. "Put her out of your mind, sweetheart. She's nothing to you."

Petra was more than happy to do as he said, and when Guy relinquished her to Rupert she threw herself energetically into the Gay Gordons reel and then set out to do her hostess duty and dance once with every male guest. It was after three o'clock in the morning when the last guests had left.

"Oh, how my feet hurt," Petra declared, flinging herself into a chair and kicking off her shoes. "But it was a good party."

"It was," Guy agreed, handing Jonathan a goblet of cognac. "One for the road."

"My thanks." Joth took it eagerly and drank deeply. "That's better. Well, you're well and truly engaged now, my dear."

"So it would seem," Petra replied, yawning. "I can hardly keep awake. I wish I could somehow magically close my eyes and find myself in bed."

"That can be arranged." Guy set aside his brandy goblet. He bent over her, lifting her easily into his arms. "We'll bid you good night, Jonathan."

"Oh, yes, right," Joth said. "I'm going home alone, I take it."

"Good night, Joth." Petra blew him a kiss from her position curled against Guy's chest.

" 'Night," he responded, and refilled his glass.

Guy strode across the hall and mounted the stairs, unhampered by his burden. "Don't go to sleep just yet," he said, shifting her in his hold so that he could open his bedroom door. "I haven't finished my evening yet." He set her down on the bed in the softly lit room and stood looking down at her. "I promise you won't have to do anything."

She smiled sleepily. "I don't think I could."

"Well, let's get these clothes off you." He went to work with deft efficiency, lifting and turning her as he needed. At the last he peeled down her silk stockings and eased them over her feet before sitting on the side of the bed and lifting her feet onto his lap,

241

massaging them with knowing fingers that brought a blissful groan from Petra.

"Try to keep your eyes open," he said, setting her feet on the bed again and standing up. She turned her head indolently, watching with wide-open eyes as he undressed rapidly, casting his clothes over a chair.

"How could I close my eyes with such a delicious feast in front of me," she murmured, opening her arms in seductive invitation.

"Lie still now." He leaned over and flipped her onto her stomach, kneeling astride her. His hands moved skillfully over her back and shoulders, kneading and stroking until her skin tingled and a deep relaxation seemed to press her deeper into the mattress. As his fingers moved down over her buttocks and the backs of her thighs, pressing into the tightness of her tired muscles, she groaned into the pillow. It seemed he left not an inch of her back untouched before she found herself lying on her back again, looking dreamily up at him as he continued to work over her arms, her belly, her thighs.

"Where did you learn to do that?" she asked as her body seemed to float, her skin warm and alive, despite the deep relaxation.

"Macedonia," he answered with a chuckle.

"No more questions." He moved back, lifting her legs, resting them on his shoulders as he slipped his hands beneath her bottom and lifted her on the shelf of his palms, his penis sliding easily within her, pressing deeply within her, filling her it seemed until she could take no more of him. He moved lazily, his hands resting on his hips as he knelt above her, bringing her with almost agonizing slowness to the brink of climax. Petra could sense the moment when the intense flood of sensation would overwhelm her and she would topple into glorious molten oblivion, but it didn't come. Guy held them both on the brink, moving occasionally, allowing her to feel him pulse within her, then holding still. His eyes were on her face, her half-closed eyes, her parted lips as the moments seemed to lengthen into forever.

And then he touched the exquisitely sensitized nub of her sex and the shock sent orgasmic waves crashing over her so that for a moment she lost all sense of herself, of her surroundings, only the deep throbbing inside her body, the liquid melting of fiber and sinew.

Guy let her legs fall to the bed and leaned over her, drawing her against him, kissing her, his tongue deep within her mouth as his penis slowly slid from her body. She clung to his neck, wanting to stay a part of him, her body cleaving to his, until finally he released her, laid her back on the bed, where she lay stone still, unable to move a muscle, her eyes closed, her breathing swift.

"I think I died," she managed to say after a few minutes.

"La petite mort," he said, speaking with some difficulty himself as he stretched out on the bed beside her. "A rare and beautiful thing." His hand rested on her belly and he drew a deep, steadying breath.

Petra rolled onto her side, kissing the damp hollow of his shoulder. "Can we sleep now?"

For answer Guy sat up, lifting her against him, putting her underneath the covers, maneuvering himself beside her, pulling the sheets up over them. "There. Sleep well, sweetheart."

But Petra was already asleep, her rich chestnut hair spread over the pillow, her cheek pillowed on her hand. Guy smiled and wondered for a moment how, given his less than virtuous existence, he had managed to please the gods sufficiently to bring this entrancing woman into his life.

CHAPTER SIXTEEN

"You look so beautiful, Petra," Fenella declared, stepping back to examine her friend's appearance.

"A perfect bride," Diana agreed. "That simple style is exactly right for you." She smoothed a fold in the narrow white velvet skirt of the high-necked, long-sleeved gown that clung closely to Petra's shape, emphasizing her slim waist and softly rounded bosom.

"Sit down, dearest, and I'll adjust the veil." Fenella shook out the filmy white lace. "Where's that silver fillet to fasten it?"

"You won't be needing that," a voice said from the doorway.

"Guy, what on earth are you doing in here?" Diana exclaimed. "Don't you know it's unlucky to see the bride before the ceremony?"

"Superstitious nonsense." Guy closed the door behind him as he stepped into the room. "That is a most enticing gown, my sweet." He bent and kissed her nape, sending goose bumps down her back.

"You shouldn't be here," Petra protested but without much conviction.

"I had to bring you these." Guy set a velvet box on the dresser and opened it to reveal the rubies nestling within. He took out a silver fillet, thickly studded with deep red stones. "This will hold the veil."

Fenella took it from him, marveling at the richness of the gems. "This is so beautiful, Guy." Reverently she positioned the circlet on top of the white lace veil that reached to Petra's shoulders. "Stunning against the white," she murmured.

Guy took a pair of ruby earrings from the box and gave them to Petra, who was sitting in something of a daze on the dresser stool. She screwed them into her earlobes and then moved her head, watching the light catch the brilliant red drops.

"And now this." He took a collar of rubies and fastened it around her neck, where it glowed against the white velvet of her gown. "Give me your right wrist."

She did so without speaking and he fastened a circlet of silver and rubies around it. "Stand up and let's see the whole effect," Guy said.

Petra rose slowly, walking to the long mirror and examining herself in the same stunned silence. "I must be worth a king's ransom," she said finally.

Guy laughed. "Not an exaggeration, but they look wonderful on you."

"Oh, my goodness, what are you doing in here, Lord Ashton?" Lady Cecilia's shocked voice interrupted them. "You mustn't be in here, really you mustn't."

Guy turned toward the lady, with an apologetic smile. "I'm breaking any number of taboos, Lady Rutherford, I do apologize. But I wanted Petra to wear the Granville rubies and I didn't want to bring them until this morning. I'll make myself scarce now." With another bow and a charming smile, he kissed his future mother-in-law's hand and left the room.

"Good heavens," Cecilia said, with a flutter of her hands. "How remarkable. The groom really should not see the bride before the ceremony. How could you have allowed him to come in, Petra?"

"I didn't exactly," Petra said with a rueful smile. "When you get to know Guy better, Ma, you'll understand that one does not allow or disallow him to do anything. He's something of a force of nature. But don't worry. I'm sure nothing bad will come of it." She kissed her mother's cheek. "How do I look?"

Her mother stood back and examined her daughter. "Quite beautiful," she said. "Those stones are glorious. I wouldn't have thought rubies would suit you with your hair, but they do, most certainly they do." She nodded. "It's nearly time to go to the church. Your father's waiting for you downstairs. Oh, dear, everything's happening so quickly. Diana and Fenella, you'll come in the carriage with me and Jonathan. I imagine your husbands are already at the church."

"I expect so, Lady Rutherford," Diana said with a soothing smile, hearing the rising note of agitation in the lady's voice. "Shall we go down now? We'll be waiting at the church, Petra darling."

"Don't forget your flowers." Fenella picked up the small bouquet of white roses and twisted the silver paper more securely around the stems before handing them to Petra. "You're not anxious?"

"No." Petra shook her head, the ruby earrings dancing. "What is there to be anxious about?"

"Nothing at all." Fenella kissed her and left the bedroom with Diana and Lady Rutherford.

248

For a moment, Petra stood alone in the middle of her childhood bedroom. Should she be nervous? But she was aware only of excitement, of anticipation. It wasn't as if there were any secrets of matrimony that she had to discover. Her mother had murmured some vague words about the wedding night and how it might be a little painful, but her husband had his rights and a wife must always yield to his demands, however disinclined she might be.

It had occurred to Petra that such a maternal warning would be more likely to terrify a virgin bride than prepare her for what was to come. Her mother had then said she should ask Diana and Fenella for details of what she should expect, and had gone her way clearly considering she had done her duty by her daughter.

She gathered herself together, checked her appearance one last time, then went downstairs where Sir Percy awaited her in the hall. "Oh, good. There you are," he greeted her as she came down the stairs. Then stared at her. "Dear God in heaven, where did those rubies come from?"

"They're the Granville rubies, Pa. Guy wanted me to wear them. Apparently they're traditional for Ashton brides."

"Well, they're magnificent stones, and

249

they suit you well, m'dear. Come, let us go and get you married." He offered his arm. Petra took it, smiling. Her father somehow was much easier to be with than her mother.

The barouche, drawn by a pair of splendid grays, their harnesses decorated with orange blossoms, waited in the driveway, the coachman, resplendent in Rutherford livery, sat on the box, a groom at the footstep, holding the door. Petra stepped up, Sir Percy followed, and the carriage moved off for the very short drive to the church at the end of the long driveway.

Diana and Fenella were waiting at the porch, two matrons of honor to follow the bride and her father up the aisle. Jonathan stood just inside, having ushered guests to their pews and seated his mother. The organ, played as always by the village organist, began and Petra and her father began the slow walk up the short aisle to the altar.

Guy stood waiting, his best man beside him. He watched Petra's steady approach and felt a rush of warmth, a sense that this time in his life he was doing absolutely the right thing. He wanted this woman, he wanted to love her, and protect her, and he was not averse to clashing wills with her either. Petra Rutherford was everything and more than he could have wanted in a bride, his match in every arena. She gave him a radiant smile as she stepped up beside him and he was hard-pressed to refrain from breaking tradition again and kissing her.

Petra let the ceremonial words wash over her, responding as necessary, clearly and without hesitation, and when the last words were spoken she tipped her face up for her husband's kiss with another radiant smile.

They walked out of the church to the welcoming crowd of villagers, many of whom had known Petra since childhood, and all of whom, Somerset folk as they were, knew plenty about Lord Ashton of Ashton Court, a stately home some ten miles from the Rutherfords' village.

Confetti showered the couple as they walked to the waiting carriage outside the lych-gate. Petra responded to the congratulations shouted from all sides and stopped several times to receive single flowers offered by individuals who were particularly close to the Rutherford family. Guy, for his part, kept smiling throughout but heaved a sigh of relief when they reached the carriage and he had handed his bride up and climbed in beside her.

"They're why you wanted the wedding at home," he said, finally understanding that this was Petra's world, as the carriage started up the driveway back to the house.

"Yes, exactly. They matter more to me than the whole of London's ton," Petra responded. "Joth feels the same. It's why he's so passionate in his commitment to his constituency."

Guy nodded, reflecting that in his own Somerset village the attentions he received from his tenants and local villagers were always polite, always respectful, but he couldn't recall a moment when he'd been aware of affection from any of them. He followed in his father's footsteps, expected his agent to run the estate, to treat the tenants well, attend to their needs, and as lord of the manor the baron could expect respect and loyalty in return.

Petra cast him a sidelong glance, wondering why he was suddenly so somber. "Is everything all right, Guy?"

He smiled. "Yes, my love, everything is fine. I just can't wait to have you to myself, and it will be hours before that can happen."

Reassured, she leaned into him, lifting her face for his kiss just as the carriage drew up outside the open front doors of the house. The entire household was gathered at the bottom of the steps to greet the bridal couple with a shower of late summer roses as they went inside.

Three hours later, Petra turned to Guy, sitting beside her at the high table in the great hall. "I would like to go home now."

Guy looked around, the feasting was over and wedding guests were now dancing and strolling around the hall and adjoining salons, drinks in hand. "Then that's what we will do," he said, hiding his own relief. "Where's your brother?" He glanced around the hall and caught Jonathan's eye across the room.

Jonathan made his way through the dancing couples to the table. "Are you ready to leave?"

"Yes, how did you guess?" Petra asked.

"Oh, just instinct," her brother said with a chuckle. "Also, I could see you were getting restless. I'll sort it out with Ma and Pa while you go and change?"

Diana and Fenella appeared just as Petra pushed back her chair to stand up. "Ready to go and change?" Diana asked.

"More than ready," Petra answered. "Oh, what shall I do about the rubies, Guy?"

"Keep them on," he said. He leaned down to whisper, "I rather fancy making love to my bride dressed only in rubies." Petra felt a warm flush suffuse her skin and a now familiar jolt of arousal in her belly. She said nothing, though, and stepped away from the table, flanked by her friends. Lady Rutherford, sitting with a group of ladies at the end of the table, saw her daughter move and swiftly came over to her. "Are you going to change now, my dear?"

"Yes, it's time we left, Ma. Is it all right if we do?"

"Of course, my dear. The party will no doubt continue without you. You go upstairs. Your friends will help you, you don't need me."

"No," Petra agreed. "We can manage perfectly well. I'll be about twenty minutes."

Upstairs in her bedroom, Dottie was waiting for her, festive in her own holiday dress of pale yellow organza.

"Oh, Dottie, I told you you didn't have to leave your own party," Petra protested. The servants were celebrating with their own wedding breakfast in the servants' hall. "I can manage with Mrs. Tremayne and Mrs. Lacey to help."

"Oh, I have to see you off proper, Miss Petra, oh, I mean, your ladyship," the girl said half laughing at her confusion. "Oh, it's going to take some getting used to."

"For me too," Petra said, laughing herself. "But I'd rather you just called me Miss

Petra as always, Dottie."

"Well, I'll be waiting at Ashton Court when you and Lord Ashton get back from your honeymoon," Dottie said. "Are you sure you won't need me on the journey?"

"Quite sure, thank you. We're first going by train to Scotland to stay with Lord Ashton's sister and she has plenty of staff, and when we go on to Italy I'll use maids from the hotels where we'll be staying. Other than that, I can manage for myself." *With the able assistance of my husband,* she reflected, but kept the reflection to herself.

"It's such a shame Guy's sister couldn't get to the wedding," Diana observed.

"Yes," Petra agreed. "According to Guy it's a hazard that goes with all those children. They've all had measles, one after the other, and Lady Elinor didn't dare leave until they were all free of it."

"Well, at least you've already had it," Fenella said. "Remember, we were all laid low in the school infirmary for weeks."

"It was quite fun once we started to feel better," Petra responded with a chuckle. "Anyway, I'm really looking forward to meeting Elinor. Guy's hopeless at giving a proper description. All I gather is that she's middling height, has blue eyes and dark hair, and is preoccupied with the children.

The duke is vague, spends most of his time in the library, except when he's hunting or salmon fishing, and is generally unobjectionable."

She stood up from the dresser stool and smoothed down her dark blue wool skirt. "I think I'm ready to go down." Dottie handed her a matching bolero jacket, which she slipped over a pale blue ruffled silk blouse. She gave her friends a rather hesitant smile. "Why am I nervous?"

"You're standing on the brink of the rest of your life," Fenella said, kissing her cheek. "It's a scary moment. I felt the same."

Petra nodded, swallowed, and left her childhood bedroom to descend the stairs to the great hall where the wedding guests were assembled. Her husband stood at the foot of the stairs. He held out his hand as she reached the bottom step and raised her gloved hand to his lips, his dark gaze seeming to swallow her whole. There were moments when the power of his full attention, the all-encompassing sweep of his gaze almost frightened her. It was as if she could lose herself in him, lose her sense of who she was, the hard contours of herself in the world as she knew it.

"Come, madam wife," he said softly. "Let us go home."

They left the overheated hall and stepped out into the late afternoon. The house stood on a cliff overlooking a bay on the mouth of the Severn River and the sea breeze was brisk and salt laden. Petra shivered.

"Don't worry, I have fur wraps in the motor," Guy said. "You'll warm up soon enough."

Petra looked at the bright red motor car standing in the driveway, a uniformed chauffeur holding the door. Its engine was already running. "I've never ridden in one of those."

"You'll enjoy it," he said confidently. "Your brother approves."

"Jonathan would," she replied, before stepping into the vehicle.

Guy reached into the dickey and pulled out a fur wrap. "Snuggle up in this." He placed it over her shoulders and threw another one across her lap. "Get in the back, Johnson, I'll drive," he instructed the chauffeur as he climbed behind the wheel.

Johnson inserted himself onto the dickey seat and the car moved away down the drive, wedding guests waving them off from the front steps.

"How long will it take to get home in this?" Petra inquired, snuggling deeper into the fur wrap.

"Ten miles, less than an hour," Guy replied. "It'll be drafty along the cliff road, but a lot quicker than a horse and carriage. Try to enjoy it, sweetheart."

To her surprise, Petra found it remarkably easy to enjoy the drive. The wind was certainly cold but she pulled the fur up to her ears and settled back to watch the coastline unfurl in front of them. The journey passed in a companionable silence, but when Guy turned the motor inland, just before they reached the seaside town of Weston-super-Mare, Petra felt anticipation creeping over her, making her skin tingle and her heart beat a little faster. She glanced sideways at Guy and saw that he was smiling faintly as he kept his eyes on the narrow road.

"What will we do when we get home?" she asked, watching his expression.

"Oh, a little of this, a little of that," he answered casually, but his smile broadened. "What would you like to do, bride of mine?"

She smiled and snuggled deeper into her fur. "Oh, a little of this, a little of that."

CHAPTER SEVENTEEN

Innes Castle, the home of the Duke and Duchess of Brandon, was a many turreted edifice seated at the far end of a long narrow loch, nestled against the rugged cliff rising from the glen. The cliff sides were thick with heather, past its peak now, in early October, but still throwing off a wonderful purple haze.

They had been journeying for almost a week, a week of wedding visits to important if distant relatives, who had not been invited to the wedding itself, a week of trains and carriages, and now they were sitting in an old-fashioned closed carriage that bumped and bounced along the uneven trails that passed for roads in this part of Scotland. Petra leaned far out of the window to get a better view of their destination. "It looks positively medieval," she commented.

"It was started in the eleventh century, I believe," Guy replied. "Hamish will give you

259

all the details if you ask him. There's nothing he likes better than to discourse on his family history, although he's spent little enough of his time up here in the wilds. He and Elinor both prefer Edinburgh when they're not in London. But they like the children to spend summers up here, and, of course, August at Innes is sacrosanct for the shooting."

"Of course," Petra murmured, sitting back in the carriage again. She clasped her gloved hands in her lap, feeling a little nervous about the upcoming meeting with Guy's sister and her family. She couldn't quite imagine a female Guy, and she was very curious to see how they were together. Elinor was two years older than her brother and had been married at eighteen. She now had eight children, which struck Petra as an astounding feat in a mere eighteen years despite the fact that such broods were perfectly normal in a true Victorian household. The queen herself had had nine children, but Petra was not alone in thinking that in the present more enlightened times women had other roles to play in life.

The carriage rattled over a stone bridge crossing a swiftly running stream and proceeded up the driveway to draw up in front of the massive doors of the castle. The doors were flung open just as the coachman let down the footstep and opened the carriage door for Petra, who stepped down onto the gravel sweep to be met by a woman hurrying from the opened doors, a warm smile of greeting on her pretty, round face.

"Petra, my dear Petra. I am so very happy to see you. Welcome to Innes." She embraced Petra, who, instantly responsive, returned the embrace. "I am so sorry we couldn't get to the wedding, but we shall make up for it, I promise you . . . Guy, so you did it at last."

"I did, Elinor," Guy said, a smile in his voice as he bent to embrace his sister. She was much shorter than he and he half lifted her off her feet before kissing her warmly on both cheeks and setting her down again. "Hamish." He held out his hand to a tall, thin gentleman standing beside Elinor. "Allow me to present my wife, Petra." He drew Petra forward, his hand warm and reassuring around hers.

Petra smiled up at the Duke of Brandon. He didn't appear to be in the least intimidating, except for a rather faraway look in his eyes, but his smile was warm enough as he bowed over her hand and welcomed her to his home.

At this moment a raucous tide of humanity swept out of the doors still standing open, surged across the gravel and engulfed Guy with shrieks of "Uncle Guy, Uncle Guy."

Petra watched in astonishment as Guy seemed to disappear under the onslaught, then reappeared with children clinging to him. He held a small girl on his hip as he laughingly fielded the others.

"Enough, brats," he exclaimed. "At least let me stand up straight." He seemed to shake them off, like a horse shaking off flies, and they fell back in a babbling semicircle around him. "Be quiet for a moment, all of you," he instructed in a voice that miraculously brought silence. He set the little girl on her feet. "I want you to meet your new aunt, Petra." He reached for Petra's hand and drew her up beside him. "For some reason at the moment I can't remember all your names, so come up one at a time and introduce yourselves."

"Oh, Guy," Elinor protested softly. "Of course you can remember their names."

Guy shook his head and crooked a finger at the tallest boy in the group. "I have a feeling you might be Adam."

The boy who was probably around fifteen, Petra guessed, laughed and came up to her and bowed. "My name's Adam, Lady Ashton. Welcome to Innes."

"Thank you, Adam." She shook hands solemnly and Adam took it upon himself to marshal his brothers and sisters and usher them forward to be introduced.

Introductions completed, the children turned their attention to Guy again, swarming over him as they went into the castle. Two massive log fires burned at either end of the cavernous hall, despite the relative warmth of the October weather. A footman came forward with a tray of filled glasses.

"Whisky, Petra, or something less powerful?" Hamish asked his sister-in-law. "It's a customary welcome here in Innis, but we are adaptable."

"As am I, Hamish. I'll drink whisky with pleasure." She took the crystal glass from the footman's tray. The children were still surging around Guy, but less vociferously, although he once again had the small girl on his hip. It was a novel aspect to her husband, Petra thought, raising her glass in unison with her hosts. If asked she would have guessed he had little time and even less interest in children. Clearly she had more to discover about him.

"Come, Petra, let me show you all the things you need to know to be comfortable at Innes," Elinor said when the whisky had been drunk. "The castle is a warren and you don't need to know your way around all of it." She linked arms companionably with Petra and led her out through a small door at the rear of the hall. "This is a quick backstairs way to your quarters. I'll show you the more formal route after dinner, but you should never need to use it unless you wish to."

Petra followed her up a narrow flight of stairs onto a broad square landing, large casement windows looking out over the loch. Elinor opened double doors to the right of the landing. "Here you are. It's where Guy always sleeps. I hope you like it." She sounded a little anxious as she flung an encompassing hand out to indicate the space.

"It's lovely," Petra said honestly. The oak-beamed room was huge, the carved four-poster deep and wide, the casements, each with a deep window seat, looked out over the loch to the heather pink cliffs on the far side.

"There's a bathroom through that door." Elinor pointed to a door on the far side. "It has a functioning water closet, but I'm afraid hot water has to come up from the kitchens. If you want a bath in the evening, just tell the staff in the morning."

264

Petra nodded her understanding. It wasn't her first social visit to a Scottish castle. There were always domestic inconveniences in the vast, draughty stone mansions. One learned to manage.

Elinor sat down on the bed and patted the space beside her. "Tell me about yourself, Petra."

Petra looked surprised. "There's little to tell. I am what you see. You know my family, nothing special about them. What do you want to know?"

Elinor was silent for a moment, then she said with a rueful laugh, "To be honest, my dear, I want to know what you have that brought my brother to the altar," she said finally. "I never thought Guy would find a woman he loved . . . or even felt enough for that he could contemplate spending his life with her."

"Oh." Petra was at a loss. "I don't know how to answer you. Except to say that we love each other."

"That's truly wonderful, my dear." Elinor frowned down at her lap. "Forgive me for asking this, but, how well do you think you know Guy?"

Petra bristled slightly. "Enough to agree to be his wife."

"Oh, I'm sorry. Please don't take offense.

I know I have no right to ask, but Guy's reputation with women . . ."

"Yes, I know," Petra interrupted. "He told me all about that himself. But I'm no naïve ingénue, Elinor. I'm younger than he, I know, but that doesn't make me a simpleton. He even told me about the lady guerrilla fighter in Macedonia. Oh, and I wonder, was there someone in Tibet, do you know? He told me he learned the art of massage in Tibet." She was laughing now at Elinor's clear puzzlement.

"It was impertinent of me to start this discussion," Elinor stated. "Clearly you and Guy have an understanding beyond anything I was imagining. But perhaps I can tell you something about my brother's growing up, which you might find enlightening, useful, perhaps at some point in the future." She paused, knotting her fingers in her lap. "I hope I'm not interfering, I know it must seem like it, but . . ." Her voice faded.

Petra was all attention. "No, not at all. Please tell me," she encouraged. "I know so little about that part of his life."

"Our father was a strange man," Elinor began. "Strange and difficult. Our mother had a wretched life. That affected both of us, but I think Guy felt it even more deeply

266

than I did. It was as if, perhaps, he felt partly responsible. Our father neglected his wife, left her sometimes for a year or more. She had no idea where he'd gone or who with, whether or when he would return. She put a brave face on it in public, but in private it was very different.

"When Guy was fifteen our father started taking an interest in him. He started to introduce him to the world he lived in, the women he consorted with. Guy told me once that our father had taken him to his first brothel for his fifteenth birthday and they had shared several women." Elinor shuddered. "It's too awful to think about. Guy was such a sensitive boy . . . . Our father was a brute. I know one shouldn't speak ill of the dead, but he was," Elinor stated with a note of defiance. "And I believe he tried to make Guy like him."

Petra nodded, thinking of Guy's taste in books, of Guy smothered in small children. She thought of how tender he could be, how concerned for her reputation despite his own with women. And she thought of his arrogance, of how controlling he could be, of the times when she'd felt he had dismissed her concerns as unimportant. And she thought of the casual, thoughtless cruelty when he'd left her, a lovesick, naïve young girl, without a word of farewell all those years ago. A lot could be explained by the malevolent influence of a bullying father on an impressionable young man.

"Thank you for telling me," she said after a minute. "It explains a lot of Guy's contradictions. Did you really think he would never marry?"

Elinor shook her head, the intensity of the last moments broken. "He never seemed to want to settle down, but he does have a duty to provide an heir, so I suppose, at some point . . . but I certainly never thought he would marry for love. I didn't think he was capable of it."

Of course Guy would have had to marry at some point. Of course the ancient barony needed an heir. She just hadn't thought about it before, Petra reflected. The reflection left a slightly sour taste in her mouth. Uncomfortable realities often had that effect, she acknowledged reluctantly.

"Well, let us go down and join the gentlemen," Elinor said, getting to her feet. "One of the maids will unpack your things while we're downstairs. It's time to send the children back to the nursery. Guy will tolerate them up to a point, but they have a habit of overstaying their welcome."

"They certainly seem very fond of him,"

Petra observed, following Elinor out of the room.

"Yes, he seems to have a natural affinity with children, but his patience is not unlimited," Elinor said with a slight laugh.

Back in the great hall they found Guy and Hamish alone, sitting on either side of the inglenook, nursing glasses of whisky.

"Oh, did you banish the children already?" Elinor asked cheerfully, taking up a piece of embroidery as she sat down in a carved oak chair next to her husband.

"Hamish found them too noisy," Guy said, reaching a hand for Petra and drawing her down beside him on the cushioned settle.

"It was time for their tea," Hamish supplied.

Elinor merely smiled and plied her needle. "We don't as a rule dress for dinner at Innes when it's just the family, Petra," she said. "I hope you don't mind."

"Mind?" Petra exclaimed. "I can't think of anything better. It's so irksome at house parties having to change one's clothes three times a day sometimes. It's been like that at several of our wedding visits on the way up here."

"Well, we don't stand on any ceremony here, my dear," Hamish stated, stretching his long legs to the fire.

It was a pleasant evening and Petra felt herself relaxing into the easy friendliness of the Brandons. Guy, too, seemed to lose the sharp edges that she had assumed were always a part of who he was. He laughed a lot, teased his sister, and kept Petra close to his side, ensuring she had everything she wanted at dinner, partnering her in the rubber of bridge they played afterward. Petra was glad, however, that she was a relatively strong player when she saw how competitive Guy and Elinor were, and how very seriously Hamish took the game.

The evening broke up quite early with Guy and Hamish set to go shooting at dawn the next morning. "I'm not an early riser, Petra," Elinor said, kissing her sister-in-law good night on the landing outside the guests' bedroom. "So ring for breakfast if you'd like it in your room, otherwise it'll be laid out in the small dining room behind the front parlor. You remember where that is?"

"Yes, I think I'll be able to find my way. If I get lost I'm sure someone will show me." Petra lifted her face for Hamish's peck on the cheek. "Good night, and thank you for a lovely evening."

The bedroom was a warm haven, curtains

drawn across the casements but pulled back around the bed. Gas lamps were turned low on the mantel above the fireplace where a log fire burned, throwing out welcome warmth to combat the chilly draft that needled its way around the window.

"It gets cold at night up here," Guy said. "Whatever the time of year." He shrugged out of his tweed jacket before turning to Petra with a wicked glint in his eye. "Allow me to play lady's maid, madam."

Petra submitted to his deft hands as he undressed her. His hands didn't linger over their task and yet somehow always managed to touch, to brush, to smooth a particular spot on her tingling skin that brought a jolt of arousal deep in her belly. "There," he said finally, wrapping her in a velvet dressing gown. "You won't get cold now." He put his hands on her shoulders and turned her toward the bathroom. "Be quick in there. And leave me some hot water."

Petra obeyed the little push and went into the small antechamber where two jugs of hot water steamed on the dresser. "There's plenty here," she called, filling the basin and dipping a face cloth into the water, burying her face in its scented warmth. Her toiletries had been unpacked during the evening and she unpinned her hair, taking up her ivory-backed brush, pulling it vigorously through the rich copper mass until it shone in the soft lamplight.

"Aren't you finished yet?" Guy appeared in the doorway. He came over to her, lifting a thick hank of her hair, burying his face in its fragrant silkiness. "Magnificent," he murmured. "I have to have you now, madam wife. Get into bed."

Petra gave him a mischievous look over her shoulder. "But I'm not quite finished in here. I have one more personal matter to attend to."

"You have three minutes," he said.

Petra was now too anxious for the evening's play to begin to indulge her sense of mischief by prolonging the time she needed to complete her ablutions. She did what she had to and went back into the bedroom, unfastening the tie of her robe.

"No, wait." Guy crossed the room swiftly, drawing her closer to the fire before untying the robe himself, pushing it off her shoulders and tossing it over an ottoman. "Let me look at you." He stepped back, his hungry eyes running over her as she stood naked in the firelight. "Turn around."

She revolved slowly, feeling the heat of his gaze almost as powerfully as the flickering fire behind her.

"Get into bed. I won't be long." His voice was low and husky, as if something had caught in his throat.

Petra put one knee up on the bed as she pulled back the covers, her movements very slow, turning her body slowly, accentuating the lines and curves of her nakedness until his breath came fast and, muttering an oath, Guy strode into the bathroom, slamming the door behind him.

Petra laughed softly. She loved to see the evidence of her power to arouse him. She slid between the crisp white sheets, pulled up the thick quilted coverlet and lay wide-eyed waiting for him. When he came back, wonderfully naked, his erect penis rising from the dark mass of hair at the base of his belly, she propped herself on her elbows and gazed greedily at him. Firelight threw a flickering glow over his skin, illuminating the ripple of muscle beneath, as he walked to the bed, his dark eyes beacons of lust.

That night he made love to her fiercely, using her body as if to satisfy some primal need of his own, and Petra responded as fiercely, her own lust deeply aroused by the simple, almost savage purity of her lover's need. And when it was over she fell back against the pillows, her body sated, her limbs weak, her breath coming fast, sweat beading on her forehead.

Guy lay, one arm flung above his head, until his own breathing had slowed. Languidly he moved his other hand to rest on her belly, his fingers sliding down to twine in the damp dark curls. "I didn't hurt you?"

"No," she said, turning her face into his shoulder, licking the sweat from his skin. "Quite the opposite."

He patted the curve of her hip. "I don't usually lose myself so completely," he murmured.

"Lose control, you mean?"

He was silent for a moment before admitting almost reluctantly, "Yes, I suppose that is what I mean."

"Do you want a child?" Petra asked, her conversation with Elinor coming into her head with a surprising urgency.

Guy's stroking hand came to rest on her hip. "Why do you ask that now?"

"Well, because even though we're married you still use those sheath things, and we've never discussed it before."

"No, we haven't, have we?" He pulled himself up against the pillows, hauling her up with him so that her head rested on his chest. "Must we talk about it now?"

He sounded plaintive and Petra couldn't help chuckling. "Have I rendered you too

274

feeble even for a conversation?"

"No, I am well and truly in control again. So, to answer your question, yes, at some point I would like a child."

"A son and heir?"

"Preferably," he said dryly. "But the timing, my love, is up to you. When you're ready to breed, then I'll stop taking precautions. I thought you might want to enjoy married life for a while, before burdening yourself with motherhood."

Petra absorbed this for a moment, then said, "That's settled then. Let's go to sleep now." She reached up to kiss his mouth before turning on her side and closing her eyes. Guy smiled, leaned over to extinguish the gas lamp and drew her curled body closer into his embrace.

CHAPTER EIGHTEEN

"Welcome back, Lady Ashton."

At the laughing voice in the doorway, Petra spun on her heel away from the window of a cheerful sitting room at the back of Granville House on Berkeley Square. "Oh, Diana, I was so hoping you'd come by this morning. Is Fenella with you?"

"No, she had a rehearsal this morning, but she'll meet us for lunch at Fortnum's." Diana cast aside her wool cape. "So, how is married life? How was the honeymoon? Tell me everything."

"I don't know where to begin." Petra pulled a bell rope by the hearth where a small fire burned brightly. "Coffee first."

She gave the order to the parlor maid who answered the summons of the bell and then held out her arms to her friend. "I've missed you both so much."

Diana embraced her warmly. "Not as much as we've missed you. It's been really boring in town since you left."

"I was only gone four weeks," Petra said, "but it did feel like being in another life."

"So, tell me all about it. How was Florence?"

"Probably just as you remember it," Petra answered, "but we did have a private guide for several days at the Uffizi and that was lovely . . . Oh, thank you, Marie." She smiled at the maid returning with the coffee. "Just leave it on the table, I'll pour."

"And how's Guy?" Diana asked the question that had been on the tip of her tongue since she'd arrived at Granville House. She sat down in the corner of a sofa and looked expectantly at her friend.

"He's very well," Petra said, handing her a cup of coffee. "At least he was earlier this morning. Right now he's closeted in his office with his secretary. Some parliamentary business that Freddie's anxious about. Freddie's Guy's secretary," she added. "He's a very earnest young man who's always wanting Guy to write another article on some national issue or other for the *Times,* or give a speech in the Lords, or propose or support some bill or other. He was waiting with a sheaf of papers for Guy to deal with almost before we walked into the house. Poor Guy barely had time to take his coat off."

"I'm guessing you found that annoying," Diana said shrewdly, sipping her coffee.

"Somewhat," Petra responded caustically.

Diana laughed. "But truly, darling, what's it like being married to Guy . . . being Lady Ashton."

Petra's flash of irritation vanished. She smiled slowly. "Well, so far it's wonderful. Guy's sister and her family were lovely, very welcoming, and Guy and I didn't quarrel once the whole month."

Diana raised her eyebrows, "How did you manage that?"

Petra shook her head. "Quite honestly I don't know. There was never anything to fall out about. But it can't last," she added. "Not once real life takes over."

"That's probably true," her friend agreed. "And on the subject of real life, there's a meeting of the WSPU this evening at Caxton Hall. Can you be there? There's a lot of talk now about getting up a march on Parliament, maybe even into St. Stephen's Hall itself." She grimaced. "If it goes onto hallowed ground it'll certainly set the cat among the pigeons."

Petra frowned. "That's taking a big step forward. It's one thing to assemble peacefully in Parliament Square, quite another to invade Parliament itself." She couldn't imagine how Guy would react to such a proposition. Or rather, she could, and it was not a pretty image. Even Jonathan would be dismayed to think of his sister participating in such an event.

"Yes, it is," Diana agreed, "but there are some members who are getting restless. They feel we're not getting anywhere with what we've done so far. Sedate protest marches, speeches at Hyde Park Corner, publishing leaflets, they feel it's too passive."

"Part of me sees their point," Petra said, setting aside her empty coffee cup. "But part of me doesn't like the idea of anything too extreme."

"Well, will you come tonight? It might help to clear all our heads if we listen to all opinions."

"Yes, I'll come." Petra glanced at the clock. "What time are we meeting Fenella at Fortnum's? It's gone noon."

"We should go now." Diana stood up, reaching for her discarded cape.

"I'll fetch my coat. Give me five minutes." Petra hurried upstairs to the vast and ornate bedroom she shared with Guy. Although she had slept in this room many times before their marriage she had never felt totally at ease there and marriage had not changed that. She much preferred the privacy of her own sitting room and dressing room, which adjoined the bedroom. Guy had his own dressing room furnished with a comfortable bed on the opposite side of the bedroom. The bed was for those nights when the master of the house chose not to sleep with his wife, she presumed. So far that had not happened.

"I'm going out, Dottie. I need a coat," she said as she entered the dressing room, where Dottie was ironing.

Dottie set aside her iron and fetched a dark wool coat from the armoire. "You'd best wear your boots, Miss Petra. It's been raining."

"Yes, thank you, Dottie." Petra took the boots and sat down to lace them up. "Do you want to go to the WSPU meeting this evening? I'm probably going myself. I think it's quite an important one."

"Well, it's not my evening off," the girl said, holding up the coat for Petra.

"Oh, take it anyway," Petra said, pushing her arms into the sleeves. "I won't be here and it's all in a good cause if you want to go."

"Then I daresay I'll be there, thank you, Miss Petra."

Petra nodded. "That's settled. I'll be back

after lunch." She hurried downstairs to where Diana was waiting in the hall.

As she reached the hall Guy emerged from the library with a young man, impeccably dressed in morning attire, on his heels. "If you would just read these papers on the matter, my lord, I'm sure you'd be interested in bringing it up in the Lords. I could write you a speech this afternoon for you to present this evening."

Guy sighed. "Yes, yes, Freddie, dear boy, write the speech and I'll consider delivering it sometime in the next week or two. Right now, I'm already running late for a lunch meeting." He paused as he saw Diana.

"Diana, my dear, how lovely to see you. How are you?" He brushed her cheek with his lips before turning to Petra, who jumped down the last step into the hall. "Are you two going out for lunch? Can I give you a lift?"

"Depends where you're going," Petra said, reaching up to kiss him. "We're going to meet Fenella at Fortnum's."

"I'm going to Westminster, but I'll drop you off in Piccadilly." He shrugged into the coat that Babbit held for him.

"The cab is waiting outside, my lord," the butler informed him. "You said you were leaving ten minutes ago."

"I had certainly intended to do so," Guy said. "But I found myself unavoidably detained." He cast a glance at Freddie, who looked sheepish as he still stood in the library doorway. "Come, ladies." He swept them both ahead of him outside into the crisp early November air.

The hackney dropped them off outside Fortnum's just as Fenella stepped out of a cab at the door. She hugged Petra fiercely. "We've missed you so much. I hope you haven't told Diana everything and left nothing for me."

Petra laughed. "As it happens I've told Diana very little, so whatever you want to know I'll tell you all through lunch. Not that there's that much to tell," she added, going ahead of them through the swing doors into the foyer. "Oh, there's Annabelle Fine, she's still with Theo Frazier. I thought they'd have parted company long before now." She smiled and waved at the couple in question, who were sitting at a round table in the middle of the restaurant.

"No, it's still on again and off again," Fenella told her. "Apparently Lady Fine is going berserk because Annabelle won't make up her mind. One minute they're talking trousseau and the next Theo's about to up sticks and leave town for foreign parts."

Petra smiled, taking her seat, leaning back as the waiter shook out her napkin, placing it on her lap. It was good to be back among her friends once again, surrounded by the comforting familiarity of the regular world, even though the closeness she and Guy had enjoyed on their four-week journey was bound to be stretched. But stretched didn't mean broken. He would have his own friends and commitments as she had hers, but there were a lot of hours in the day, and particularly the night, when they would be alone together.

"So what is anyone going to eat?" she asked, picking up her menu. "French onion soup, I think, with lots of melted cheese." She looked up over her menu and an expression of distaste crossed her face. "That woman is everywhere. Was it too much to hope she'd have gone back to where she came from while we were out of town?"

"Who?" Diana followed her eyes to a corner table. "Oh, the Delmont woman. Actually I haven't seen her around for a long time. She must have just come back to town. Have you seen her recently, Fenella?"

Fenella shook her head. "No, but then I haven't exactly been looking for her."

"She's hard to miss if she's in your vicinity," Petra stated. She still remembered

Clothilde's sugary voice telling her how Guy had said she had little to recommend her. She didn't believe he'd said such a thing for a moment, but it still stung. For some reason just knowing the woman was in the same room as she was made her skin prickle.

"Well, you're well and truly wedded and bedded to Guy Granville," Diana declared. "And there's nothing she can do about it. Anyway, it looks as if she's found a new man to keep her warm at night."

"He's very young," Petra observed, and then briskly changed the subject. "So, what time does the meeting start this evening?"

"Nine o'clock. Christabel is speaking, so it's bound to get a bit fiery." Diana sliced her calf's liver thinly.

"Well, if we're planning to invade Parliament, it's certainly going to set some fires burning," Fenella observed. "How do you think Guy will react if you're arrested occupying St. Stephen's Hall, Petra?"

"I have no idea," Petra said. "But not well, I suspect."

"You don't have to do it, dearest, you know that," Diana said swiftly. "If it's going to upset Guy you should sit this one out."

Petra shook her head. "No, I'm not doing that. If that's what the Union is doing then I'm part of the Union and I'll go along with them. Guy might come around, he often surprises me." She concentrated on her lunch, keeping to herself the reflection that Rupert and Edward would probably be cheering their wives on, if not marching at their sides, while the best she thought she could hope for was Guy's silence on the subject.

The opportunity to test the waters came that evening. On her return home from lunch, Babbit greeted her with the news that his lordship had sent his apologies but that he would not be dining at home as he would be having a private dinner with the Lord Bishop of Bristol. He would not be late home, however.

Petra's first thought was one of relief, she'd be able to go to Caxton Hall without having to discuss the matter with Guy, but then she realized he would probably be at home waiting for her when she came back. Well, she shrugged, her private affairs were her own. If there had to be a confrontation, better sooner than later.

"It's always so cold and drafty in here," Fenella complained as the three women entered the red brick building that housed Caxton Hall. The meeting room was already filling rapidly with women, many clustering around the tea urns on a long table at the back of the room.

Petra waved at Dottie, who was drinking tea in a knot of young girls in the cloth hats and coats and sturdy shoes of working women.

"Let's see if we can get seats close to the front." Petra weaved her way through the groups to the front of the hall where Christabel Pankhurst was already standing at the dais in front of a table piled with papers. She went up to the table, greeting the woman with a cheerful smile. "It looks like quite a crowd tonight, Christabel."

"Oh, Petra, so you're back in town." Christabel returned the greeting as she rubbed her hands together vigorously. "It's always so cold in here. Let's hope the room will warm up with all the bodies. Is that Diana?" She indicated Diana, who was talking with a woman by the wall. "She always has a flask of something warming on her."

Petra laughed. "Tonight's no exception . . . Diana," she called over the buzz of voices.

Diana excused herself and came over to the dais. "Good evening, Christabel. Are you ready to rouse the troops?"

"I was hoping for a nip from your flask first," the other woman said, laughing. "Dutch courage."

"Since when have you ever needed that?" Diana handed over a silver flask. "Finest cognac, I think you'll find."

"Oh, I brought some too," Fenella said, coming up behind them. "I was going to get some tea. Anyone want a cup?"

"I'll help you," Petra plunged back into the chattering throng, heading for the tea table, Fenella on her heels. They returned to the dais carrying two cups of tea each and after a few more words with Christabel while they spiced up the dark brew in their cups took their seats in the front row.

The atmosphere of this meeting was different from usual, Petra thought. There was a buzz of excitement, of anticipation, but also of trepidation. They were planning a march like any of the others they had taken but this one meant invading the hallowed halls of Westminster itself. While the building was open to the public with the right entrees, the wives and families of members of Parliament, and anyone with official business, the protocols for admission and conduct were rigid. These women were intending to shatter those protocols forcibly.

When they finally left Caxton Hall, the three women were silent as they walked down Palmer Street in search of a hackney. Finally Petra said, "Something's changed, hasn't it? There's a different feeling in the air."

"Determination," Fenella suggested. "Impatience. We're not making enough progress. The government's no closer even to listening to us."

"It's time to get their attention," Diana stated. "And an invasion of St. Stephen's Hall will certainly do that."

"Can you imagine the expressions of all those self-important dignitaries and politicians faced in their holy of holies with a sea of irate banner-waving women who won't be quiet?" Petra asked on a bubble of laughter. "If it wasn't so deadly serious it would be hilarious . . . oh, there's a cab." She stepped into the road, waving a hand at an approaching four-seater hackney.

It was half an hour later that she stepped out of the hackney in Berkeley Square. It had made sense to drop Diana and Fenella off first so it was past eleven o'clock when she put her key in the door. It was opened before she could turn it in the lock.

"What have you been up to, madam wife?" Guy inquired, smiling at her. "I expected to find you ready and waiting for me."

"I was out with Diana and Fenella," Petra said lightly, stepping into the hall as Guy

288

closed the door behind her.

"Ah." He leaned back against the closed door regarding her closely, before leaning forward and taking both ends of her purple-, green- and white-striped scarf and pulling them gently. "WSPU business, I take it."

"Yes, at Caxton Hall. Christabel Pankhurst was speaking," Petra responded, keeping her tone light and casual. "It was a lively meeting." She made to move away from him and for a moment he kept hold of the ends of her scarf, keeping her where she was, before letting her go.

"A warming cognac?" he suggested, moving toward the library.

"Yes, please." She followed him into the room, letting the door close behind her. "So how was your dinner with his lordship, the bishop?" She curled up in the corner of the sofa.

"Pleasant enough," Guy responded, handing her a brandy goblet. "He has a notable fondness for claret. His nose blends beautifully with his cassock."

Petra laughed. "Did he want anything in particular?"

"Oh, Bristol Cathedral needs funds to renovate parts of its roof. He was hoping I would see if I could find a source of government money that could be diverted for that purpose."

"Did you talk to Joth about it? All things to do with Somerset are in his remit in the Commons."

"Your brother joined us after dinner. He sends his love, by the way, and wants to come to dinner this weekend."

"Oh, lovely. I haven't really seen him properly since we got back." Petra yawned. "I'll set something up for Saturday evening."

"Come, it's time for bed. You can hardly keep your eyes open." He took her glass from her, setting it aside before taking her hands and pulling her up from the sofa. "Go on up, I'll follow you in a few minutes."

Petra, yawning, left him to turn down the lamps in the library and made her way upstairs. She was sitting on the edge of the bed in her petticoat, peeling off her stockings, when Guy came into the bedchamber.

"Where's Dottie?" he asked. "It's not her evening off."

"Oh, I told her I wouldn't need her tonight. I saw her at the end of the meeting and she was going to the pub with some other girls," Petra said easily, tossing her silk stockings aside.

"Your maid is a member of the Union?" There was a note in his voice that made Petra sit up straight.

"What if she is? It's her business."

"I find it hard enough to accept that my wife is a member of the WSPU but I certainly will not permit members of my household to be involved in that political issue. It causes disagreements among the staff and leads to all sorts of trouble. Babbit won't stand for it if he finds out." He walked into his dressing room, closing the door behind him with a click.

Petra stared at the closed door. He had never shut it before. It seemed like a statement of a kind. And not a reassuring one.

CHAPTER NINETEEN

Petra awoke in semidarkness the next morning with a faint sense of unease. She lay for a moment in the half world between sleep and wakefulness probing the feeling. Turning her head on the pillow she felt a wash of relief. Guy's head was on the pillow beside her and he appeared to be still asleep. She had fallen asleep the previous evening before he had emerged from his dressing room and now realized that her sleep had been disturbed by the fact that she hadn't heard or felt him get into bed beside her. Reassured, she turned on her side and went back to sleep.

When she next awoke it was broad daylight, the curtains drawn back across the window to let in the autumn sun. Guy was standing in his dressing gown beside the bed, holding a cup of tea, which he set down on the bedside table.

"Good morning, sleepyhead. Your tea."

Petra reached her arms above her head in a luxuriant stretch. "Come back to bed. It's lonely without you."

He shook his head, bending to kiss her. "Don't tempt me. I have the country's work to do."

She put her arms around his neck in a tight clasp, rolling onto her back so that he fell forward onto the bed beside her. "Are you sure I can't tempt you, my lord?"

He groaned. "All too easily. For such a little thing you make remarkably strong magic, Petra." He reached behind his neck to unclasp her hands. "But not this time. I have an important meeting to attend."

Petra yielded, pulling herself up against the pillows as he stood up. "What's the meeting about?"

"Ah." The smile died in his eyes and he turned away from the bed. "I don't wish to spoil our present amity so if you don't mind I'll decline to answer that." He walked to the bathroom.

Petra's unease flared anew. She frowned at his retreating back and decided to bite the bullet. "Does it have anything to do with the WSPU?"

For answer he gave her only the sound of running water. They couldn't go on tiptoeing around the subject. Last night, he had openly declared his opposition to women's suffrage and had all but forbidden her maid from participating, but nothing definitive had been said. It was clear as day now that any open discussion would be acrimonious and Petra couldn't decide whether she was ready for that or not.

She drank her tea, considering her next move. There were men who supported the idea of enfranchising women. There were men who marched with the suffragists. Surely, given time and calm tempers she could get Guy at least to see why it meant so much to women like her. Surely they could agree to disagree on something so vital.

Guy came back into the bedroom and went directly into his dressing room. Petra got out of bed and began to pick up her discarded clothing from the previous evening. Usually she would have rung for Dottie, who would have brought her tea and tidied up the bedroom, but she thought it unwise for Guy and Dottie to be maneuvering around each other at the moment. She shook out her crumpled stockings, laying them over an ottoman, following them with the rest of her undergarments.

"Do you never wear a corset?" Guy asked suddenly, appearing from the dressing room, knotting a tie at his throat.

Petra looked down at the heap of under-clothes on the ottoman and then up at him in surprise. "No, of course not. Why are you asking this now? You've never mentioned it before."

"It didn't seem appropriate to express a preference on your choice of undergarments before I gained a husband's prerogatives," he said.

"And dictating whether I wear a corset or not *is* a husband's prerogative?" she asked, momentarily dumbfounded.

He shrugged. "Not dictating, no, of course not. But, as I said, expressing a preference."

Petra stared at him, astonished. "Do you know what such constriction does to one's insides?"

"I know what it does to a woman's out-sides," he commented with a smile that she found infuriating. "And I have to say, my dear, that in general I approve."

The image of Clothilde Delmont's elegant hourglass shape popped unbidden into Petra's head. Every inch of the woman was molded by a corset, the outthrust shelf of her bosom, the minute, nipped waist, the curve and projection of her hips and rear, all designed to draw the predatory male eye, a tantalizing feast put on for his delectation.

"You're not a modern man at all, Guy," she snapped. "You have the most outdated ideas. You're not even that old to be so old-fashioned."

His expression darkened and there was an unmistakably dangerous spark in his eyes. His voice was frigid as he said, "You're on very thin ice, my dear. I suggest you take a step back from whatever line you're about to cross."

Petra felt suddenly cold. She turned away and went into her own dressing room, carefully leaving the door slightly ajar, unwilling to exhibit a display of anger that could have been accused of childishness by slamming it as she wanted to. She sat down on the daybed fighting with her fury. Somehow these two bones of contention were connected. His opposition to the WSPU and his outdated desire to see her constricted, constrained, dominated by the whalebone prison of a corset.

How could he possibly want that? She heard the bedroom door close and waited a few more minutes before venturing from the dressing room. The bedroom was empty. Petra began to pace the room, muttering to herself as she gave her outrage free rein in the safety of solitude. It was absurd that they should be fighting over such fundamental issues now. The time for that was before they got married, not after. She had known what he was like after all. Why had she been so blind to the real dangers of his naturally controlling instincts? She had blithely thought she could manage them . . . *manage Guy.*

And that was a piece of idiotic arrogance, she thought. Guy wasn't manageable. She'd assumed she'd be able to work around any truly impossible beliefs and behavior and that somehow love and lust together would lift them above any mundane differences of opinion and belief. But these issues were far from mundane, they were essential to what she believed and the only way she could honestly live her life.

After five minutes her pace slowed and her anger died, but it was replaced by a fierce desire to convince Guy that he could not order her life as he pleased. An up and down fight wasn't the answer, she wouldn't win it. Neither would he, but the damage to their marriage could be irreparable. And it certainly couldn't be allowed to fall apart because of a corset.

Except of course that the whole corset business was merely a symptom of what was really the issue. Guy's assumptions about a husband's prerogatives. It was the first time she'd heard anything about those. She'd certainly never heard Diana or Fenella discuss them. And then she remembered what Elinor had told her. Presumably Guy's father had had his own ideas on the subject and had imparted them to his son. Confrontation was definitely not the way to get her own views across.

Somehow she had to diffuse the situation. What was needed was a subtle approach, a lighthearted way to make her point. She rang the bell for Dottie, turning over ideas in her mind.

Dottie bustled in a few minutes later bearing a tea tray. "Oh, you've had your tea already," she said when she saw the empty cup on the bedside table.

"Lord Ashton gave me a cup before he left," Petra said. "But I'd like another cup. How was your evening?"

"Oh, very nice, Miss Petra, thank you," Dottie replied, picking up the clothes on the ottoman and taking them to the laundry hamper in the dressing room. "I felt a bit uneasy like when Miss Pankhurst talked about marching into Westminster. I don't know that I want to do that."

"No, and you shouldn't do anything you don't want to," Petra said as the maid returned to the bedroom. "And, Dottie, I think it would be best if you didn't talk about the meetings or anything to do with the Union in the servants' hall. Not unless you're talking to someone you know supports the cause."

Dottie looked a little alarmed. "If you say so, miss. Is there a problem?"

"I understand that Mr. Babbit is not a supporter and he could make your life uncomfortable if he knew that you're a member of the Union," Petra explained awkwardly.

"But you're a member, miss, and I work for you," Dottie said, frowning.

"Yes, I know. And of course I won't let anything unpleasant happen to you. It would just be better for the time being to be discreet." Petra hated hearing herself counseling her maid to hide her political affiliations but she also knew that she could protect Dottie only so far when it came to life in the servants' hall, where Babbit ruled supreme. She could make sure the girl didn't lose her job, she could make sure she had impeccable references, but she couldn't protect her from her fellow servants or the butler's tyranny when she wasn't around.

"I'll be careful, Miss Petra. Will you be going out this morning?"

"Yes, in an hour or so." Petra wandered

into the bathroom. An idea was formulating, an amusing way to get Guy to see things her way. She just had to manage to enlist the help of two particular women.

Just before noon, Dr. Louisa Garrett Anderson was contemplating leaving her surgery at the Royal Free Hospital in the Grays Inn Road for a lunch break when she was informed that a Lady Ashton wished to see her if she could spare her a minute.

Surprised, Louisa went into the waiting room herself. "Petra, what brings you to this part of the city?"

Petra jumped up from the hard wooden chair. "I need to ask a favor, Louisa. If you can't give me that then I need some advice. I can wait for as long as you like if you have lots of patients."

"The surgery's closed for an hour for lunch," Louisa said. "I was about to get something to eat. D'you care to join me?"

"Absolutely. Where do you go around here for lunch?" The Grays Inn Road was not a part of London with which she was familiar. Grays Inn was one of the four inns of court, exclusively inhabited by the legal profession and the hospital.

Louisa laughed. "Certainly not the Savoy, or anywhere like it. But there's a café on the corner, popular with junior law clerks. They do a good cheese and bacon sandwich, or steak pie. Cheap and cheerful for the impoverished young men slaving away for the barristers."

"Where do the barristers eat then?" Petra inquired, following Louisa back into her office.

"Oh, they have their own watering holes," Louisa said dismissively, putting on a serviceable tweed coat. "They don't welcome women, particularly women alone." She crammed on a close-fitting wool hat. "If they don't want me, I don't want to be there."

"Quite," Petra agreed. Louisa and her mother, Elizabeth, the first woman ever to qualify as a doctor in England, were active suffragists as well as medical professionals and Petra knew both through her work with the Union.

The café was noisy, smoky and smelled of grease, none of which seemed to trouble Louisa, who seemed a well-known figure there, greeted by customers and waitress alike. Petra followed her friend's lead and took a seat at a stained wooden table for two against a wall that seemed to drip condensation.

"The food's much better than you might

imagine from the surroundings," Louisa whispered, pushing across a dogeared menu. "The day's specials are on the chalkboard above the counter."

Petra looked over at the board. Split pea soup with ham, and spotted dick for pudding appeared to be on offer. "The soup looks good," she said after a doubtful glance down at the menu, which featured sausage, egg and chips as well as the recommended ale pie and cheese and bacon sandwich.

"Yes, I'll have the same," Louisa said briskly, unbuttoning her coat. She signaled to the lone waitress. "Two of the soup special, Maude, please, oh, and a half pint of cider." She glanced at Petra. "What are you drinking? If you don't feel like strong tea, cider or water's your best bet."

"Just water, then," Petra replied, settling back on her chair, thrusting her gloves into her coat pockets.

"So what favor can I do you?" Louisa asked, eyes bright with curiosity. She listened as Petra explained, her eyes widening, laughter bubbling as Petra finished. "Oh, that's an outrageous but wonderful idea, Petra," she declared. "But how will your husband take such a lesson? Will it amuse him?"

"I certainly hope so," Petra said, dipping

her spoon again into the surprisingly good soup. "But to be honest I'm taking a bit of a risk. I think, I hope, he'll see the funny side. But I also want him to understand how important it is."

"Well, I certainly support that," Louisa said. "When do you want to do this? I don't have surgery on Friday afternoons."

"This Friday then? Unless Guy has something else he has to do."

"Let me know if he does. Otherwise, four o'clock?"

"Perfect."

Petra left Louisa half an hour later, having spurned the spotted dick, and went to the lingerie department of Marshall & Snelgrove to recruit her last participant in her plan. Rachel Young, another fellow member of the Union, ran her department in the elegant store with a friendly efficiency that belied the passion with which she held her political beliefs. She was well aware that if her outside work activities became generally known she would be dismissed from her post without references, a bleak prospect for a woman of a certain age.

"Lady Ashton, what can we do for you today?" She came across the floor as soon as she saw Petra step out of the elevator cage.

"I'd like to consult you, Mrs. Young," Petra said, glancing around. The floor was quiet, customers sparse. "Can we go into a fitting room? It's rather private."

"Of course. This way." The woman led the way to the back of the department and through a curtain. She unlocked the door to a cubicle and stood aside to let Petra precede her.

When they emerged some twenty minutes later, Rachel went straight to a display of corsets, both long and short. "The S-curve is the one we want." She selected a garment with a slight moue of distaste. "I do dislike selling these, but customers want them. I can hardly keep them in stock." She held it up. "This should fit you. Do you want to try it now?"

"No, I trust your eye, Rachel."

"Then I'll bring it to Berkeley Square at half past three on Friday."

Satisfied with her afternoon's work, Petra went directly home. Ordinarily she would have discussed her plotting with Diana and Fenella but she felt somehow that this was strictly between herself and Guy. A purely domestic matter. She didn't want to expose him to her friends' judgment, she realized. And they would judge him. It was one thing for a stranger to be critical, but quite another for friends.

At home she greeted Babbit as he opened the door for her. "Lord Ashton and I will be dining alone tonight," she informed the butler. "I think it would be nice to have dinner served in the library in front of the fire. Could you ask Alphonse to come and see me in my sitting room."

Babbit bowed and Petra made her way to her own cozy parlor, not bothering to go up to her bedroom first to get rid of her outdoor clothes. The chef, like most of Guy's staff, had been in service to the Granville family for many years. He was slightly suspicious of the new Lady Ashton and Petra had gone out of her way to ask his opinion and generally acquiesce to his menu suggestions, but she had a very specific request for this coming evening.

"You sent for me, my lady?"

"Yes, Alphonse. Thank you for coming." She smiled and gestured to a chair. "Please, sit down. I'd like to discuss tonight's menu."

Alphonse glanced pointedly at the clock on the mantelpiece as it struck four. "After the soup, I am preparing poached turbot with baby shrimp in brown butter, madam. It's a favorite of his lordship's. I am intending to follow that with roast pheasant in a game sauce, and to follow, a mushroom fricassee —"

"That all sounds splendid, Alphonse." Petra interrupted him. "But I think three courses will be plenty this evening, well, four if you count cheese. We will forgo the fricassee. For cheese I would like you to prepare Welsh rarebit. Lord Ashton is very partial to Welsh rarebit. And for dessert, marron glacé. I happen to know that that is one of his absolute favorites."

"If you say so, Lady Ashton." Alphonse stood rigidly at attention, his expression impassive. "Will there be anything else?"

Petra swallowed a sigh. It seemed she hadn't yet been granted full acceptance as the mistress of the house. "We shall dine *a deux* in the library at half past eight. Will that suit you?"

"Indeed, madam. If that will be all." He bowed, turned on his heel and stalked from the room. How not to make friends and influence people, Petra thought. It wasn't as if she'd really interfered with the man's dinner. But he was a sensitive soul and a superb chef, whom Guy would be devastated to lose. She went in search of Babbit to discuss wines for the evening. At least the butler didn't resent her suggestions. Not that she had many. The vast Granville cellars were still a mystery to her.

CHAPTER TWENTY

Guy entered his house that evening a little warily. No one could say the morning's parting with his wife had been amicable although somehow they had managed to keep from saying anything regrettable, but he'd be foolish to imagine the matter was over. He had no idea what to do about Petra's involvement with the suffragists. He didn't know how to outright forbid it. As a husband he had the right to prevent his wife from causing embarrassment to either of them. And it would certainly embarrass him to have his wife known for her suffragist activities. It was one thing for her to believe in the cause, she was entitled to believe what she chose, but it was quite another to act in a manner detrimental to either her or his own position in society. He thought for a bad moment of what his own father would say if he were alive at having a daughter-in-law marching the streets of London flourishing a political banner.

"Is Lady Ashton at home, Babbit?" he asked, surrendering his coat, cane and hat to the butler.

"Yes, m'lord. She's in the library."

"Thank you." Guy crossed the hall and opened the door to the library.

Petra was as usual curled up in a corner of the sofa, a book in her lap. She was dressed in a loose silk robe, more suited to the boudoir than the library. "Ah, you're back. I'm so glad." She uncurled from the sofa and came over to him, putting her arms around him, lifting her face for his kiss. "I was hoping you wouldn't be late. I've planned a quiet, intimate evening, just us. Dinner by the fire in here and afterward . . ." Her smile was languidly seductive. "Afterward . . . well, I'm sure we can think of something to amuse us."

He kissed her mouth, relishing as always the supple sensuousness of her lips, the soft fragrance of her skin and hair. "Did you just come out of the bath?" he asked, lifting his head, smiling down at her, his hands clasping her waist beneath the thin silk.

"As it happens," she said, leaning back in his hold. "I wanted to be ready for you."

Desire flickered in his eyes as his body responded to her words, to the feel of her in his hands. "Give me ten minutes, my sweet. I have no wish to sully this perfection with my day's grime." He gave her a gentle push back onto the sofa. "Don't move."

Petra smiled to herself as he hurried from the room, little prickles of anticipation lifting her skin. As she had hoped, Guy readily responded to her invitation, putting aside all bones of contention, and that was how it was going to be this evening. Love and lust, the twin peaks of their marriage. No valleys, no crevasses.

Guy came back within fifteen minutes, relaxed in a velvet smoking jacket with wide silk lapels. He carried a tray with an ice bucket and fluted glasses, which he set aside before bending to kiss her. His skin, freshly shaved, smelled of citrus cologne. "Champagne, my love?"

"Please." She watched as he deftly twisted the cork and filled the fluted goblets with the pale pink bubbles. Guy knew how much she enjoyed pink champagne.

Guy sat beside her on the sofa, giving her one glass before taking a sip from his own. He lifted her chin with a forefinger and kissed her, the cool bubbles of wine sliding from his mouth into hers. It was the most delicious feeling and Petra almost laughed with delight as the effervescence slid over her tongue.

"That's a most novel way to drink wine," she said. "Let me do it to you." She took a sip from her own glass, then moved her mouth to his, her lips parting as she kissed him. Guy moved his free hand to cup the back of her head, holding her steady as his tongue moved inside her mouth, tasting the inside of her cheeks, running over her teeth, exploring the sweet wine-infused cavern. A knock at the door brought them both upright. Petra felt her cheeks warm and flushed. She lifted the book from her lap and buried her head in it. Guy laughed softly and bade the knocker enter.

"May we set the table for dinner, my lady?" a parlor maid inquired, holding an armful of table linen.

"Yes, yes, of course," Petra managed from behind her book. She could feel Guy's quiver of laughter as he sat so close to her and struggled to contain her own.

Guy moved to the far side of the sofa and pointedly crossed his legs, taking a sip of champagne before reaching for a copy of the *Gazette* on the side table.

The parlor maid spread the snowy cloth on a gate-legged table and folded the napkins while a footman came in with a tray of cutlery. They worked swiftly and silently, while Petra and Guy sat seemingly absorbed in their reading matter side by side on the sofa.

"Are you ready for the soup, my lady?"

"Yes, thank you." Petra lifted her head from her book as the door closed behind the servants. "We'd better eat soon," she said. "Otherwise . . ."

"Otherwise, you wicked woman, I shall have no choice but to ravish you right here and now and to hell with dinner," Guy stated. "What do you do to me, Petra . . . you leave me with no willpower at all."

"Oh, I like the idea of being ravished," Petra said with a grin. "Is that a promise for later?"

Guy made a move to seize hold of her and she jumped up, dancing away from him, laughing. Guy was on his feet just as the door opened and a footman carrying a silver tureen came into the room. Muttering an oath Guy turned sharply aside toward a bookcase, pretending to be deeply engaged in the spines of the leather tomes on display.

"Thank you, Neil. I'll ring when we're ready for the next course." Petra tried to sound dignified, in her best lady of the house manner, but she could see the speculation in the footman's eyes. He bowed and left the room.

"Do come and sit down, Guy, and eat your soup." Petra took her own seat at the table in front of the fire. "Alphonse will get so upset if we linger over the soup and his turbot gets cold."

Guy took his seat opposite her and dipped his spoon into his bowl of chicken consommé. He glanced across at his wife, who was demurely spooning her own soup. "To be continued," he said.

Her eyes danced. "Oh, I hope that's a promise."

"It might even be a threat," he responded, his dark gaze a swirl of liquid smoke.

Petra pushed aside all doubts and misgivings and let the evening's momentum carry her forward. It seemed that Guy too was prepared to set aside any bones of contention in the interests of a succulent evening where sensual promise simmered beneath everything they said to each other, the suspense and anticipation building with each mouthful of Alphonse's dinner, each sip of rich dark wine.

When the table had been cleared and they were finally alone, Guy sat on the sofa and beckoned to Petra. "Come to me, madam wife."

She crossed the room to the sofa and he drew her down onto his knee, shifting her

312

so that she lay back with her head against his shoulder, her legs stretched across the sofa. His fingers moved to unbutton the tiny pearl buttons of her silk robe, his hands slipping inside. "Ah," he murmured on a sigh of satisfaction, "I had hoped you would be naked beneath this." He cupped the soft rounds of her breasts, a fingertip teasing first one nipple then the other, bringing them both to hard peaks. He stroked down her body, playing a tune on her rib cage, before circling her navel. His fingers dipped lower, twined in the dark tangle of hair at the base of her belly, slid lower, teasing the full lips of her sex, opening them as one finger tantalized the swollen opening of her vagina before sliding within her, moving with wicked intent as a liquid warmth spread through her loins, weakening her limbs, a pulse throbbing fiercely against his probing finger.

And just as the wave was about to break over her, it all stopped. He withdrew his hand and matter-of-factly rebuttoned her robe.

"What . . . what's the matter?" Petra stammered, too stunned by anticlimax to form a coherent thought.

"It's as hard for me, my love," he said, his smile teasing her as he kissed her lightly.

"But sometimes, deferring delight is a powerful spur to greater heights. Trust me." He tipped her off his knee and stood up. "Go upstairs now and I will join you in bed in half an hour."

Petra looked at him for a moment, unsure of what was happening, but his smile was reassuring as he said, "Go, do what you have to. I promise it will be worth it."

Pulling her robe closer about her, Petra left the library. The house felt cold as she crossed the hall to the stairs after the warmth of the library fire. She hurried up the stairs to the bedroom, glad to see a fire kindled in the hearth there, the curtains drawn against the night, the lamps softly lit. She threw off the robe and climbed into the deep feather bed, her hands moving over her body of their own accord, keeping alive the spark that had been kindled downstairs.

"Wait for me," Guy's voice broke into her reverie. He closed the door behind him and turned the key in the lock. He came over to the bed, tossing his own robe over a chair. "Don't you even think of doing my work for me, madam." He knelt over her, taking her hand in a firm grip, guiding it to his penis. "Work your magic there, while I get on with what I was doing."

Petra chuckled weakly. Her husband was

in his managing mode and she was perfectly happy to be guided by him. In this area at least.

Sated, lost in the deep afterglow of love, Petra lay curled against her husband, her body throbbing pleasantly. "If that was ravishment, my lord baron, please feel free to do it any time," she murmured, kissing his nipple, moving her hand down his body to cradle his now flaccid penis. "Shall I wake it up?"

"Have mercy," Guy groaned into her hair. "I need time to recover."

Petra laughed softly. "Actually so do I. I can barely move a muscle." They lay quietly for a while watching the firelight flickering on the ceiling before she said, "If I asked you to be home on Friday afternoon, do you think you would be able to be?"

"Why do you want me here?" Guy asked sleepily.

"Oh, I have a little surprise planned," she murmured, trying to keep her voice lazy and neutral, as if his answer didn't really matter.

"This Friday?"

"If you could?"

"Well, your surprises, my love, tend to be irresistible, if tonight's is anything to go by," he said. "So, yes, I can arrange to be home

315

this Friday afternoon."

"Four o'clock?"

"If you say so." He rolled her on her side, molding himself around her like spoons in a drawer. "Go to sleep now."

Petra closed her eyes, feeling his breathing deepen as he held her close. Her last waking thought was the hope that she wasn't about to tear this wonderful closeness apart.

"My lord, may I have a word?"

Guy, on his way out of the door the following morning, paused and tried to disguise his annoyance at his secretary's hesitant yet always impossible to ignore pleading tone. "Make it quick, Freddie. I have things to do this morning."

"Yes, my lord. It's just something I thought I should bring to your attention." Freddie stepped back, gesturing to the door to the office.

Guy sighed. Obviously it was not going to be a quick word if it couldn't be had in the hall. He turned aside and went into the office. "Well, Freddie, what's so important?"

"Well, I know you've been taking an interest in the activities of the Women's Social and Political Union, sir," Freddie began. "I know you've been to several meetings recently at Westminster about the issue of universal suffrage."

"Yes, so what?" Guy's tone sharpened. He hadn't involved his secretary in his interest in the movement's doings. It fell too close to home with his wife's open involvement in the Union to be discussed objectively.

"I hope I'm not speaking out of turn, my lord . . ."

"Oh, cut to the chase, Freddie, for God's sake," he exclaimed. "I don't have all day."

"Well, I heard that there are plans for a large march on Westminster."

"It wouldn't be the first time," Guy said, but with an acute sense that something unpleasant was in the offing.

"As I understand it, my lord, this time the marchers intend to enter Parliament, to enter St. Stephen's Hall with their petition."

"What?"

"I have it on very good authority, sir. And as I believe Lady Ashton —"

"My wife has nothing to do with this," Guy interrupted fiercely. "And her affairs are no concern of yours."

Freddie looked stricken as he realized his faux pas. "No, my lord . . . of course not. Forgive me, I didn't mean to speak out of turn."

Guy frowned. He was seriously put out that his staff had obviously discussed his wife's annoying commitment to such a contentious political issue. He didn't want to discuss it further but he needed information. "When is this march to take place?"

"I believe soon. I can confirm the exact date with my source, but it's definitely to be within the next several weeks," Freddie told him, looking increasingly uncomfortable. He was only doing what he thought was his business but he had the unmistakable impression that Lord Ashton was far from appreciative.

"Find out and let me know." Guy turned on his heel and left the office. He still hadn't the faintest idea how to deal with Petra's affiliation to the Union, not to mention her active participation in the protests. He was not fool enough to imagine he could forbid her having anything to do with the Union. She would ignore him and he would have to respond. The consequences were unthinkable. Neither did he think she would respond well to a request that she leave the Union, or, at the very least, play only a passive role. He knew his wife well enough by now to know where she drew her lines of autonomy. And, in truth, he respected her for it. It was just damned inconvenient in this instance, but he would have to find a way to deal with any active participation in the invasion of Westminster, which, he strongly suspected, was what she had in mind.

He shuddered at the thought of the scene in St. Stephen's Hall, the sergeant at arms and his men wrestling with a horde of women suffragists, trying to evict them without causing physical injury. There would be police, bystanders, newspapermen and photographers. Lady Ashton was a prominent society figure, married to an influential member of the peerage. There was no way she could escape notice and her inevitable arrest would be on the front pages of every newspaper and scandal sheet in town. It didn't bear thinking about.

CHAPTER TWENTY-ONE

"Are you going to Westminster this morning?" Petra asked her husband as he finished dressing on Friday morning.

"Not immediately, Freddie requires my presence," Guy said with a mock sigh. "The dear boy is on a hobby horse about the land bill and he will insist I give a speech on the matter. I have to go over it with him before I find myself saying something in the Lords I might regret. Then I'm engaged to lunch in the Peers Dining Room. But never fear, I will be back at four o'clock." He came over to the bed where she still sat against the pillows drinking her morning tea. "For this mysterious surprise." He bent over to kiss her. "Won't you give me a hint?"

Petra shook her head vigorously. "Not a smidgeon. Have a good morning and enjoy your luncheon." She slid out of bed, blowing him a kiss as he went to the door. "Until this afternoon." The door closed in his wake and she went to the window, looking out on a brilliantly bright morning. The trees in the square were a mass of red and gold, the sky a cloudless blue. It promised a perfect day.

How would it end? She still had not said a word to Diana or Fenella about her plan, but now wondered if it would ease her nervousness to share it. What if it was truly harebrained and would cause more harm than good? Was she certain her husband's sense of humor was strong enough to see the funny side? What if she was about to make a colossal mistake?

Guy had seemed preoccupied since their intimate evening two days earlier, but he hadn't seemed out of sorts particularly. It was just that she thought occasionally she had caught him regarding her rather speculatively, an almost calculating look in his eyes. It was disconcerting because if she asked him about it he merely laughed and offered some vague explanation that had nothing to do with her.

She spent the morning on tenterhooks, not even the company of her friends helped. "You've hardly eaten any lunch, Petra," Diana pointed out as a waiter removed Petra's barely touched plate of duck confit. "That dish is one of your favorites."

"Yes, is something the matter?" Fenella asked, leaning over the table with an air of concern.

"No, nothing at all," Petra denied. "Everything is perfect, I promise. I suppose," she added, "I might be a bit preoccupied about arrangements for the march."

"Everything is nearly in place," Diana said, taking a spoon to her chocolate mousse. "We're just waiting to hear from the Manchester folk as to how many to expect from there. Emmeline is in charge of that contingent."

"I like her idea of putting the word out to the world in general with the wrong date," Petra commented. "That should at least prevent any attempt to stop the march before we get to Westminster."

"You can always trust Emmeline to be devious," Diana said on a note of admiration. "We'll catch them completely unprepared."

"And there'll be several hundred at the least," Fenella put in. "If we can make five hundred it will really cause a stir."

"Oh, I think we'll cause a stir however many women storm St. Stephen's Hall," Petra declared. "We'll probably all be arrested."

"Probably," Diana agreed. "Rupert and

Edward will stand bail for us all, including you, Petra, just in case . . ." The sentence trailed off.

Petra grimaced but said confidently, "Guy will stand up for me. He'll hate to do it, but he will. What happens afterward is anyone's guess." She glanced at her watch. "It's nearly three o'clock. How could the time go so fast? I have to go, I'm meeting someone at home at half past." She gathered up her things, kissed her friends, and hurried out of the restaurant, hailing a cab at the door.

Rachel Young arrived promptly and was shown upstairs to Petra's dressing room. She laid the parcel she was carrying on an ottoman.

"Take off your coat, Rachel." Petra was wearing a dressing robe over a chemise and drawers. "Would you like a glass of sherry?" She poured a glass for herself from the decanter on the dresser.

"Perhaps after the demonstration," Rachel said. "I am working after all, even if it's a somewhat unorthodox fitting."

Petra laughed a little, but it lacked conviction. Louisa arrived soon after with a portfolio under her arm. She knew Rachel from the Union and willingly accepted a glass of sherry, asking Petra quizzically, "Do I need Dutch courage?"

"No, of course not," Petra replied, taking a gulp of her own sherry. "Guy has a sense of humor."

Guy arrived at home just as the clock struck four. "Is Lady Ashton in her parlor, Babbit?"

"No, my lord, she asked that you join her in her dressing room," Babbit said without expression, taking his lordship's coat and hat.

Guy raised a quizzical eyebrow and took the stairs two at a time. He opened the door to Petra's dressing room and stopped on the threshold. Whatever he had expected it wasn't his wife in dishabille, and two other women, both of whom looked solemn and businesslike.

"This is a surprise," he said. "Good afternoon, ladies. Petra?" He looked at his wife for an explanation.

"Guy, may I introduce Dr. Louisa Garrett Anderson from the Royal Free Hospital."

"Dr. Garrett Anderson." Guy inclined his head in a small bow. "I know of your work, and of your mother's, of course."

"And may I introduce Mrs. Young. She is head of the lingerie department at Marshall and Snelgrove."

"Mrs. Young." Guy gave her the same

courteous nodding bow. His curiosity was piqued but he was beginning to get an inkling of what his determined and impetuous wife was up to.

"Sit down, Guy," Petra said, taking his hand. "We want to show you something. Would you like a glass of sherry, or there's whisky, if you'd prefer?" She indicated the decanters on the dresser.

"Am I going to need it?" he asked, taking a small armchair beside the dresser.

"Maybe," Petra responded, shrugging out of her dressing gown.

Guy tapped his mouth with a fingertip as he examined his scantily clad wife. "Whisky, then."

Petra poured a measure and gave him the glass. "Now for the demonstration." She stood in her chemise and drawers, looking expectantly at Rachel.

Rachel fitted the long S-shaped corset to Petra's slight frame, straightening the rigid whalebone rib cage, pulling it down over her hips before she began to lace it.

Louisa had opened her portfolio and took out a series of anatomical drawings which she held up for Guy to examine. "As you can see, Lord Ashton, when the top laces are drawn tight the woman's breast is pushed up and forced outward and the ribs are compressed, crushed, you might say. As the lower laces are tightened the internal organs including the lungs are also compressed, the stomach is displaced, pushed above the waistline, as is the liver, as this drawing illustrates. This leads to the digestive distress from which many women suffer. In addition, with the lungs compressed, breathing becomes shallow and the S-curve causes the spine to become misaligned, which results in pain and crippling displacement in later life. As you can see from this drawing."

Guy listened to this matter-of-fact explanation and looked at the illustrations as they were proffered without a flicker of expression as Petra struggled to catch her breath with Rachel's final tightening of the laces. Then he took a sip of whisky and stood up, going to the armoire, opening it and after a moment's thought selecting an evening gown of deep red taffeta. "If you would be so good as to help Lady Ashton with this gown, Mrs. Young."

Petra could think of nothing to say and it wasn't for either of her companions to comment on his lordship's response to the demonstration. She submitted to Rachel's assistance with the evening gown, still struggling with the discomfort of the corset, wondering what her next move should be.

When Rachel stood back, having fastened the last tiny button on the gown, Guy said with cool courtesy, "Thank you for your time, ladies. Allow me to show you out." He opened the dressing room door with a bow.

Rachel and Louisa had no choice but to accept their dismissal and with a murmur of farewell to Petra left the dressing room. In the hall beyond Guy summoned a hovering footman. "Escort the ladies to the door, please, and hail a cab for them. I give you good afternoon, Dr. Garret Anderson, Mrs. Young." He bowed punctiliously, then turned on his heel and went back into the dressing room.

"I'm not at all sure what that little demonstration was intended to achieve, my dear Petra," he remarked, closing the door behind him. "But it gives me the opportunity to demonstrate something of my own. Come to the mirror." He took her waist and turned her to face the long pier glass. "Look at you, how graceful and elegant you are." He turned her sideways to show her profile. "Don't tell me you can't see the difference the corset makes. It gives you stature."

"Which I lack," she retorted, spinning round to face him. "I grant you the semblance of elegance and grace, but that's all it is, a semblance, a manufactured look produced by artificial garments made of cords and whalebone invented by men to create just for them their ideal shape of a woman." She spun back to the mirror. "Look at me. I look like Clothilde Delmont. Is that what you want, Guy? Is that really what you want? Because if so, why the hell did you marry *me*?"

"Because you're not Clothilde," he said softly into the pulsating silence.

Petra's mouth opened, then closed as she struggled for words. She was ready to fight and with that soft statement he had cut the ground from beneath her feet.

"I don't know how many times I've told you that you need never give Clothilde a second thought, Petra."

"Yes . . . I know," she stumbled. "But then you go and do something like this, trying to make me look like her."

"Nonsense, you don't look remotely like her, corset or not," he retorted. "You have a lot more in common with the Macedonian guerrilla than the vicomtesse."

"Oh," Petra said. "Did she ever wear a corset?"

"Good God no. I don't think she ever wore anything but britches and a jerkin," he said.

328

Petra grinned. "That sounds more my style, I've always wanted to wear britches."

Guy looked pensive. "I can think of certain scenarios where that might be appealing."

Petra fumbled with the buttons at the back of the crimson gown. "Get me out of this, Guy, quickly." His simple statement had sent the familiar electric jolt of arousal into her belly and she struggled to catch her breath, which had little to do with the corset's constraint.

"Must I?" he teased.

"If you don't want me to expire on the spot."

"That wouldn't suit my plans at all." He spun her around and unfastened the tiny buttons at the back of the dress, then attacked the laces of the corset, observing, "Mrs. Young certainly believes in tight lacing."

"No, she doesn't, she hates selling these abominations," Petra told him, hurling the despised garment to the ground. "Look at the marks it's made." She lifted the bottom of her chemise and gingerly touched the deep welts on her skin. "And I only wore it for a few minutes."

Guy was too familiar with the disfiguring aspects of corset wearing to respond, saying instead, "I assume then that Mrs. Young is a member of the WSPU, like Dr. Garrett Anderson."

"Yes," Petra said simply. The last thing she wanted was a discussion of the Union now, when somehow her relationship with her husband had emerged unscathed from her little demonstration, which, with hindsight she freely admitted to herself had been a mistake. She now saw that she'd put Guy at a disadvantage and any other man would have been embarrassed. Guy was just above and beyond such irritatingly human weaknesses.

Petra was in her parlor the following afternoon answering letters and a pile of invitations when a knock on the door brought Diana and Fenella into the room, together with Diana's dogs, two magnificent South African Ridgebacks.

"This is a nice surprise, and very well timed. I'm getting bored with this." She gestured to the correspondence littered on the writing table.

"We're taking the dogs to the park. Will you come?" Diana asked cheerfully.

Petra bent to stroke the dogs, who were greeting her enthusiastically. "Yes, I could do with the fresh air. I'll just fetch my coat and meet you downstairs."

Five minutes later the three women were walking briskly toward Hyde Park. They entered at Cumberland Gate and Diana bent to unclip the dogs' leads, letting them run free. "So I have news," she said as she straightened. "The march is to take place next Monday, but word is being spread that it will be the following Friday."

"On Monday?" Fenella exclaimed. "But that's so soon. Can they get everything together in just three days?"

"Apparently so," Diana said. "Speed is vital if we're to keep it a secret until the last minute. We're hoping that the powers that be will be persuaded that it's not for another week so we'll catch them unawares." She bent to pick up a stick and threw it for the dogs in the general direction of the Serpentine.

Petra bent to take a soggy stick from the jaws of Hercules, who stood panting and drooling at her feet. "That'll be quite an achievement. The Union has grown so much it's becoming a real political nuisance. If they get the chance to disrupt the march they will. It'll be quite a coup if we can pull it off." She hurled the stick toward the lake.

"Has Guy said anything?" Fenella asked, hurling another stick for Hera, who was looking expectant after her brother had chased the one Petra had thrown.

"Not in so many words," Petra said thoughtfully. "But I know he's waiting for something to happen. It's very unnerving. I catch him looking at me now and again as if he's trying to read my mind."

"Why don't you ask him?" Diana questioned.

"Because I don't want to open the whole can of worms," Petra responded. "And quite honestly I don't think I could lie convincingly. I'm not very good at it at the best of times and Guy would see right through any deception. I prefer to just get the whole march over with. There'll be plenty of conversation after that. At least, I hope it'll be a conversation," she added with a grimace. "I've never seen Guy really angry."

"He might surprise you," Diana offered. "He doesn't come across as unreasonable at all. Although he is clearly used to being in charge all the time."

"That is certainly true. Anyway, what are the details for the actual march?"

"As I understand it, we assemble at Caxton Hall at ten o'clock on Monday, take up our banners and just process in a quiet and peaceful manner to Westminster, hoping that we can get to Parliament Square before they have time to marshal the forces to stop us. Emmeline and two or three others will bang on the door to St. Stephen's Hall and demand entrance. If the sergeant and his men try to block their way then they'll push forward and the rest of us will be right behind them, a bit like a battering ram at the siege of a castle."

Diana laughed, her eyes glinting with excitement. "It's going to be wonderful. This time we'll make sure they hear us."

"What do we do when we get inside?" Petra asked.

"Chant our demand for suffrage, just that, over and over, and wave our banners. Nothing more aggressive."

"It'll make enough of a stir as it is," Fenella observed. "Will Parliament be sitting on Monday?"

"Not until the afternoon, of course, but there should be enough members around in the morning to find our presence disrupting." Diana turned her step toward Mount Street. "I need to get home. I promised to go to Caxton Hall this evening to help with the posters. Can either of you join me?"

"Not tonight," Fenella said. "I have a rehearsal in Chiswick. Edward's written three one-act plays and he wants to put them on together at the Music Box. It'll be an exhausting evening, but I can come and help tomorrow morning."

"Petra, how about you?" Diana asked.

Petra shook her head. "Guy's going to be in for dinner and I'll get all flustered and muddled if I try to make up some reason why I'm suddenly going out for the evening. Can you manage without me tonight? I can come tomorrow morning too."

"I'll see you both then." Diana raised a hand in farewell and went off with the dogs toward Cavendish Square.

CHAPTER TWENTY-TWO

Guy was in his office when Petra came home and when he heard her voice in the hall went out to greet her. "Can you spare me a few minutes, Petra?"

"Yes, of course." She looked askance as she followed him back through the library. "Is it something important?"

"Something I want to discuss with you." He closed the door after her, gesturing to a chair.

"Nothing unpleasant, I hope," she said warily. It was unlike Guy to sound so businesslike.

"No, I trust not." He sat down, leaning back in the big leather chair behind the desk. "I want to have a house party at Ashton Court."

Petra nodded, saying nothing.

"Do you feel up to hosting such an event?" Guy asked directly.

Petra frowned. "Why wouldn't I?"

He held up his hands defensively. "Don't misinterpret, Petra. I rather assume you haven't had any experience in such matters and I want to be sure you feel comfortable. It's quite an undertaking and the guests will for the most part be politicians, members of the cabinet, the prime minister himself, I hope."

Petra found herself bristling at her husband's assumption that she was not up to one of the most essential tasks of a society hostess. "I can assure you, Guy, that I am perfectly capable of organizing and hosting a country house party, however erudite the guests. I'd like it, though, if you'd invite my brother. He may be a junior member of Parliament but I don't see why his career shouldn't benefit from having you as his brother-in-law."

"Of course Jonathan will be welcome." He offered a rueful smile. "I do appear to have offended you, my dear girl, and I really didn't mean to. I don't want to impose too much upon you, that's all."

"We're married," Petra stated. "Shared social obligations aren't an imposition. If you want, need to invite these men to Ashton Court then I shall be delighted to welcome them. And you needn't worry, I know what's expected of a hostess and I'm more than capable of fulfilling those expectations."

"I don't doubt it," he said, somewhat surprised at her vehemence. "Forgive me if it sounded as if I did."

"My mother may have neglected some aspects of my upbringing," Petra stated, "but not the social duties of a chatelaine. She did rather assume I'd be married in the end and would need such skills." She wasn't quite sure why she was so put out, it wasn't an unreasonable assumption of Guy's, given what he knew of her family, but it seemed to cast reflections on them and while she considered herself entitled to criticize them as much as she wished, it was no one else's business. Joth, she knew, felt the same way.

"My mistake, I'm so sorry," Guy said. "Can we forget I made any apparent aspersions about your upbringing, please." His smile was penitent. His wife was rarely touchy but this was obviously a sore point. One not to be forgotten in future.

Petra shrugged in agreement, asking briskly, "When do you want to have this house party?"

"I thought the last weekend of the month, a Friday to Monday."

Petra nodded and stood up. "Give me a guest list and I'll see to the invitations." She paused at the door. "It doesn't sound like the kind of company Diana and Fenella and their husbands will particularly enjoy, so I won't invite them."

"If you say so," Guy said easily. "I leave all the details entirely up to you, my sweet."

Petra left him, reflecting that in three weeks the memory of the women's invasion of Westminster would still be very fresh and she could well imagine that her friends would prefer to avoid a social encounter with their bêtes noires so soon. As for herself, well, she would just have to brazen it out. How Guy would choose to handle the awkwardness remained to be seen. She couldn't deny, though, the prickle of apprehension at the prospect.

"Good afternoon, Lady Ashton." Freddie had just entered the house when she crossed the hall on her way upstairs.

"Good afternoon, Freddie. Isn't it a lovely day?" she greeted him with a smile. "His lordship's in his office."

"Thank you, ma'am." He bowed, holding his hat to his chest, waiting politely for her to start up the stairs before going into the library and through to the office.

"Good afternoon, my lord."

"Freddie . . ." Guy looked up from his papers. "I wasn't expecting to see you this

338

afternoon."

"No, but I have some information that I thought might be of interest," his secretary said.

"Oh?" Guy looked a question mark.

"I heard from a reliable source, sir, that the suffragists' march on Parliament is to take place a week this Friday. You said you wished to know."

Guy nodded. "Yes, indeed, I did, thank you, Freddie. Have you heard anything else? How big it's expected to be . . . ?"

"Not exactly, my lord. But rumor has it that the London protesters will be joined by members of the Union from Manchester and other cities."

"Mmm." Guy pushed back his chair, his expression thoughtful. "Since you're here, there are some notes I've made on common land rights on my desk. Take a look at them and see if you can make a decent speech out of them." Distracted, he left the office, collected his hat and cane from the attending footman in the hall and went to Westminster to see if he could find Jonathan, who, he reasoned, might know something more about his sister's plans.

He ran Jonathan to earth in the Commons bar, drinking with a trio of friends. "Granville, what brings you to this side of Westminster?" Jonathan asked jovially. "May I get you a drink?"

"Whisky, please," Guy responded. "I wanted a word with you if you can spare it."

"Of course. Annie, two whiskies please." He signaled the woman behind the bar before gesturing to a table and chairs in the window. "Shall we sit over there?"

Guy followed him and they sat down, waiting until the barmaid had brought their drinks before he asked, "Do you know anything about this proposed women's suffrage march on Westminster, Jonathan?"

Jonathan looked wary. "Not really," he said carefully. "Petra doesn't usually tell me the details of these protests in case it puts me in an awkward position."

"Considerate of her," Guy muttered into his glass. "So you don't know anything about a planned invasion of Westminster?"

Jonathan looked startled. "An invasion? No, no one's said anything to me about that. I heard that another march was being planned for some time soon, but just the usual protest in Parliament Square."

Guy sipped his whisky. "I suppose I'll just have to ask her point blank."

"Petra's a very bad liar, sir."

"Yes, I know." He drummed his fingers on

the table. He didn't like the idea of confronting her, putting her on the spot, forcing her to tell him something she didn't want to divulge. And he knew he would get it out of her if he was determined. But it seemed like bullying and didn't sit well with him.

"Are you totally against the idea of universal suffrage, sir?" Jonathan looked at him closely.

"I am against your sister, my wife, taking any part in activities designed to force His Majesty's government to take actions against the will of Parliament and the well-ordered running of this country," Guy stated with some force.

Jonathan frowned. "But if it were acceptable to the government you wouldn't be against the idea of universal suffrage?" he asked hesitantly. "Against women having the vote? The principle itself, I mean?"

"As far as I'm concerned, right now that's not the issue. My problem is to keep your sister from breaking the law and causing an untold amount of trouble and embarrassment." He drained his glass and stood up. "Thank you for the whisky, Jonathan." He strode from the bar leaving his wife's brother staring after him wondering what if anything he could do to stop whatever collision was about to happen between his sister and her husband.

Guy decided not to confront Petra directly for a few days, there was time before the march was to take place for him to set Freddie to discover the details. Besides, he had the whole weekend ahead of him and maybe Petra would let something slip. But the weekend passed pleasantly with no mention of suffrage, universal or otherwise. He had engagements of his own on Saturday morning so he wasn't aware of his wife's activities at Caxton Hall, and the dinner party they hosted that evening went off smoothly. He had the feeling once or twice that Petra was going out of her way to prove herself an impeccable hostess, which made him feel guilty and willing to indulge her triumphant air at the evening's end.

Monday dawned bright, sunny and chill.

"You're up early," Guy observed in surprise as he emerged from the bathroom to find his wife consulting with her maid over her dress for the morning. Petra tended to enjoy leisurely mornings over tea and the *Gazette* and *Times* before preparing to take on the day.

"I have a dressmaker's fitting at nine thirty this morning." Petra's voice was a little muffled as she headed into the bathroom. "I don't even have time for a bath."

Guy shrugged and continued with his dressing. "Are you coming down for breakfast?" he inquired as he prepared to leave the bedroom.

"No, Dottie will fetch me a piece of toast. I'm meeting Diana and Fenella after the fitting and we'll have coffee and crumpets at Fortnum's, probably." It wasn't a complete lie. It was certainly an intention, although they all doubted it would be possible.

Guy nodded, dropped a kiss on the back of her neck and headed downstairs to the breakfast room. Petra heaved a sigh of relief. The next time she saw her husband it was going to be in very different circumstances.

"Shall I fetch the toast, m'lady?"

Petra shuddered. "No, thanks, Dottie, I feel sick, I couldn't eat anything." She pushed her arms into the sleeves of a tweed coat. She wanted to look as unremarkable as possible and any of the rich furs in her wardrobe would not do for this morning.

"I think I should come and show my support," Dottie said doubtfully.

"No, absolutely not," Petra declared, taking the girl's hands in both hers. "Just go about your work as usual and don't let on to anyone that you know anything. There's no point stirring up trouble for yourself when it's not necessary. Just think that I'm going to be there for both of us." She smiled reassuringly and Dottie nodded, unable to conceal her relief.

Petra hurried downstairs, casting a quick glance at the closed door to the breakfast room as she sped past, and attained the pavement with a sigh of relief. She hailed a passing hackney and only seemed to breathe normally when the door was closed and the vehicle had turned onto Mount Street.

CHAPTER TWENTY-THREE

"Looks like something's going on at the Hall, ma'am," the hackney called over his shoulder. "Quite a crowd gathering."

"Just let me out here," Petra instructed, reaching into her purse for change. "This'll do fine. Thank you." She handed him a few coins and jumped down to the street, hurrying in the direction of the commotion.

Women, for the most part wearing the colors of the Women's Social and Political Union, seethed around the entrance to Caxton Hall, waving posters as organizers stood on boxes trying to form orderly groups out of the mass.

"Over here, Petra." Diana hailed Petra from a group forming on the other side of the street. "We're in the first group with Emmeline, so we'll be among those knocking at the entrance to St. Stephen's Hall." Her eyes shone with excitement and passion. "Can you see Fenella anywhere?"

"Not yet." Petra took the poster a woman thrust into her hands as she stood on tiptoe to see better over the crowd. "Oh, there she is. Fenella . . . Fenella," she called, cupping her hands around her mouth as a megaphone.

Fenella waved a hand in acknowledgment and pushed her way through the crowd to where her friends stood.

"Have a poster." Diana thrust one into her hands. "We're going to start in a few minutes and hope everyone will somehow fall in after us in some orderly form."

"There's so many of us," Petra said in awe. "No one can ignore a protest this big."

"We'll just make sure they don't." Christabel Pankhurst appeared beside her mother, Emmeline, a militant gleam in her eye. "I intend to knock a few helmets off if any policeman tries to stop me."

"That'll get you convicted of assaulting an officer of the law," Fenella pointed out. "A bit extreme, don't you think?"

"If we're going to fight this fight we have to use every tool at our disposal," Christabel declared. "Either you believe in it or you don't. There's no point in half measures."

"I think we should try to be as peaceful as possible, my dear," Emmeline said, trying as always to persuade her daughter to keep her more extreme inclinations in check. "Violence doesn't really achieve much."

"Sometimes it's a last resort," Christabel stated. "Let's get started." She raised her poster high above her head, gestured with her free hand to the group around her and set off toward Westminster. Gradually the throng fell in behind them and the mass of women processed to the Houses of Parliament, chanting and singing, drawing a crowd of spectators as they went.

A small police force was assembled in Parliament Square. The WSPU had marched peacefully many times to the doors of Parliament and presented several petitions at St. Stephen's door, all of which had been refused by the sergeant at arms, and there was no reason to assume this protest would be any different. Until Emmeline and Christabel hammered on St. Stephen's door and as soon as it was opened pushed forward, brandishing their posters, the crowd surging behind them in a tidal wave of chanting women that drove back the sergeant at arms and his own small group of parliamentary officers.

The crowd of women poured into St. Stephen's Hall, with sheer force of numbers pushing through the men trying to form a barricade. From there they stormed the Central Lobby, which stood midway between the Commons and the Lords at the heart of the Houses of Parliament. They stood on chairs and benches, waving the banners, shouting their demands for "Freedom" and *"Votes For Women."*

Petra lost sight of Diana and Fenella in the crush. She was concentrating on keeping her own footing in the melee even as she struggled to keep her poster aloft. There were more policemen now and they were seizing women, hauling them off chairs, carrying them toward the open doors, almost throwing them out into the square.

Guy was sitting in the salon of the House of Lords, drinking coffee and reading the *Times,* when he noticed a stirring of the generally peaceful, almost sacrosanct air of the paneled room. A footman hurried in and murmured something to the barman, who murmured something to the Duke of Mortby, sitting at the bar nursing a glass. The duke sat up abruptly, turned on his stool, saw Guy and came over.

"Granville, heard the commotion?"

"What commotion?"

"Something in Central Lobby. Women all over, I gather, shouting and makin' nuisances of themselves. Positive disgrace. Police involved and all sorts."

Guy closed his eyes briefly on a wave of frustration. How had Freddie got it so wrong? Why had he himself been so complacent as to let this happen? He'd been warned and he could have wrung the truth out of Petra. Now he had no doubts at all that his wife was somewhere in the commotion in Central Lobby.

With a word of excuse he left the duke and the salon and swiftly made his way along the Peers Corridor to Central Lobby. He could hear the clamor as he hastened down the corridor. Two parliamentary officers stood at the door leading to the lobby. They had the air of men prepared to defend entrance into a castle under siege.

"Let me by," Guy ordered and one of them opened the door exposing the uproar within. At first Guy stood in the doorway, the officers at his back, trying to make sense of the scene. There were women everywhere, standing on chairs, on plinths with the various statues adorning the space, on the long benches along the walls. The slogan chanting was incessant, the posters now being wielded as weapons against the policemen struggling with the protesters.

Guy finally found his wife in the chaos

and for a moment he had the absurd urge to laugh. Petra was standing on a chair, using her poster to fend off a broad-shouldered officer who was attempting to pull her down. She looked, he thought, like a diminutive gladiator fighting off a lion. Then he saw a man holding up a camera pointed at Petra on her chair and he lost all desire to laugh. Swearing under his breath he pushed his way through the seething horde looking for the photographer who seemed to have disappeared into the melee. A member of the gutter press, no doubt. They'd be all over this story and pictures of the protesters would be plastered across the front pages of the evening papers.

He reached Petra still on her chair and still fighting off the officer with her poster. "Excuse me." He pushed the man aside without ceremony. He leaned forward, caught Petra around the knees and hoisted her over his shoulder.

She dropped the poster with her sudden change of position, and reared up against his shoulder, "Put me down, Guy." Her demand fell on deaf ears as he shouldered his way back through the crowd. The two officers at the door to the Peers Corridor had remained in the open doorway, staring in dumb astonishment at the scene in front of them. Hastily they moved aside as Guy marched past them with his burden. "Shut the damn door," he snarled, stalking halfway down the corridor before setting Petra roughly on her feet.

She spun round on him, hazel eyes flashing with outrage. "How dare you, Guy. You have no right to interfere."

"No right," he exclaimed. "No right to prevent my wife from making an appalling spectacle of herself, from dragging my name through the gutter press. How *dare* you expose yourself and *my* family in such a shameless display."

"Oh, that's all you care about," she threw at him. "*Your* family, *your* name? This battle is so much more important than your trivial concerns, *Lord Ashton.*"

"*Trivial concerns.*" He stared at her in disbelief, his dark eyes filled with anger, his expression a hard mask. Petra took an involuntary step back. She had wondered what his real anger would be like and it frightened her a little. He didn't look like himself.

"It's politics," she said, trying to stand her ground. "Politics are more important than personal concerns. It's not right that half the population should essentially belong to the other half and have no say in how their country is run, or how they run their own lives."

Guy said nothing. He continued to fix her with that same disbelieving fury and in the face of his silence Petra could think of nothing else to say. The noise from beyond the corridor seemed if anything to be growing louder and more out of control. She wondered what was happening to Diana and Fenella.

Guy moved suddenly, taking her arm in a hard grip, still saying nothing as he propelled her down the corridor to the House of Lords's private entry and out into New Palace Yard, away from the commotion outside the St. Stephen's entrance. He didn't loosen his hold until they were inside a hackney, away from the photographers' cameras and the police, who were loading women into Black Marias in Parliament Square.

Nothing was said on the short drive to Berkeley Square and when they reached the house, Guy jumped down first, held Petra's arm as she stepped down and kept hold into the house. His expression a grim mask, he didn't acknowledge a for once startled-looking Babbit and steered his wife to the stairs and up to her own parlor, where he closed the door behind them and finally released his grip.

Petra was disinclined to break the silence and stood by the window, waiting, her gloved hands tucked into her coat pockets, aware of the lingering feel of his fingers on her arm.

Guy threw another log on the fire. He straightened and stood for a minute with his back to her, his hands braced against the mantel shelf. The silence was almost menacing and Petra found herself holding her breath waiting for him to speak.

Finally he did, turning slowly to face her. "I am so angry, Petra, that I can hardly trust myself to be in the same room with you. At some point I will have to decide how to deal with this but I don't want to do or say anything I'll regret, so for the moment it'll have to wait. Will you give me your word that you will not leave the house again today?"

"Why?"

"You have to ask?"

She considered. No, she didn't have to ask. But she wanted to know what had happened to her friends and she wanted to stand her ground with her husband as far as she could. "Very well, I'll stay in the house today, but I intend to write some letters. I assume you have no objections to that?"

"No, of course not. I don't mind who you write to or who visits, I just ask that you remain inside."

"As you wish."

Guy nodded and went to the door. "I'm not going out myself so I'll be in the library or my office, if you need me." He left, closing the door softly behind him.

Petra wondered why she would possibly need him in the present state of affairs. He was far too intimidating in this incarnation to engage in a civilized discussion of the issue that she felt so passionately about, and a shouting match wouldn't do either of them any good.

She sat down at her writing desk to write to Diana and Fenella, wishing she knew whether they'd found themselves in the dock at the Old Bailey for trespass or disorderly conduct, or even assault on a policeman. Quite a few helmets had been knocked off in the affray but she'd been too busy defending herself to see who had been involved. Perhaps they'd slipped away and were now sitting in Fortnum's wondering where she was.

Tears pricked behind her eyes and she blinked furiously. She hadn't realized how greatly Guy's anger would upset her, but she felt strangely unmoored, as if she'd lost an essential support. She stared at the blank sheet of vellum, trying to summon a coherent sentence but she hadn't got very far when a brisk knock at the door brought Diana and Fenella, agog with their own adventures and anxious to hear their friend's experiences of the morning.

"What happened to you?" Diana asked, casting aside her coat and striped scarf. "One minute I saw you jumping on a chair and the next I was dodging away from an officer. When I looked again, you'd disappeared."

"Guy happened," Petra stated. "He came and carried me away. It sounds ridiculous, I know, but I couldn't do anything to stop him. How did you get out of there unscathed?"

"I ducked out when they were arresting Christabel, she was making such a racket and everyone's attention was focused on her, she'd already knocked one policeman's helmet off and was kicking another one as he tried to carry her out to the Black Maria," Fenella said. "I felt a bit of a coward cutting and running like that, but I thought it better to live to fight another day."

"Absolutely," Petra agreed, feeling slightly

better herself about her own ignominious departure from the fight. "But now, I don't know what's going to happen. Guy is livid and I don't know what to do with it." She gave a helpless shrug. "He won't talk to me because he's too angry."

"Oh, my dear, that's so hard." Diana was instantly sympathetic.

"Yes, there's nothing like a good knock-down, drag out fight to clear the air," Fenella added. "In my experience it's always better to have things out."

Petra smiled faintly. What worked for Edward and Fenella was not for every marriage.

"Let's go to Covent Garden for a late lunch. I'm famished," Diana said. "I was too nervous to eat breakfast and it's already two o'clock."

"You two go. I can't," Petra said. "Guy asked me to stay inside and I said I would."

"He's keeping you a prisoner?" Fenella asked, shocked.

"No, not in the least." Petra shook her head. "He asked a favor and I agreed. He's not going anywhere either. I think we have to stay under the same roof until we can come to some kind of resolution. Does that make sense?"

"If it makes sense to you, darling, that's

356

all that matters," Diana stated. "We can stay with you if it'll help."

Petra shook her head again. "No, this is just between myself and Guy. You go and find some lunch. I'll let you know how things work out."

After they had left she abandoned her writing desk and stood at the window overlooking the garden, winter bare now except for a bright splash of red from a camellia blooming against the rosy brick of the garden wall. She turned as the door opened again and Guy came in.

"Freddie has prepared the invitations for the house party," he said, dropping the handful of engraved and embossed white cards in a fan on her writing desk. "If you'll sign them this afternoon they can be hand delivered this evening."

His expression was neutral, his tone cool and distant. Petra took a breath. She'd had half an idea in the light of the morning's debacle that Guy would think again about the house party. But, of course, she should have known better. Backing down was not her husband's way.

"I'll do them now." She went over to the desk, dipped her pen in the ink and signed her name on the ten cards. Ten couples was a large party and without exception the guests were all members of the government. Men for whom, for the most part, universal suffrage was anathema. None of their wives to her knowledge had shown any active interest in the Union and Petra could see an excruciatingly uncomfortable weekend ahead.

She handed the cards back to Guy, who stood waiting behind her chair. "What will you do if my presence this morning becomes known?" Her voice was more tentative than she'd hoped it would sound.

"Oh, believe me, my dear Petra, it's all over town by now," he said with the same lack of expression. "There are newspapermen lurking outside with cameras already."

"We could throw a bucket of water over them from the upstairs landing," Petra suggested, realizing too late how totally inappropriate an attempt at humor was in present circumstances.

Guy looked at her in disbelief. "Are you utterly witless? Have you no idea what this means?"

"Yes . . . yes, of course I do. I'm sorry, I shouldn't joke about it. I'll keep away from the street and any cameras until this all blows over." She hesitated, then took a deep breath. "I'm sorry this makes things awkward for you, Guy, but I'm not giving up the Union."

"You are my wife and I can do little to change that," he said coldly. "But don't expect any support or acknowledgment from me, public or otherwise. That's all I have to say at the moment." He slipped the signed cards into his coat pocket and left the parlor.

Petra swallowed a knot of tears. Did he mean that he would change the fact of their marriage if he could? It seemed to be what he'd meant. Was that his last word? There was to be no resolution, just this yawning gap between them? Somehow she had to go on as normal, maintaining her public position as Lady Ashton while pursuing her private political passions at the same time without her husband's even tacit support. She didn't see how she could do that and have a marriage in anything but name.

CHAPTER TWENTY-FOUR

"How are things now with Guy, Petra?" Jonathan asked his sister as they settled into a first-class carriage in the train to Bristol a week later.

"Chilly," she responded, taking a corner seat.

"I don't suppose he enjoyed seeing his wife's picture splashed across the front page of the *Times*." He put his attaché case onto the overhead shelf. "That was sheer bad luck, considering that Diana and Fenella managed to stay incognito."

"And it wouldn't have mattered with them, anyway," Petra said bitterly. "Their husbands support the Union and wouldn't be seriously put out."

"They're also not members of Parliament," Jonathan pointed out, taking the corner seat opposite his sister. "You must admit their situation is rather different."

"Perhaps, but the issue of suffrage is more

like a matter of conscience, it should rise above mundane concerns like dignity and family name," Petra declared with a return of her customary energetic passion. "It's such a noble and vital cause. If men of power like Guy supported the cause then it wouldn't be necessary to protest in the way we are. If Asquith becomes prime minister in a Liberal government shouldn't we expect some movement toward suffrage reform? You'd support it, wouldn't you?" It wasn't a rhetorical question.

"Yes, I would, and I do," Joth said with a sigh. "But I don't like the Union's methods of persuasion."

"They're the only ones left to us," Petra stated. She stared out of the window at the passing countryside, neatly fenced fields, cattle grouped under clumps of trees, the silver thread of a river. It was all so peaceful on the surface. She sat up straighter and said firmly, "Let's not talk about this anymore. Why aren't you staying at Ashton Court for the weekend?"

"Because it's time some member of the family showed their faces on our own estate," Joth said. "And I can ride over from Rutherford Court every morning and back again after dinner. I can't miss any of the political discussions."

"No," Petra agreed. By including her brother, a very junior member of Parliament, in every aspect of the weekend, Guy had been doing him a great favor. His presence would make him more noticeable to the men at the top of government, those who really ran the country.

"I'd like to stay on the spot, of course," Joth went on. "But I have duty to the family as well. Ma and Pa haven't been near the house since your wedding. I've been trying to persuade them to celebrate Christmas there at least, give the tenants the usual party, have the tree for the village, all the old traditions. But I don't know if they will."

"You, my dear, need to find a wife," his sister stated. "Then you can put Rutherford House to its proper purpose. Fill it with children, celebrate every major holiday, revive the Christmas pageant, a proper Boxing Day. The tenants and villagers would be in seventh heaven."

Jonathan said nothing but a little smile hovered on his lips. "There is someone," Petra crowed. "I knew it, you've been too busy to visit me for weeks. Who is it?"

"Not yet," he said, putting a finger to his lips. "I'll tell you when I'm ready."

"Or do you mean when the lady is ready?"

"Perhaps I do."

Petra had to be satisfied with that, but the news of her brother's present and prospective happiness cheered her up. It gave her something else to think about other than her own present misery. And maybe the weekend wouldn't be as hideously awkward as she feared. Maybe the change of scene might make Guy a little easier to talk to . . . might give them back some of their old ease, the loving touch that she now knew was so essential to her happiness. She settled back for the long journey, watching the countryside as the train huffed its way toward the bustling port city of Bristol, steaming into the station three hours later.

Petra followed Joth to the platform and waited while he hailed a porter to fetch their bags from the luggage compartment. She had come a few days early to Ashton Court to arrange the details for the Friday to Monday, a necessary duty of any good hostess, one that in any other circumstances she would have taken on cheerfully. Guy would follow on Thursday, when he would expect everything to be in order.

It would be, of course. Whatever the state of affairs between herself and Guy she would not fail to play the part of Lady Ashton, perfect in every detail. As she looked around the platform, she stiffened suddenly. The unmistakable figure of Clothilde Delmont, statuesque and elegant as always, stepped down from a first-class carriage, her hand firmly held in that of an equally elegant gentleman standing on the platform. He embraced Clothilde and they exchanged a brief kiss of greeting, before he turned to a liveried footman behind him, gesturing to the luggage compartment. A woman, clearly a maid from her sober dark coat and hat, descended after Clothilde and busied herself straightening her mistress's fur stole.

Now, what had brought Clothilde to Bristol? Petra wondered. Was it pure coincidence? That seemed hard to believe. People didn't just go to Bristol on a whim. But someone had met her, so perhaps she had good friends in the city. It seemed a little unfashionable though for someone of the vicomtesse's stature.

"Do you know who's with Lady Delmont?" she asked Joth when he returned with the porter and their luggage.

Her brother followed her gaze. "I wouldn't have expected to see Lady Delmont here," he commented. "Oh, but that explains it. That's Lord Harrington with her. He has a house just outside Bath. I heard a rumor she was showing a particular interest in him."

"As his mistress?" Petra was intrigued.

Jonathan shrugged. "The lady usually finds a protector when she needs one and I've heard tell she's been without since Guy finished with her."

"Why's she here at this particular time?" Petra mused. "I'd have thought there was more than enough in town to keep her amused."

"Who's to say? Come on now, your motor is waiting outside."

"Motor?"

Jonathan chuckled. "Apparently Guy sent word that you were to be met by his motor, not the barouche." He flung an arm around his sister's shoulders and steered her toward the station entrance. "You should be at Ashton Court within the hour."

The driver in a chauffeur's livery stood at the door of the sleek motor vehicle on the cobbled drive outside the station. He tipped his hat and opened the low-slung passenger door. "Welcome, Lady Ashton. We'll have you home in no time."

Petra kissed her brother goodbye and stepped into the car. The chauffeur tucked a fur lap robe around her. "There's a hot brick for your feet, m'lady."

Her booted feet encountered the brick, its warmth instantly soothing. "Lovely, thank you." She waved goodbye to Joth and as she did so caught sight of Clothilde and her escort emerging from the station. Clothilde paused and looked directly at Petra. In the gloom of late afternoon Petra felt rather than saw clearly the malice in those lavender-blue eyes. She felt the hairs on her nape lift for an instant, as she realized the woman was making her way across the cobbled forecourt toward her.

"Lady Delmont? What brings you to Bristol?" She greeted her with a bland smile.

"Oh, a private matter," the lady responded. She leaned toward Petra. "Are you perhaps rusticating in the country, Lady Ashton? I understand there was something of an embarrassing spectacle in town the other day. The newspapers appeared to find it amusing, but I doubt Lord Ashton appreciated it." Her smile flickered, reminding Petra of the darting tip of a snake's tongue.

"How very well informed you are, Lady Delmont," she returned. "But perhaps you don't know everything. I bid you good afternoon." Pointedly, she turned her head to the front as the car rumbled out of the forecourt leaving Clothilde still standing on the cobbles.

Petra's renewed sense of cheer had disappeared the moment the woman had approached her. The malice in her eyes as she'd taunted Petra with Guy's reaction to the *spectacle* his wife had created plunged her anew into misery. For all her bravado she couldn't deny that in this matter Clothilde Delmont knew how her former lover would react all too well.

CHAPTER TWENTY-FIVE

Guy stepped off the train on an overcast Thursday afternoon and made his way directly to the front of the station, expecting to find his chauffeur and motor waiting for him. He was not prepared for the sight of his wife, standing beside the open door of the vehicle, looking impatiently toward the station entrance. His heart lifted at the sight of her; Berkeley Square had seemed strangely desolate for the last few days. He had tried to untangle the mess of his feelings, his anger fueled by his sense of Petra's disloyalty that she had not given a thought to the position her actions would put him in, clashing with his knowledge deep down that she was her own person as well as his wife and was entitled to hold her own opinions, whether they suited her husband or not. And in absolute truth, he had to admit that he held no strong opinions against the idea of universal suffrage. Until

Petra had come into his life it had never been an issue at the forefront of his mind. He certainly hadn't met any female advocates of the cause in his own social circles.

"I thought I'd come and meet you," she said unnecessarily as he approached the car. She lifted her face for his kiss and he pecked her lightly on the cheek.

"You didn't need to do that," he said, tossing his bag into the dickey.

"No, I realize that," Petra said dully, climbing back into the car. Somehow she had hoped that surprising Guy might surprise a warm reaction from him. A false hope, clearly.

Guy felt a wash of guilt at her crestfallen expression. He didn't want to behave the way he was behaving, he wanted to crush her to him, feel her in his arms, slight and warm and so responsive. He wanted to hear her ready laughter, her quick-witted banter, her loving responses. He'd had enough time in the last few days to realize that matters between them couldn't continue in the same vein. There had to be some resolution. He reached out a hand and took hers, enclosing it lightly in his own. She looked at him, startled, a hopeful question in her hazel eyes.

"This evening," he said quietly, conscious

369

of the chauffeur sitting in front. Petra nodded and slid down in the seat a little, allowing her head to rest on his shoulder, and they passed the drive in a silence that was almost companionable although redolent with the unspoken waiting in the wings.

Guy waited until after they had eaten a subdued and somewhat stilted dinner before facing the issue head-on. "Why didn't you tell me that you were planning to take part in that protest, Petra?"

She looked at him in surprise. "How could I have done? You would have tried to stop me."

"How do you think I would have done that? If you were determined to do something against my wishes, regardless of my reasons, what action could I take to prevent it?"

"I don't really know," she said, realizing for the first time the truth of that. "I . . . I didn't want to upset you and I suppose I thought that if you didn't know about it you wouldn't be."

"How the hell did you think I wouldn't know about it when you're invading Westminster and getting your face and name splashed across the front pages?" he exclaimed, his anger rising again. "At least if I'd been expecting it I could have done

370

something to avert the publicity. Instead I'm left on the back foot looking like a blind fool."

"I didn't think of it like that," she said. "It's such a vitally important matter, Guy, I didn't see anything else around it, just the need to force the government to at least acknowledge the issue. I'm so sorry if it seems to you that I was deliberately causing you embarrassment. I truly didn't think of it like that."

"It seems to me you didn't think at all," he responded curtly.

"How else are we to get the government to listen to us?" she asked. "We've tried asking politely, we've tried delivering petitions, the only response we get is a blanket refusal even to debate the subject."

Guy was silent for a moment. He knew the truth of her statement. The government was not prepared to consider women's suffrage.

"We would be overjoyed to discuss it in a civilized fashion," Petra pressed. "But we're dismissed like overexcited children wanting an impossible toy. It's not right, Guy. I can't back away, I'm sorry. But I promise I will tell you before I take part in any further action."

Guy rubbed his eyes wearily. "Then I suppose we'll have to leave it there," he said. "There's no point going around in circles."

"What do you have against women voting?" Petra asked abruptly. "You've never given me a straight reason."

"I don't know why you'd want it," he responded. "Women are welcome to give their opinions and the government is always willing to listen. What point is there in your having the vote?"

"Women won't settle for being mere supplicants," she stated. "You must see the difference between having an equal voice and having to rely on a man to speak for you."

He shook his head. "I'm too tired to argue the points with you tonight. Let's go to bed. We have a busy weekend ahead." He opened the door for her, gesturing she should precede him.

He made love to her that night for the first time since the invasion of Westminster and it brought some return to normality between them, enough at least for them to present a united front when their guests arrived the following morning.

Petra was as charming and efficient a hostess as she knew how to be and Guy was her equal as a host. Politics were not discussed when the whole party was together. It was as if the men considered it taboo around their wives, although Petra couldn't fail to notice the occasional speculative glance sent her way when the general conversation touched lightly on the government, but it was only ever a fleeting moment. For the most part she concentrated her attentions on the ladies of the party, who required some form of entertaining while the men were participating in a shooting party on Saturday morning, playing billiards or closeted for many hours in the library discussing detailed political issues.

Only once was Petra forced to bite her tongue in the drawing room after the ladies had withdrawn from the dining table, leaving the gentlemen to their port and cigars, and the wife of Viscount Barber brought up the subject of the WSPU. She expressed her disgust for the behavior of women of their own social standing who dared to shame their sex by blatantly breaking the law and behaving in a manner more suited to a peasant mob than the affluent wives of powerful and influential men, and it became rapidly clear that she was not alone in her opinion. None of their remarks seemed addressed directly to Petra, so she assumed her own participation in the Union was not generally known. Probably the ladies didn't read the news sections of the papers, she thought with some derision. Their interests would be focused on the engagements and the court pages.

She maintained her hostess smile, poured tea and coffee, passed around sweets and engaged in social chitchat as if it were all that mattered in her world.

Guy was still playing billiards when she went up to bed, and she had turned the lights down low and was feigning sleep when he finally came up. She didn't think she could bear to discuss anything about the drawing room conversation with him, and it was all she could think of at the moment, her complete bewilderment at the pathetic apathy of her own sex. She didn't think he was fooled by her pretense at sleeping, but he had the delicacy not to invade her silence. He was up at dawn the next morning for the day's shoot and Petra murmured a sleepy goodbye when he bent to kiss her on his way out of the bedroom.

"You and the women will be joining us for lunch by the lake," he said. "Babbit has the lunch organized and carriages will bring you all at noon."

"Yes, Guy," she confirmed in a tone of exaggerated patience. "I've gone over all the arrangements with Cook and Babbit. We shall be waiting for you in the lake pavilion.

Have a successful morning."

He hesitated a moment before saying, "If I haven't already told you how much I appreciate your doing this, Petra, I'll say it now. You are a superb hostess. You have everything at your fingertips."

"Even suffragists can be capable hostesses," she murmured, keeping her eyes firmly closed. If she'd hoped for a response she was disappointed as she heard the door close behind him.

Petra lay back against the pillows. Things were still far from right between them. If they had been, the old Guy would have responded to her teasing provocation in some lighthearted way. She sighed, contemplating the rest of the day to be spent entirely in the company of politicians' wives. A day of pure tedium, she thought, but tomorrow there would be some leavening. Guy had invited some of the local prominent families for lunch which would dilute the company somewhat. And after that it would all be over and who knew what the immediate future would hold.

She lay down again, closing her eyes. She knew exactly what she wanted the very immediate future to hold. A day at the seaside, alone, revisiting a childhood haunt and the rich memories of carefree days. Ashton

Court was only a few miles from Weston-super-Mare, at the mouth of the Severn Estuary. The pier was a children's paradise, with its theatre and magicians and little trinket stalls. There was usually a band playing either on the pier or in the bandstand on the beach. It would be too cold to swim, but the sandy beach was always lovely. She could get fish and chips from the little café on the beach and eat them in the beach pavilion. A day just to herself where she could let her thoughts go where they would and maybe find some peace in the present turmoil of her mind.

Just before noon Petra and her guests climbed into carriages and pony traps and were driven across the estate to the lake with its open-sided pavilion. Babbit was supervising footmen, who were laying out lunch for the guests. There was a brisk breeze coming off the lake but no one seemed troubled by it. The women were all dressed in furs and several braziers had been lit in the pavilion. Hot soup simmered on trivets over spirit lamps, and platters of cold roasted chickens, ham, and game pies covered the long white-clothed tables. Bottles of wine were arrayed on a table to one side, together with decanters of sweet sherry, whisky and cognac for

376

those who needed spirituous warming.

The shooting party arrived soon after, their guns carried by the gamekeepers and their assistants, who also carried the morning's spoils. Petra was not in favor of shooting innocent creatures but knew it was an unpopular viewpoint in this society and once again kept her opinion to herself. Jonathan was one of the shooting party and looked very pleased with himself as he took a glass of whisky from a footman and came over to greet his sister.

"I bagged three pheasants and two hares," he announced, taking a chair beside her, close to one of the braziers. "It was a good morning. Guy certainly knows how to look after his game."

"Well, his estate manager does," Petra corrected, taking a sip of sherry.

"That's ungenerous," Jonathan chided. "It's Guy who gives the orders. If he didn't care, neither would the estate manager. Poachers would be rife and the gamekeepers wouldn't pay attention."

Petra laughed. "I'm sorry. I just don't see the appeal in killing the poor creatures, particularly the pheasants, when they're born and bred and looked after on the estate before they let them loose just so that they can shoot them."

"What are you taking issue with now, madam wife?" Guy came over to them, looking as pleased with himself as Jonathan. His tone was lightly teasing but his dark eyes were sharp.

"Petra's never approved of shooting," Joth said.

"I don't see the point of raising the birds just to shoot them dead," Petra stated.

"That's certainly a legitimate point of view," her husband said. "But as with so many things, we must agree to differ."

Petra heard the note of sharpness in the statement and bit her lip, turning her head aside to hide her dismay. The gap still yawned between them. Guy's expression, however, was even, unperturbed, he was clearly much better at maintaining a façade. Perhaps she had imagined the sharpness but she knew she hadn't. Any more than she could ignore the conviction that the foundations of her marriage were not as steady as they used to be. One violent kick and the foundation would give way and the whole glorious edifice come tumbling down about her ears. With an effort she forced her attention back to her guests, who were seating themselves at the long tables.

Petra was in her dressing room that evening

dressing for dinner when Guy came in holding his onyx cuff links. "Can you fasten these, Petra, my fingers are all thumbs for some reason."

Petra turned on her dressing stool and obliged. "I shall be glad when this evening is over," she confessed.

"You've shown remarkable self-restraint. I'm sorry to have subjected you to such a fusty group."

"It's not their fustiness I object to," she responded, opening the jewel box on her dressing table.

Guy let the statement lie. He reached over her shoulder and closed the lid of the jewel box. "I'd like you to wear the rubies this evening."

She looked up at him. "Any special reason?"

"Not exactly. I'll fetch them. They're in the safe." He went back into the bedroom.

Petra frowned at herself in the dressing mirror. Wearing the rubies would be a statement, a statement of her position as a Granville, the wife of Baron Ashton. She was certain that that was what Guy intended to demonstrate. The stones were a stamp, a brand that assigned her place in the world. It wouldn't occur to any of the guests at Ashton Court that evening that their hostess, resplendent in the family gems, was a passionate suffragist intent on disrupting the social order as they understood it. But if Guy hoped that dressing his wife in the outward manifestation of her social place would weaken her passionate ideals he was very much mistaken.

Guy came back with the casket that contained the rubies nestled in velvet. He fastened the necklace and helped her with the bracelet, but when he handed her the silver-and-ruby fillet for her hair, Petra shook her head. "No, that's too formal, Guy. It's not as if we're going to one of the queen's drawing rooms. I prefer a more casual style for my hair, particularly when we're dining at home." Dottie had arranged the rich chestnut mass twisted in a loose knot on her nape, artfully stray tendrils drifting over her forehead and about her ears.

"As you wish." He shrugged and placed the ornament back in the casket. "It looks very pretty. By the way, I thought we might get up some foursomes for bridge after dinner."

"That should keep people occupied," Petra agreed. "At least those who don't want to play billiards." She stood up, smoothing the skirts of her turquoise damask dress as Dottie draped an Indian silk shawl over her elbows. She took one last look at her reflection in the long mirror. The rubies dominated the image, blood red, deep fires glowing in their depths. They were as gorgeous as they were intimidating, dangerous almost. But that was fanciful. "Shall we go down?"

Guy offered his arm. He was acutely aware of how fragile the present truce was. Occasionally Petra's customary warmth and bubbling good humor would show itself, but not for long. In its place was a somewhat chill composure as she performed her hostly duties to perfection. But once the weekend was done and there was no longer a need for the pretense there would have to be a real reckoning, however bloody it turned out to be.

"Tomorrow will be less of a trial," he said as they went downstairs. "Some of our neighbors are amusing and in general not particularly interested in politics."

"As long as the status quo remains," Petra responded.

Guy set his lips and made no response.

Chapter Twenty-Six

Petra awoke to the sound of church bells from the village church situated on the grounds of Ashton Court just inside the gates at the end of the driveway. She stretched and yawned in her warm nest beneath the covers, listening to the peeling bells summoning the faithful. She felt peaceful, rested, filled with a sense of well-being as if she'd had a night filled with delightful dreams. She hadn't felt like this since the invasion of Westminster and even that memory couldn't pierce her present delicious sleepiness.

Guy leaned over and kissed the tip of her nose. "Matins at eleven."

"Everyone?" Instinctively she reached her arms around his neck, pulling him down to her. For the moment the distance between them disappeared and all was as it should be.

"Most probably." He moved his mouth to

hers, flinging one leg across her thighs as he came over her. He pushed up her nightgown with one hand, sliding his hand between her thighs, smiling against her mouth as he felt her warm, moist readiness. Still co-cooned in the aftermath of sleep, he joined his body with hers, moving lazily inside her. Petra responded with a soft murmur of contentment, inhaling the sleep warmth of his skin, feeling her body respond of its own accord to this deliciously indolent union.

For long moments afterward they lay wrapped together in the warmth until Guy groaned and rolled away from her, kicking aside the covers. He stood up and stretched as Petra gazed at his naked body, relishing the ripple of muscle beneath the taut skin, the long, powerful thighs and the smooth planes of his back and belly. He moved to pick up his dressing gown from the end of the bed and shrugged into it, turning back to the bed as he did so.

"That is one very lascivious look, madam," he observed.

"I can't help it. That is one very lascivious sight," she returned, pulling the pillows up behind her head as she reached for the bell to ring for Dottie and her morning tea.

Guy laughed and went into the bathroom. Petra listened to the sound of bathwater running and contemplated the day ahead. The luncheon was an open house affair, invitations issued to all the neighboring gentry, and guests would begin to arrive from church at the conclusion of the eleven o'clock matins.

"Good morning, my lady." Dottie greeted her with a tea tray and a bright smile. "It's another lovely day, quite warm for the time of year." She set the tray down and went to open the curtains, letting in golden morning sunshine. "What will you wear to church?"

"Oh, something plainish," Petra said, reaching for her teacup. "The pink shantung dress and jacket with the black trimming, I think, and the black felt hat with the pink ribbon."

Dressed accordingly an hour later she went downstairs to breakfast with her houseguests. Guy had already breakfasted and was closeted in the library with the prime minister and the chancellor of the exchequer for the last political discussion of the weekend. But just before eleven o'clock the entire house party gathered in the hall to walk together to the church for the Sunday morning ritual.

The Ashton boxed pew was not large enough for the entire party but the prime minister, the chancellor and their wives were all accommodated with Lord and Lady Ashton. Petra kept her eyes open with difficulty during a long and tedious sermon and it was with relief that she walked out of the church with her husband to greet the rector at the door. After a few minutes' conversation they walked back to the house and Petra hurried upstairs to change her church attire for an afternoon dress, reflecting that the rules of dress in the country were more arduous than in town. In London she rarely changed her daytime dress until the evening.

She was in the drawing room talking with a group of newly arrived luncheon guests when Babbit announced, "Lord Harrington and Lady Delmont."

Petra spun around to face the drawing room doors. It had not occurred to her for one instant that she would be receiving Clothilde Delmont at Ashton Court, but now she realized she should not be surprised. She knew she was staying with Lord Harrington and his lordship, as a near neighbor, of course would be automatically included in the open house invitation.

She stayed where she was by the fireplace watching as Guy left the people he was talking to and went to greet the new arrivals.

Why hadn't he warned her? *Why* had he invited his former mistress in the first place? He didn't have to include Harrington and his guests. Of course, he'd invited the woman to his own engagement party, she thought with a surge of anger. How *dared* he do this to her again?

She watched as Guy took Clothilde's hand. It looked as if he was going to brush it with a conventional kiss but Clothilde leaned in and presented her cheek, giving him no option but to give her the kiss that indicated a close friendship at the very least. Plastering a smile on her lips, Petra walked across the room, aware of a slight buzz around her. Of course, most of the guests would know of the erstwhile relationship between their host and Lady Delmont.

"Lady Delmont. Welcome to Ashton Court." She held out her hand, the smile still on her lips.

Clothilde's gloved fingers barely brushed Petra's hand. "Lady Ashton. How kind of you to invite me."

Petra wondered if the smile would set on her face. She had the feeling it was probably more of a grimace. She glanced at her husband, who stood as composed as always, exchanging small talk with Lord Harrington. He met her glance, however, and there was something in his dark eyes that she couldn't interpret. Was it a warning? She gestured to a footman with a tray of glasses. "Sherry, Lady Delmont?" Then she turned and walked away, back to the group she had been with earlier.

Lunch was served on small tables in the conservatory, warmed by the sun pouring through the glass roof. Petra had decided against a seating plan. She wanted to encourage informality and allowing her guests to choose their luncheon partners was a good way to do that. She and Guy, of course, would not sit together. Clothilde maneuvered herself next to Guy and engaged him in conversation that to Petra's jaundiced eye seemed deliberately to exclude anyone else at their table.

She was, however, aware of Guy's eyes on her much of the time although once again she couldn't tell what he was thinking. He maintained a cool courtesy and as far as she could tell managed to conduct a conversation with Clothilde while also engaging other members of the party at his table. He would not be impolite, she knew, but nevertheless she felt her own anger rise as she cast surreptitious glances in their direction. It was obvious to the blindest person that there was a special relationship between

Guy Granville and Clothilde Delmont. She touched his arm too often in emphasis, fluttered her extremely long dark eyelashes, and laughed prettily when he spoke. For a moment Petra could find it in her to feel sorry for Guy as he tried to deflect the woman while maintaining a courteous façade. But then she thought that he must have been expecting this, he'd invited her after all. And whatever excuse he thought he had for doing so, nothing would ease her angry disappointment.

At the end of the meal, the guests wandered away from the tables, some into the garden, others into the salon, others to the billiard room or the smoking room. Petra saw Clothilde in the garden, her hand resting possessively on Guy's arm as he attempted to pour cognac for the prime minister, who stood in the same conversational group by an ornamental pond where a marble fish spouted a fountain of water. Petra walked over to them.

"It's such a lovely mild afternoon. Would anyone like to play croquet? The croquet lawn is set up." She indicated the smooth, velvety green lawn with its hoops just beyond a low ornamental hedge.

"Oh, I detest that game," Clothilde declared, "hitting a ball through hoops, so childish."

"Not the way I play it," Petra said. "I've always found it a viciously competitive game. My brother and I and our friends used to spend hours knocking each other's balls out of play. It frequently ended in tears."

"I find country life so boring," Clothilde said with a derisive smile. "What on earth do you find to do here, except for silly lawn games?"

"Oh, there's always the seaside," Petra said cheerfully, picking up the gauntlet with savage pleasure. Clothilde was standing very close to the edge of the pond. One surreptitious push and . . .

She continued in the same cheerful tone. "Weston-super-Mare is only a few miles away. There's plenty to amuse one there."

"The seaside?" Clothilde looked incredulous. "Only children enjoy the seaside."

"Not necessarily," Petra returned. "I happen to love it. In fact, I'm going myself to spend the day there later this week, probably on Wednesday," she heard herself say, although she hadn't fixed on a day until this minute. She glanced at Guy. It was the first he'd heard of this plan and his eyebrow twitched a query.

"I find the sea air very relaxing, it helps to

clear my mind, chase away the cobwebs," she continued brightly.

Guy could hear the brittle edge to her voice and read the anger in her hazel eyes. "Sea air can be bracing," he observed with a bland smile, at the same time moving his arm away from Clothilde's hand.

"The puppet show on the pier is always wonderful," Petra continued in the same tone. "And the theatre at the end of the pier often has wonderful music hall performances. I doubt you'd appreciate them, though, Lady Delmont. I'm sure you'd consider the humor beneath you." Her voice was sharp with contempt. "If you'll excuse me, I must see how many croquet players I can gather."

With another smile, she moved away, congratulating herself on having had the last word. It was a small satisfaction but in the circumstances she would take what she could get. Guy had said almost nothing during her exchange with Clothilde, his expression giving nothing away. If she'd expected any overt indication of her husband's support, she was disappointed. She wondered what he would have said had she actually given in to the urge to give Clothilde that tiny little push.

She glanced back and saw that Guy and

Clothilde had moved away from the group by the pond and were deep in conversation, or rather Clothilde was talking with an intimate dip of her head as if imparting some seriously private news. Her anger flared and it was only with great difficulty that she managed to keep herself from interrupting the tête-à-tête.

"It must be so difficult for you, *mon cher,*" Clothilde said, her lavender eyes liquid with sympathy. "To have to stand aside as your wife takes part in such vulgarity. Believe me, Guy, I know how such a public embarrassment must distress you. What could she have been thinking, to drag your name through the mud for such a ridiculous reason. Women don't need to vote, they assert their power behind the throne, as the saying goes. Why, a clever woman can make a man do anything she wishes him to do."

"That's true of you is it, my dear?" he inquired silkily, a strange smile on his lips.

Clothilde missed the tone and the smile. "Well, of course it is," she said, looking up at him from beneath long, black lashes. "But I would never cause you such hideous embarrassment. Politics are so unfeminine and I know how much you appreciate delicacy in a woman. I do hope you have no regrets." She touched his arm in a gesture of sympathy.

"Regrets about what, my dear?" he inquired in the same silky tone.

"Oh, I think you know," she said with an arch smile. "I must say I was surprised that you would consider such a social nonentity as a wife, but maybe little Petra has some unseen tricks up her sleeve." She gave a tinkling little laugh as if at some absurdity.

"So you consider an interest in politics to be unfeminine, Clothilde?" he inquired, still smiling.

"Of course it is. Such mundane, boring matters have nothing to do with the real business of women. We play our own games, *mon cher,* and men enjoy them."

"As your playthings?" Guy inquired, his eyes dark slates.

"Oh, not exactly." Clothilde's laugh trilled again. "As our play*mates,* I think you would say. It is a partnership. We give you what you want and cause you no discomfort and in return you take care of our needs and desires. A perfect arrangement, don't you agree?"

"Symbiosis, indeed," Guy said. "If you'll excuse me . . ." He offered a small bow and walked off across the lawn in the direction of his wife's voice coming from the croquet lawn. He stood for a few minutes watching over the low hedge as she played, partnering her brother against two other pairs of guests. Petra enjoyed competitive games of the croquet variety, but manipulation, games of deceit, she wouldn't know where to begin, he thought, smiling unconsciously as she hit her own and then her brother's ball to strike the central finishing post and immediately danced a little jig of triumph.

Had he once enjoyed Clothilde's manipulations? Had he once appreciated her subtle deceits as she managed her life and those in it according to her own wishes? He had always known what she was up to, but it had amused him and now he couldn't for the life of him think why. There was something so fresh and clean about his wife's way of living her life. She believed in universal suffrage and she would fight for it. She hadn't warned him in advance, and for that he was entitled to his annoyance, but for her convictions . . . ? Maybe not.

Blithely unaware of her husband's self-reflections, Petra nursed her anger at his apparent complicity in the presence of his erstwhile mistress, but there was no opportunity to express any of her feelings, even after the luncheon guests had left. The house was still full of the weekend guests who must be entertained. But finally the interminable evening came to an end. Dottie had gone to her own bed and Petra sat in her dressing robe on the end of the bed and waited for Guy to come upstairs.

Guy couldn't help but be aware of his wife's suppressed anger whenever they were in the same room during the evening. She was icily polite to him, while maintaining her hostess charm with their guests. He steeled himself as he went upstairs to join her after seeing the last of his male guests to the foot of the stairs on their way to bed.

"All right, let's hear it," he said as he came in, his hands raised, palm forward in a gesture of defense.

"I don't understand, *why* would you invite her . . . after the last time."

"I didn't," he returned. "I had no idea she was staying with Harrington. It was unspoken that the open house invitation would include any guests under his roof. You know that as well as I do, Petra."

"You didn't *know* she was here?" Petra asked, incredulous.

"No, how should I have?"

She shook her head in bewilderment. "Well, I did, and she certainly knew *you* were here."

"How can you know that?"

"I saw her on Bristol station the day Joth and I arrived. Don't tell me it was pure co-incidence that Lord Harrington was in the country. He's known for hating it. He hardly ever leaves London except during hunting season."

"Which is now," Guy pointed out mildly.

Petra was silent for a moment. Then she said, "You really didn't know?"

"Of course I didn't. Do you think I would have sent Harrington an invitation if I had known?"

"I don't know. You invited her to our engagement party."

"And you know why I did that." He sounded impatient. "I now am a married man and I would not consider it appropri-ate to invite an ex-mistress under my roof when my wife is present."

"Oh, but if I weren't here . . ."

"Don't be ridiculous. I refuse to have this conversation, Petra. Go to bed. I'm going to read in the library for a while." He walked out, closing the door behind him with a firm click.

Petra felt angry tears welling and blinked them away fiercely. Not only had Guy dismissed her own righteous anger but had actually taken offense himself. Maybe he hadn't known Clothilde would find her way into his marriage, but he could at the very least acknowledge how uncomfortable that made his wife feel.

She turned out the lamps and got into bed, then got out again and relit Guy's bedside lamp, turning the wick down low. She wasn't going to let him accuse her of being petty as well as ridiculous. *Oh.* She thumped the pillow, threw it on its other side and thumped it again before flinging herself down and closing her eyes.

She heard Guy come back sometime later as she lay sleepless in the dim lamplight. She closed her eyes and listened as he moved around the room, discarded his dressing gown, turned out the lamp and slid carefully into bed beside her. He lay still for a moment, then said softly into the darkness, "I know you're awake." He pushed out an arm, sliding it beneath her and rolling her against his body. "I am so sorry. I was so angry with Clothilde myself that somehow it got transferred to you. You had every right to be angry and upset."

She nestled her head into the hollow of his shoulder. "I know I shouldn't let her upset me, but she tries to and I don't seem to be proof against it."

"Don't you trust me, Petra?"

"I trust you absolutely," she declared, pressing her lips to the side of his neck.

"Then let's get some sleep. This will all be over by tomorrow afternoon."

"Thank the Lord for that, sir," she murmured, feeling his skin ripple with silent laughter.

The following morning an early hunt took many of the guests, both men and women, out following the hounds just after the sun came up. Petra excused herself from the hunt, as she was not an avid horsewoman, unlike Diana and Fenella, and spent the morning ensuring that all the arrangements were in order for the guests' various departures. The enormous hunt breakfast with its copious supplies of wine and whisky was a cheerful farewell and finally she and Guy waved off the last of the guests on their way to the London train from Bristol.

"I feel as if I've run a marathon," Petra said, turning back to the welcome silence of the now empty hall.

"In a way you have," Guy said. "I've never hosted a weekend of that kind before. I confess I hadn't realized how exhausting it was going to be."

"You've never hosted one before?" Petra was astonished.

"I've never had a hostess before," he pointed out. "A man needs a wife, an accomplished wife, I might add, to manage such an event."

"Mmm. A mistress won't do, I suppose."

"No," he agreed. "But there are many other events where they can be useful." He laughed, seeing her expression. "My love, if you insist on provocation, you must expect to have it answered."

Petra sighed. "I suppose so." She flopped into a deep armchair in the drawing room. "Will you ring for tea?"

Guy did so before saying, "What's this about going to Weston on Wednesday?"

"Oh." Petra considered for a minute. "I hadn't planned on doing so until I heard myself say it. But yes, I am going for the day. I love it there and it's been over a year since I walked along the sands. It was always one of Joth's and my favorite days out when we were children." She hesitated a moment, before saying, "I need some time to myself, Guy. I have a lot to think about . . . priorities," she added with a vague gesture.

"Two heads wouldn't be better for that?"

Petra shook her head and said again, "I need to spend some time with myself."

"Perhaps we could both benefit from the time without distraction to work on what we consider important," Guy responded, his tone now cool and impersonal.

Petra was saved from a response by the arrival of the parlor maid with the tea tray.

CHAPTER TWENTY-SEVEN

"I'll drive you to Weston in the motor?" Guy said on Wednesday morning at the breakfast table as Petra cracked the shell on top of her boiled egg. "What time do you want to leave?"

"Oh, I don't need to be driven," she said quickly, sprinkling salt onto the egg. "You have things to do this morning. Besides, I'd like to drive myself in the gig. It's only a few miles."

There was a moment's silence before he said, "As you wish. But you must take a groom with you."

"No, that's not necessary," she stated, determined not to give in on this issue. "I am quite capable of driving a gig alone. I'll leave it with the pony in the stable at the Ship Inn. They know me there."

Guy wondered if it was worth a fight. It was one he would win, because his servants would not disobey his direct orders, but he suspected it would be a Pyrrhic victory.

"May I ask then that you be home by mid-afternoon?"

"Yes, but why?"

"Because I will be concerned for your safety," he said simply. "The lanes are narrow and there'll be more traffic later in the afternoon. Wednesday is market day in Kingston."

Petra scraped the last of the egg white from its shell. "I will be home by four o'clock." She reached for the butter dish and spread butter liberally onto her toast. "Good enough, sir?" She raised an ironic eyebrow.

"Good enough."

Petra took the reins of the gig an hour later, shook them encouragingly, clicked her tongue, and the pony between the traces started off down the driveway. It was another beautiful late autumn morning, the oak trees along the drive richly burnished in gold and red and for the first time in days, it seemed, she drew a deep breath of relaxation, feeling the tension run away. The lanes were quiet and the main road into Weston had little traffic. Wednesday was market day and the traffic would have been heaviest earlier in the morning. It would be bad again late afternoon, as Guy had

401

pointed out, as customers and stall holders made their way home, but Petra had every intention of keeping her promise about being home by four o'clock.

She guided the gig into the stable yard of the Ship Inn on the town's sea front and jumped down, handing the reins to a stable hand, who hurried to take them. "I'll be back later this afternoon. See that the pony's fed and watered," she instructed before making her way into the inn.

"Good morning, miss. What can I get you?" The innkeeper behind the counter in the saloon bar greeted his customer cheerfully as he polished the stained counter with his apron. "It's Miss Rutherford, isn't it? Haven't seen you hereabouts in a year or more."

"It's Lady Ashton now, Mr. Jackman," Petra told him with a smile. "And I'd like coffee, please."

She sat down at a table in the mullion-paned window overlooking the promenade above the beach.

"Well, I never did," the innkeeper said. "Wait till I tell the missus. She usually knows all the gossip hereabouts." He poured coffee. "Fancy a nice bit o' fruitcake with this? Our Matty bakes a right good 'un."

"Yes, thank you." For some reason Petra

associated the sea air with food, candy floss and toffee apples, cockles and whelks soaked in vinegar, and, of course, fish and chips. They were all part of the ritual experience of a day at the seaside.

Refreshed after coffee and cake, she left the inn and walked across the road to the broad promenade that ran along the seawall for the length of the expanse of what at high tide was golden sandy beach below. But the tide was out now and the dark rippled sand gave way to mud flats that stretched across the bay to the open sea. The beach here was notorious for its extreme tides, at low tide damp sand and mud seemed to extend to the horizon, stranded boats leaning sideways in the mud. It was a good time to collect the cockles and whelks at the edge of the flats and Petra watched the local folk bent to the ground as they walked, filling their buckets with shellfish as greedy seagulls circled above, looking for an opportunity to raid a bucket or snatch a cockle from an unwary hand. Fearless and threatening, they were considered as bad as rats by the local people with their constant ferocious hunting and continuous screaming.

She strolled along the promenade, the gulls shrieking and swooping overhead, still filled with that deep relaxation, the wonderful feeling of being alone, responsible for nothing and no one, only herself. And now she had the time to think clearly about how to reconcile her own powerful support for universal suffrage with Guy's equally powerful opposition. After much thought she had decided that her husband was entitled to feel let down that she had not warned him that she would be taking her public support for her cause onto his own ground. And she was resolved that in future she would always inform him of any civil actions the Union was going to take. But what would that do to her marriage?

How was it possible to feel such deep love for a man who held views diametrically opposed to her own? No, stronger than that, views that she now found abhorrent. Views that denigrated her as a person in his world. Guy would deny that, of course, but Petra knew she was right.

She had reached the end of the promenade and turned back toward the pier and the pavilion. Her mind was clear but the answer remained a conundrum. Thrusting her hands deep into the pockets of her jacket she walked the length of the pier, absently noting the stalls that were open, that the puppet show was still performing a vigorous Punch and Judy, and the theatre at the end of the pier was showing a variety show every day until the end of November.

The smell of frying mingled with the pungent aroma of vinegar made her realize that she was hungry and it had to be lunchtime. The smell wafted from a small kiosk located at the beginning of the pier, just where it met the promenade. She increased her speed, walking quickly toward the scent, thinking now only of the delights of vinegar-soaked fried cod and thick chips wrapped in newspaper.

There was a queue, which was usual, and Petra took her place at the back, looking around at the beach just below. Some children were playing with buckets and spades in the damp rippled sand, others exploring the rock pools left high and dry by the receding tide, their shrill voices rising in competition with the screaming gulls. The cluster of shellfish pickers were still at their gathering. The queue moved forward and she moved with it, still watching the scene on the beach. It would be too cold to swim even if the tide were in, but the beach would look completely different, water lapping golden sand instead of the expanse of damp dark sand and black mud with its green and brown patches of seaweed and toppled, stranded boats. In winter, she knew, the sky would be gray and black, seeming to join seamlessly with the dark wet sand and the dark brown mud, but today the sky was clear and brilliant blue, the sun pouring yellow light onto the scene.

She had reached the head of the queue without realizing it until the person behind nudged her elbow. "Oh . . . sorry," she apologized quickly. "Cod and chips, please. Salt and vinegar."

She waited, salivating, as the man in his blue-striped apron dropped a piece of battered cod into the steaming fryer. He fished it out, dumped it on a sheet of newspaper on the counter, ladled a huge quantity of crisp chips on top and liberally doused the whole in vinegar with a hefty shake of salt. "There y'are, miss." He folded the newspaper over to form a packet and handed it to Petra. "Sixpence halfpenny."

She took the hot, greasy parcel and tossed sixpence halfpenny onto the counter, turning away with a word of thanks, climbing down the few steps that led to the beach. She found a rock resting up against the seawall and sat down, inhaling the fragrance of her lunch mingled with the salt tang of the sea air.

"Well, I can't imagine what Lord Ashton would say if he could see you now," a familiar voice said from above her.

Petra felt a cold anger at the invasion of her privacy. Of all the people to disturb her peace on this day, this woman was the worst. She twisted to look up and behind her. Clothilde Delmont stood on the wall looking down at her. "What are you doing here?" Petra demanded making no attempt at politeness.

"You said you'd be here today," Clothilde said, surveying the steps down to the beach warily.

"How did you get here?" Petra asked, looking around. "Is Lord Harrington with you?"

"No. His carriage brought me." She looked around with an air of disdain. "This place is the height of vulgarity. I can't believe Guy would patronize it. Is he here?"

"No, he's at home." Petra broke off a piece of fish from the newspaper and popped it into her mouth, licking her fingers before selecting a fat chip. "If you want to talk to me you'll have to come down here. I'm eating my lunch."

"How disgusting," Clothilde declared, cautiously stepping down to the beach. She was as always the picture of elegance in a dark blue suit, a pale blue ruffle–necked blouse beneath. Her high-heeled yellow kid

407

shoes made no concessions to the terrain and the heels sank into the sand.

A bright-eyed seagull perched on the seawall, watching the newspaper in Petra's hands, his clawed feet gripping the wall, his fierce beak opening and closing as he shrieked at her.

"I should take the shoes off, if I were you," Petra suggested through a mouthful of fish. She wore flat, open-toed sandals herself, with a colorful patchwork skirt and ruffle-edged green waisted jacket. Perfectly appropriate clothing for an autumn day at the beach. She was beginning to enjoy this tête-à-tête, if it could be called that. Lady Delmont was at a disadvantage for the first time since Petra had laid eyes on her, and for once she was not intimidated by the other woman's elegance. It was so out of place.

"Shoo it away," Clothilde demanded, flapping a hand at the seagull with a shudder. "Dreadful creatures." The gull merely rose on its toes, opened its large wingspan and shook its wings, emitting a shriek.

"It'll only come back," Petra said unhelpfully but with absolute truth. "Did you want to talk to me?" She stood up from her rock. Clothilde towered over her at the best of times, and remaining seated merely made it worse. "Let's walk along the beach a little, the sand's firmer where it's damp." She moved farther onto the beach toward the faint silver glimmer of sea on the horizon. After a moment Clothilde followed her, picking her way delicately. The seagull flew low over Petra's head and in a moment was joined by two others angrily squabbling.

Petra continued to eat from her soggy newspaper, relishing each vinegary mouthful. "Well, go on, Lady Delmont, I'm listening," she prompted.

Clothilde grabbed at her wide-brimmed hat as a breeze swept in from the sea. "You will not keep him, you know that," she stated. "He finds you amusing at the moment. It's the way he is with all his affaires de coeur but he always come back to me in the end."

"I don't believe he's ever married one of his lovers before," Petra pointed out mildly.

"Oh, you tricked him, but it means nothing to him, you'll see that soon enough. I wouldn't marry him if he begged me. He's not capable of being faithful and neither am I, which is why we will always come back to each other. I know him as you cannot possibly, you're no match for Guy, Petra, and he'll realize it soon enough. And when he does he'll —"

"Have a chip," Petra interrupted, thrusting the newspaper parcel toward Clothilde. "They're very good and might sweeten your temper."

"You're a fool and a . . ."

The abrupt movement of the newspaper into the open brought a flurry of wings and a loud shrieking which broke into whatever she'd been about to say. The two huge white birds screaming like banshees hurled themselves down between the two women. For a moment Petra could see nothing but feathers and beady eyes as she flailed her hands against the terrifying melee of dagger-sharp claws and open beaks in her face. One minute she was holding out the remnants of her fish and chip parcel to Clothilde and the next it was snatched from her hand.

Clothilde gave an unearthly scream, flapping her arms wildly, blinded by their wingspan as the two birds fought over their prize inches from her nose. Still screaming almost as loudly as the seagulls, arms still windmilling, she turned and took off without thought across the beach, her head down, not looking where she was going in her panic as other gulls joined the fray, swooping down on her, their wings batting violently just above her head.

Petra ducked and weaved as the birds fought above her and saw that Clothilde,

410

shoeless now, was running hell for leather toward the waterline. She saw that the original pair of fighting gulls had been joined by three or four others, all fighting for scraps from the now shredded newspaper, circling above the terrified woman, darting and weaving, seeming to be encouraged in their attack by her frantically waving arms. Petra could only imagine how frightened Clothilde must be, she was fairly shaken herself, but the other woman's predicament was worse than her own had been. It took her another bemused moment to realize where Clothilde was heading and cupped her hands around her mouth, bellowing, "Clothilde, stop. Turn around."

The other woman took no notice, even if she'd heard, and Petra was uncertain about that. Kicking off her sandals Petra did the only thing she could think of and raced after Clothilde, still shouting at her to stop.

The gatherers along the sand's edge stopped at the commotion, looking around them. When they saw what was happening they too began to shout at the fleeing figure. Almost everyone on the beach but Clothilde Delmont knew the dangers of the mud flats.

Petra reached the edge of the rippled sand where the mud began. Clothilde's shoes lay discarded on the sand, at least she'd had the sense to get rid of them, but sweet heaven, what was she to do now? It was a desperate question and the answer equally so. Still shouting at Clothilde to stop running, she gathered up her patchwork skirt, and gingerly took a step forward, feeling the mud seep around her toes. As she took another step she heard another voice, calling behind her.

"For God's sake, Petra, stay where you are."

She looked over her shoulder. Guy was racing down the beach toward her. He held a life ring, one of the many hooked onto poles left by the Coast Guard lifeboat crews along the sands. Petra couldn't imagine what good it would do in the present crisis, and she couldn't for the life of her imagine what Guy was doing here or how he could have appeared so suddenly. She ignored his command and stepped forward again, carefully, trying to step as lightly as possible on the surface of the mud flat. It was still shallow and sucked against her ankles.

A few yards ahead of her she saw that Clothilde had at last stopped, but she wasn't moving at all, just standing stock still and Petra realized that the deeper mud had snared her. It was thick, viscous and deadly.

She shaded her eyes against the sun and looked to the horizon. The silvery glimmer of the sea caught her eye and a cold dread ran down her spine. The tide, the notoriously fast tide of Weston, was coming in.

Desperately she took another step toward Clothilde, then another. She could hear Guy behind her. *"Stand still,"* he shouted. "I'm coming."

Petra couldn't imagine what good it would do if they were both stuck. She looked around. A stranded dinghy lay half on its side a few steps away. At least it was solid. She tiptoed sideways, and by some miracle the mud loosened around her toes as she lifted her heels as high as she could. Another step, and then another, and she could grasp the side of the dinghy. She was safe now. All she had to do was swing herself up and into the boat and wait for the incoming tide to lift it out of the mud. But Clothilde was several yards away and stuck fast with a rapidly rising tide.

"I can't move," the Frenchwoman called, sounding numb.

"Of course you can't," Petra retorted, too angry with their predicament to offer sympathy. "Didn't you hear me calling to you to stop? Of all the bloody stupid things to do. You don't run toward the water, you run

413

away from it. Don't you know anything?" Fear infused her anger but when she saw the terror in Clothilde's eyes her anger died. The poor woman hadn't known which way was up under the gulls' attack and she wouldn't know the dangers of this beach anyway.

"Help me," Clothilde begged in a voice of such terror that Petra forgot everything that lay between them. She looked sideways and saw that Guy, also shoeless, was only a few feet away, still holding the life ring. Considerably heavier than she, he was having more trouble getting to the dinghy, but somehow he twisted his foot onto its side so that he was walking only on its edge and with a curious set of hopping movements fought through the mud. At last he was able to grab the side of the boat and haul himself forward until he was beside Petra.

"The tide's coming in," Petra told him succinctly.

"Yes, I saw."

"What are you doing here anyway?" She couldn't help herself from asking the question despite the urgency of the situation.

"I missed you and I needed you," he stated flatly.

"Oh." There seemed no answer to a comment that filled her with warmth. Instead

Petra leaned over to look into the boat. A thick rope lay coiled along the bottom. "Do you think she could catch the rope if we threw it to her? Then we could pull her through the mud."

Guy looked grim but he didn't answer, instead turned toward Clothilde, who still stood frozen so far and yet so close to them. "Clothilde, I'm going to throw you a life ring," he called, his voice calm. "Catch it and slip it over your head. The tide is coming in."

"But if she's stuck firm the tide won't float her off, it'll drown her," Petra said in an undertone.

"That's not helpful," Guy snapped, the moment of warmth forgotten. "Get in the boat and uncurl the rope." He gave her an undignified boost over the side of the dinghy and she fell in a heap on the bottom.

"Ugh." Petra righted herself. The bottom was covered in a greenish sludge. She examined the rope. It was wet and coiled tightly. She perched astride one of the thwarts and pulled it toward her.

Guy held the life ring ready to throw but Clothilde stood paralyzed, the mud halfway up her calves, the silk folds of her blue skirt stuck to her legs. "You have to catch this, my dear," he called in a kind, almost gentle

415

voice, quite unlike the one he had used with Petra. Despite Petra's correct dismissal of the usefulness of the ring, he knew that it would give Clothilde some sense of hope and with any luck shake off her paralysis. He measured the distance with his eye and then sent the ring in an arc through the air. Clothilde raised her arms to catch it. A seagull cried, she screeched in alarm and the ring fell into the mud at her feet.

"Can you pick it up?" Guy asked in the same gentle voice, hiding his frustration. He glanced toward the horizon. The silver line was now an unmistakable wave of water moving toward the beach.

Clothilde bent a little, reaching down to grab the ring as it lay in the mud. She seized it. It was thick with mud and she looked at it helplessly as if unsure what she was to do with it.

"Put it over your head," Petra yelled, and startled at her sharpness Clothilde did so, shuddering as the wet, muddy thing encircled her body.

Petra's fingers were bleeding as she struggled with the last wet coil of the thick rope but at last she had it. "Here." She handed one end to Guy, who still stood outside the boat. "If she can grab hold of that, we can both pull her in. I'll stay in the boat and

416

pull from here."

Guy nodded, casting another anxious glance at the fast approaching wave. He could hear it now, a subdued but unmistakable rushing surge of sound. "Hold on to this as tightly as you can." He looped the rope around his hand, leaned as far forward as he dared and tossed it toward Clothilde.

Somehow, this time she caught it. "Now," Petra called, "tie it around your waist so that if you drop it, it won't be lost." Clothilde obeyed, her fingers all thumbs, but at last it was done. The first little rivulets of water crept across the mud toward her.

"Now, Petra," Guy said, hauling on the rope, hand over hand.

Petra took a firm stance in the slanting boat and pulled with all her strength. Clothilde didn't seem to move at first, and then, as Guy gave another almighty heave, the mud gave up its hold with a great sucking sound and she was dragged across it until Guy got his hands around her and lifted her bodily into the boat.

She lay on the sludgy bottom, a pitiful sight, mud and tears streaking her perfect complexion.

"What now?" Petra asked as Guy pulled himself over the side into the dinghy.

"Now we wait." He looked out to where

417

the line of waves was coming ever closer.

"Once the boat floats we'll have to swim to the sand," Petra pointed out. "Can you swim, Clothilde?" She held out her bloody hands to pull the woman into a sitting position.

Clothilde shook her head. She seemed to have lost the power of speech during her ordeal. She shivered and Guy pulled a handkerchief out of his jacket pocket before taking off the jacket and draping it around Clothilde's shoulders.

"It shouldn't be too long now," he told her, trying to sound reassuring before turning to Petra. "Let me look at your hands."

Petra extended them palms up in silence. Guy spat on his handkerchief and wiped away as much of the blood as he could. "They're scrapes rather than cuts," he declared. "Keep dabbing at them and the bleeding will stop."

Petra watched the tide racing in. It was astonishing how fast it came. She knew all the stories of unwary people caught by the tide on this beach and the many lifeboat rescues, and she'd read the stories of those who'd died in the mud, but still the speed of the oncoming tide shocked her. Within fifteen minutes of Clothilde's rescue the dinghy was beginning to float and small waves were lapping at the sand twenty feet away. There was no sign of the treacherous mud beneath the blue-green water.

"Instead of swimming, why don't we see if we can row the dinghy closer to the shore?" Petra suggested. "Once we reach the sand, you can help Clothilde to walk onto the beach. I don't mind bringing the boat back to its mooring and then swimming back across the mud."

"You'll do no such thing," Guy stated. "Your heroics, madam wife, are over for the day." He leaned sideways, resting on the palm of one hand against the thwart, and kissed her mouth. He glanced at Clothilde, who now sat on the second thwart, huddled in his jacket.

"What in the devil's name were you doing here, Clothilde?"

Petra kept silent. She had the feeling that Guy was about to dispense with his customary courtesy.

Clothilde said nothing, but turned her head away, looking toward the beach. Guy unhooked an oar from one of the rowlocks and reached across for the other. He turned the little boat and began to row to the beach. Just as the boat was about to run aground again, but this time on sand, he said somewhat curtly, "Get out here, Petra, and go to the Ship. Get a room, order mulled wine, and get out of those clothes. I'll join you within the hour."

"But . . . but . . ." She looked expressively at Clothilde.

"Would you just for once do as you're told."

There was a note in his voice that made Petra swing herself over the gunwale into the calf-deep water, her feet finding the sandy bottom with relief. She waded to shore, holding up her skirt, although it was already soaked through above her knees. On the dry sand, she looked back at the dinghy. Guy was holding it steady with the oars and he was talking.

Petra suddenly thought that she did not want to hear what he was saying to Clothilde. Much as she despised her, she couldn't help but feel a stab of compassion for the Frenchwoman. She was soaked and filthy, barely recovered from a terrifying ordeal, and Guy didn't look as if he had a smidgeon of sympathy for her.

She trailed back up the beach, retrieving her sandals on her way, and walked back along the promenade to the Ship Inn. The landlord was still behind the saloon bar and he stared at his bedraggled customer when she entered.

"Good Lord, ma'am. What's 'appened to you?"

"Mud," Petra said concisely. "My husband will be here soon and he looks as bad as I do. Do you have a room free where we can clean up a little? Oh, and Lord Ashton wants a jug of mulled wine as well as hot water and a fire in the room."

"Right away, m'lady. How'd you get caught in the mud? You and 'is lordship know these parts well enough."

"Someone needed rescuing," Petra said. "But all's well that ends well. So, if you could show me to a room upstairs . . ."

"Right this way, my lady. And I'll send a maid up to you right away." He bustled ahead of her up a creaky staircase and opened a door on the first landing. "This is the best room in the house, ma'am. I'll have the fire lit in no time."

"Thank you. And don't forget the mulled wine." She smiled at him and when he'd left leaned against the closed door for a moment feeling the quiet normality of the room settle around her. It was large, with a four-poster bed, a deep inglenook fireplace and an oak settle with a chintz cushion. There was no attached bathroom, but the inn was several centuries old and presumably lacked such niceties. She pushed herself away from the door as someone knocked.

A maid came in with two jugs of steaming hot water; behind her was a leather-aproned manservant with an armful of wood. Petra found a seat on the settle, careful to keep the folds of her wet and muddy skirt away from the crisp chintz cushion, and watched as the fire began to blaze.

"I'll get the mulled wine going, ma'am," the maid said, dropping a curtsy. "I'll do it up here, shall I?"

"Yes, please." The inglenook was begging for a trivet and saucepan of hot spiced wine on the fire.

"Should I help you with your clothes?" the girl asked tentatively. "I could sponge off the skirt for you and press it. Have it good as new by morning."

The prospect of spending the night in the inn was suddenly very appealing. It was a place with no connotations, no ill memories, a place where she and Guy could be themselves, with no distractions from their own personal issues. What better place to sort out those issues that had to be sorted if they were to have a proper marriage?

"Is there a shop somewhere you could buy me a dressing gown?" she asked the girl, digging her purse out of the deep pocket of her jacket. She took out three guineas.

"Yes, ma'am. There's Judy's on the High Street. She has some nice things. I could run there now for you."

"Thank you." Petra handed her the guineas and as soon as the girl had left stripped off her sodden outer garments and, dressed only in her chemise and drawers, poured hot water in the basin on the washstand and sponged as much of her as she could get to. The heat was wonderfully refreshing and relaxing. Feeling much more comfortable she wrapped herself in the bed coverlet and returned to the settle by the roaring fire, wondering what had happened to Clothilde. Would Guy bring her to the inn?

She had her answer a few minutes later when Guy came in without an alerting knock. He gave a sigh of relief as he looked around the warm, inviting room. A fragrant pot now simmered gently in the hearth, two earthenware mugs warming beside it.

"You look comfortable," he said, crossing over to her with long strides. "What an abominable afternoon." He kissed her, then said, "I want to hold you but I'm filthy and wet and you look so warm and comfortable, and dry," he added.

"Where's Clothilde?"

"On her way back to Harrington Hall with

Harrington's driver," he said shortly. "And that, my love, is the last time the woman's name will ever pass between us. Is that clear?"

"Crystal," she said, deciding she didn't want to pry further. Whatever had happened between Guy and the Frenchwoman would not have been pleasant for either of them, she guessed. "If you have the motor, what are we to do with the pony and trap?"

"Douglas is taking them back to Ashton Court now." He stripped off his shirt. "Pour some of that wine, sweetheart. I am perished."

"Did you have to swim to shore?" She knelt by the fire, ladling the hot wine into the mugs, sticking a cinnamon stick in each one.

"As luck would have it, the dinghy's owner came out for a late afternoon's fishing on the high tide and took it from me on the beach. A couple of guineas satisfied him as a loaner's fee and I escaped total immersion." He took the mug and inhaled deeply. "Ah, I've been dreaming of this for hours."

"I think we should spend the night here," Petra stated, looking at him through the steam curling from her own mug.

"Do you?" He looked around the cozy room. "Apart from the obvious, is there another reason?"

"Yes." She cupped her hands around the mug. "We have to find a way through this morass. I love you, Guy, with all my heart, but I won't change my convictions, my loyalties, I can't possibly. And you won't change yours, but perhaps, here, in this neutral space we could try to find a way to love and live with each other despite."

Guy looked at her for a long moment. "As it happens," he said slowly, "I find that under my wife's influence my convictions seem to have undergone a change."

Petra stared at him, her hazel eyes wide. "Do you mean —"

"I mean that until you entered my life I had not really given much thought to the idea of women and the vote," he interrupted. "I couldn't really see why you would want it, but Clothilde explained it to me."

"Clothilde?"

He nodded. "It was not her intention, quite the opposite, I believe, but I found the argument against her argument quite convincing."

"Oh. That sounds very convoluted," Petra said hesitantly.

"It's actually very simple," he responded, a slow smile spreading from his eyes to his mouth. "Oh, my darling love, I don't want

425

to change one tiny iota about you. Everything about your redoubtable, stubborn, unconventional, reckless, competent, combative, loyal and loving self informs my lifeblood. I can't imagine what kind of life I was living before you came into it."

Petra felt a little spurt of inner warmth that had little to do with the mulled wine. She looked at him, wondering if what he was saying could be true. "You would support universal suffrage?"

"I have every intention of doing so," he responded. "I'll discuss it with Asquith and Campbell Bannerman when we return to London. Damn, now what?" He turned to the door at a brisk knock.

"Here's the dressing gown, ma'am." The maid looked at Guy in his shirtless state and looked away hastily, blushing. She put the parcel on the bed and turned back to the door. "Is there anything else, my lady?"

"Is there by any chance a gentleman's haberdashery in Weston?" Petra asked on a bubble of laughter. "His lordship has need of a dressing gown too." She held out her purse. "Take what you need from there."

"I'll send Robbie the barman, my lady." The girl took the purse and scuttled away.

"Here, you'd better have this." Petra unwrapped herself from the coverlet, passing it to him before she ripped open the tissue-papered package, shaking out the folds of a sturdy woolen dressing gown. "Not the height of fashion, but it'll certainly do." She pushed her arms into it and tied the girdle at her waist. "Oh, I feel almost human again. And I'm starving. Can we order dinner up here?"

"I might have an order of my own first," Guy said, peeling off his sodden trousers and undergarments. He pulled back the bedcovers. "Get in. It's playtime." He patted the sheet, looking at her with narrowed eyes. "Must I fetch you, wife?"

"Well, that could be fun on another occasion," Petra said, considering. "But not today." She leaped onto the bed, untying her robe, flinging her arms wide. "Ravish me, my lord."

"With the greatest of pleasure, my lady."

ABOUT THE AUTHOR

Jane Feather is the *New York Times* best-selling author of more than thirty historical romances. There are now more than 11 million copies of her books in print. Jane was born in Cairo, Egypt, and grew up in the south of England. She currently lives in Washington, D.C., with her family. Visit her online at JaneFeatherAuthor.com.

The employees of Thorndike Press hope you have enjoyed this Large Print book. All our Thorndike, Wheeler, and Kennebec Large Print titles are designed for easy reading, and all our books are made to last. Other Thorndike Press Large Print books are available at your library, through selected bookstores, or directly from us.

For information about titles, please call:
(800) 223-1244

or visit our website at:
gale.com/thorndike

To share your comments, please write:
Publisher
Thorndike Press
10 Water St., Suite 310
Waterville, ME 04901